JUSTIFIED DECEPTION

Our most influential
& supporting neighbors
Thanks for your
support
Craig Reiners

C . R . REINERS

ISBN: 1548954977
ISBN 13: 9781548954970
Library of Congress Control Number: 2017911371
CreateSpace Independent Publishing Platform
North Charleston, South Carolina

To my wife, Mary, for everything.

CHAPTER 1

She made the soft whimpering sounds he liked and clawed at his back—but not too aggressively. As she lay there on her back, he pumped and jerked like a wild animal. She closed her eyes and whispered his name on cue, yet her thoughts flew to another place and time. Their tiny two room farmhouse in northwest Jiangsu County was all she and her father shared. He was a rugged farmer, who used to call her Sparrow. She would come running home from school, ponytail flying, and find him working his small rice paddy on six *mu*, less than one acre. His back was permanently stretched to the earth as if he were a growth coming from it. Seeing his daughter, he would straighten his spine and lift Sparrow high into the heavens as she would delight in laughter. This was twelve years ago, yet it seemed like forever.

Mr. Mao Ling leaned forward to kiss her cheek and neck. The strong body odor mixed with the overpowering chemical smell of mao-tai on his breath nearly made her gag. But who was this man she had entertained seven times in the past month? Certainly not a businessman from Beijing or Shanghai, for his scruffy shoes, long dirty fingernails, and country dialect placed him more as an office worker for a small company outside the city limits of greater Nanjing. And how could he afford her for a mere half hour? Each visit cost 2,500 renminbi (RMB), including the overpriced drinks—easily one month's pay for a mid-manager at one of the many foreign joint-venture enterprises on the city's southwest side. Yet he repeatedly showed up at the Wild Bunch Cabaret and requested her, the proprietor's most expensive woman. Each time in the bar before their tryst, she had seen Mr. Ling's companion pay her employer in large bills. The companion always remained downstairs. Short and a bit stocky, perhaps midthirties, with a fleshy face and longish, slicked-back hair, he had thick eyeglasses. He dressed in the Western style. He always sported an expensive tie, dark double-breasted suit, and cheap shiny black shoes. He was quick to smile. He always seemed to be backslapping the other well-dressed patrons. He seemed to know everyone. He never ventured upstairs to the private rooms.

When Mr. Mao Ling, whom she heard others refer to as "the Chairman," finished his business with her, she would watch them both depart through the double glass doors to a waiting black limousine with darkened windows. The men never turned to wave good-bye.

CHAPTER 2

It had been a humid late-summer evening when she first stepped onto the portico of the Cabaret in Nanjing. The factories of this industrial city spewed out their unwanted particulates into the atmosphere, where the sun reflected a yellowish haze. Most of the joint-venture firms ran adjacent to the Yangtze River, and their effluent mixed with garbage to form sheen on the water's surface. She was met by the club's madam. They walked through the lower level, which was primarily just a large bar and an open floor with multiple tables and chairs. The floor was sticky. Trash and cigarette butts were everywhere. The lighting was poor. They made their way to the stairs in the back, which led to the girls' rooms. These were both for their professional work and to serve as their quarters. Sparrow was to share with another girl, also from rural China. Sparrow gritted her teeth as she concluded there was no turning back now.

Sparrow was emptying her suitcase when her new roommate knocked and entered. The girl was younger than Sparrow, most likely sixteen or so. Her hair was partially dyed red. She had piercings in her lower lip and one eyebrow. She did not look Sparrow in the eye as she spoke in a dialect from rural northern China. Sparrow found her speech difficult to follow. The northern girl was attempting to welcome Sparrow, but her diction was disjointed and the message was lost as the girl's mind wandered from topic to topic. What she did pick up was the girl's father had been arrested for theft and her mother had passed away years ago. The local communist-cell leader in their small community would visit her in the farmhouse and rape her at least once a week. She was beaten and told to remain quiet.

After nearly a year of the beatings and the unwanted sex, she began to formulate an exit plan. One late afternoon in the fall, the cell leader arrived at the farmhouse, and she was nowhere in the three-room structure. The cell leader sat on the stoop and lit an unfiltered cigarette. He opened the one sorghum beer he had brought to enjoy after the tryst. He was looking around the decrepit farmyard with its one sow and having his second sip when she startled him from behind with a creak of a floorboard. She had the hoe held high above her head and expected to come down on the base of his backbone, but he had just turned enough that the blow caught him over the eye and ear. He instinctively covered his head with both arms. She came down with another blow, but this second one glanced off his forearm. Blood from the first hit covered the stoop, mixing with the spilled sorghum product. The third blow with the sharpened hoe landed at the base of his skull, and his screaming stopped. The northern girl told the story with absolutely no emotion. She continued with the tale of leaving the farm and finding her way to the city, where a distant relative was to help her. When she finally made it to Nanjing, she found the uncle almost more destitute than she. As a result, the Wild Bunch Cabaret proved her only option. She had worked here over the last six months.

Sparrow was as taken back by the story of misery as she was by the deadpan delivery from the girl. Sparrow shared her story of her father's meteoric rise in the Party, only to be disgraced by a devious rival. For some odd reason, Sparrow felt she could trust this country girl and shared how her father was killed by the triad.

Organized crime in China, which had its origins in the eighteenth century, had become much more brazen of late. The Triad, Sparrow had learned, translated to "triple union society," which referenced the union between heaven, earth, and man. Triad members were sworn to thirty-six oaths of obedience. Violating any of those codes resulted in death. Their primary sources of income came from narcotics and human trafficking. She learned the Nanjing Triad had a number of the senior political and business leaders beholden to them in one fashion or another. Many of these men frequented the cabaret.

Over the next few weeks, the northern girl would give Sparrow hints on how to survive at the brothel: which men to avoid, if possible, which men would offer gratuities, and which men held powerful positions. Sparrow learned quickly, despite her difficulty with the northern dialect. The two young women formed a strong bond. Both had a history of misery. Both were searching for something more. Sparrow felt the northern girl had her back.

On Sparrow's first-month anniversary at the cabaret, her roommate was killed. Details were difficult to come by. Sparrow was later able to piece together part of the story. One of the Jiangsu County Triad leaders, known for his temper, had gone too far and killed her young roommate in the brothel. He had cut her femoral artery after rough sex, and she had bled out in one of the private rooms. This was bad for business, and the proprietors had banned the triad leader from the club. Sparrow suspected he may have been one of those involved with her father's torture and murder. She would learn everything about the man—his routine, his partners, and his weaknesses.

The triad's hotshots preferred to relax at the cabaret. The local police were paid off, the girls were young and pretty, and for every renminbi they spent at the establishment, the triad recognized the necessary kickback into their own pockets for protection. Visiting Western men were initially drawn in by the flashy red strobe lights across the rather gaudy facade. Officers from the nearby air-force base found the club a great distraction from their normal routines. Members of the Party's hierarchy found the place a safe haven from the minions who worked for them.

CHAPTER 3

Over the first several months of her employment, Sparrow was simply one of two dozen girls at the club. She entertained numerous clients, including visiting Western businessmen, Party officials, local government men, and some officers from the nearby military base. Her life was a living hell. Most of the customers, after forking over such a significant sum to the proprietors, had a sense they owned her for their time together. They would lose all sense of decency behind the closed doors. In most cases she had to act extremely subservient. Twice she was beaten. One time a soldier, who she believed was a lieutenant, had difficulty with his male organ and decided to blame her for his shortcomings. He struck her on the side of the head, and when she fell, he grabbed her by the hair and slung her against the wall. She was knocked out. The officer stormed out of the room and demanded a refund from the club, which he did not receive. On another occasion, this time with a junior local politician, Sparrow apparently fell short of convincing the client of his bedroom prowess. This guy beat her with a club. She survived with welts and bruises on her back and arms. This time she yelled out, and the club's security rescued her and escorted the underperformer out the door.

There were a few kind men, usually the older ones. Some of the Western businessmen would actually tip her—usually something like RMB 200 or about $27. One customer would repeatedly come in just to hold her and tell her of his crappy life at home. One guy took nude photographs and that was all. It usually wasn't that mundane. Many customers expected her to do everything in the bedroom their wives or girlfriends would not. Sparrow provided this service with clinical precision overlaid with theatrical flair. She had many repeat customers.

One serious downside to her feminine sensuality was the club's bodyguards. The bodyguards took it upon themselves to have her whenever there was a lull in customer demand. They never tipped her and often were rougher than they needed to be given her small frame. This abuse continued the first six months she worked at the cabaret. As her clientele grew and the house escalated the price for a half hour with her, her internal status and value with the owners allowed her a degree of exclusivity and choice.

Sparrow's acumen grew with each passing week. Her customer base became solidified. The prices charged by the cabaret for her services increased. The in-house security people were instructed to leave her alone. Regular customers were entranced not only by her beauty but also by what seemed to be her genuine interest in them. She wanted to know about their occupations, their families, their victories and their fears. She made each patron feel like he was someone very special to her. The clientele began to open up to her more than they would with their wives. Sparrow's value to the cabaret grew exponentially. She was bringing in more revenue than another four girls combined. She was given her own room, with a closet. She was given unprecedented access to the entire club, including the finance-and-accounting section, where the cash was counted. She earned the right to come and go from the premises as she wanted. She purchased better clothes and beauty aids and a few sex toys.

This relative freedom was spent learning. She understood the economics of the brothel. She recognized powerful men and how they wielded that power. She studied human behavior—that of the clientele, the proprietors, and the girls. She studied the competition in town. She shared tea with a number of the mid managers of the brothel. The lowly maintenance man taught her how the basement boiler operated. She learned of the vetting process used for new customers. She became friendly with the brothel's security people and the local police.

Over time, Sparrow would learn one of her regular customers was a very important man in Nanjing. He was often referred to as "the Chairman" in a business context and sometimes as "the Dragon" in a political context. This powerful man held senior joint-venture board positions in both Nanjing and Wuhan. He was the eyes and ears of the Party in boardrooms across multiple industries, including manufacturing and service providers.

As her amorous skill set improved, the Chairman gravitated to her bed over all others. After a few months, the Chairman requested Sparrow to be exclusively his. Of course he would pay for this exclusivity to the proprietors of the Wild Bunch, which was accepted graciously. This arrangement allowed Sparrow to be relatively free four or five days a week. She used this time wisely. She studied martial arts and politics. She read. She learned from all those around her. She engaged the Chairman in meaningless banter to start and then increasingly began to have meaningful dialogue with him. She was quick to stroke his ego, not only in the bedroom but for his intellectual prowess as well. Other girls at the cabaret became jealous, but Sparrow ignored them. She had her sights set much higher than the Wild Bunch Cabaret.

As her image grew with the Chairman, she was given money for proper clothes and shoes. She was given access through him to the arts. She read extensively. She became exposed to visiting Party members at banquets, where she captivated men with her intellectual curiosity coupled with her stunning looks. She had her hair and nails done professionally. She rode in limousines to state events. Said simply, she became eye-candy with a brain, on the arm of one of the most influential men in the province.

Sparrow also focused on the style of others—how they moved and how they behaved in certain situations. She became a student of all human behavior, and she was good at it. All the nuances of power and privilege were not lost on her. She recognized every muscle twitch and every eye movement. She practiced in front of a mirror. She studied how people spoke in the north of China, how they spoke in the southern provinces, and how they spoke on the coast. She was a sponge, learning every single day.

Sparrow befriended the older maintenance man, who at one time was a provincial martial-arts champion. At least three times a week she would join him in the cavernous basement and practice the ancient art after his shift was completed. As she became more adept, he added a weapons component. After several months of intense instruction and practice, she became highly proficient. The older man thought she was learning for self- defense and was taken back with her interest in offensive maneuvers as well. During this time, Sparrow focused on her physical body. She would spend over an hour stretching each day, followed by extensive and focused strength training. Her older mentor found her synchronized movements more like a ballerina, albeit a lethal one.

One of her earlier clients was a young captain who was enamored with her beauty and bedroom skills. She showed genuine interest in weaponry, and while off-duty, he would instruct her on the use of small arms and knives. She in turn returned the favor with sexual favors beyond anything he could have imagined. She became an expert in both handguns and mortal blades.

Once she became the exclusive courtesan of the Chairman, the proprietors of the establishment held little control over her. She stayed in a private room upstairs, paid for by the Chairman. Official cars would swing by to take her places. At just shy of twenty years old, she had made it to the top of the club's hierarchy. Sparrow had much bigger plans.

She was intrigued by the Western joint-venture businesses in the southwest quadrant of the city. The joint venture's investments included automobile manufacturing, steel mills, foundries, and consumer products. The infrastructure in that part of the city was undergoing major renovations. The capital investment in plants and equipment exceeded what she witnessed elsewhere in the entire province. Western businessmen from Europe, the Middle East, and North America were often seen at the best restaurants and hotels. A few of the more junior people could also be found at the Wild Bunch Cabaret in the late evening. Her mentor, the Chairman, lived in this world of money, power, and unlimited possibilities.

Sparrow found a retired Chinese teacher to instruct her on English. She gained access to the library at Nanjing University. Her focus on learning was more than intense; it was her passion. She decided to further expand her world and learned to drive, a highly unusual job for a young woman in China. Her English-speaking skills improved. The driving skill, coupled with her language skills, allowed her to apply for open lead driver positions at one of the highly regarded joint-venture companies.

CHAPTER 4

Two years later Sparrow had earned her limo license and finished a state-mandated curriculum for those associated with the new state-sponsored joint-venture businesses in the special tax-free zone of the city. Not co-incidently, she had maneuvered the system to become the lead driver for the Nanjing malt-plant executives. The malt plant sat southwest of the city's core. The massive complex used locally grown barley and imported barley to produce malt for the beer and distilling businesses flourishing across China. The plant's footprint was along the north side of the mighty Yangtze River, which originated in the Tibetan Plateau. The Yangtze is the third-longest river in the world after the Nile in Africa and the Amazon in South America. The massive river, easily five kilometers wide at this point, supplied the complex with the water necessary for processing. It also served as the plant's effluent disposal unit. Waste water from processing mixed with raw sewage flowed back into the river through multiple iron-cased pipes. Government officials charged with environmental controls tended to look the other way when free passes to the whorehouse were supplied by mid managers.

The malting complex could be seen from miles away. It was nearly a self-contained city in and of itself. Large dormitories for several hundred workers were flanked by massive warehouses for finished product stored in super-sacks and burlap bags. The nine processing units, each the length of a soccer field, stood ninety meters high. Inbound barley arrived by barge and truck. The barges, typically three abreast and six long, were unloaded into covered conveyors that snaked up the riverbank to the plant. Trucks of every type waited in long lines outside the gates of the complex. Armed security guards made themselves quite visible. Four chimney's from the sizable coal boilers belched black soot and smoke 24-7. The on-site water-treatment plant included holding ponds the size of one hundred Olympic-size pools. The administrative building was ten stories and ominous in its own right. A well-tended garden in front of the admin building sported two flagpoles—one for the company's flag and the other for the People's Republic. The red PRC flagpole was noticeably higher.

On her first day on the new job, she drove the Chairman who was surprised to see her working the daytime state job, yet knowing her skills as his personal courtesan made him extremely pleased.

The relationship with the Chairman grew over the next several months. He became almost a surrogate father in terms of exposing her to the world, teaching her on how the government really worked and having her join him for various business meetings around the sprawling metropolis of Nanjing. This was not a father-daughter relationship by any stretch of the imagination. He still expected sex, but now that she was so accessible, it became less frantic with him. Learning was terribly exciting for her. The sex remained her price of admission to a much-larger world.

She enrolled in the Nanjing University with the Chairman's endorsement. She was a part-time student. She only focused on finance. Her objective was straightforward—understand how funds moved legally and illegally across cyberspace. Male instructors tended to give her more one-on-one time, and her inquisitiveness, coupled with her hourglass figure, gave her access to the institution's computer lab. She found the black notebook, which the Chairman always carried with him, particularly interesting. Often he would be on his cell phone, refer to the little black book, and recite a string of letters and numbers. As she spent more and more time with him, these coded communications were done openly with her in the same room or in the state's automobile. From her schooling, she recognized these as passwords and passcodes for moving funds between accounts. She memorized the complicated codes and could regurgitate the bank-account numbers. Knowledge was power. This critical information would fund her plan. The Chairman had personal accounts in Nanjing, Beijing, Hong Kong, and one offshore in the Bahamas.

Using her access to the computer lab at the university, Sparrow accessed the Chairman's secret accounts. The Chinese accounts were in his name, and the offshore account was simply numbered with various proprietary access codes, which she now possessed. Gaining access across the web to these accounts was exceptionally easy and straightforward given the codes she had memorized. The grand tally across the four private banking accounts was staggering. This upper-level manager in the Chinese government had RMB 23 million in the combined three Chinese accounts. There was an additional US$7.05 million sitting in the Bahamas. If her math was correct, this equated to US$9.05 million. She also noted routine deposits direct from the joint-venture companies he currently served on. There were a few withdrawals. Knowledge was power, and Sparrow's long-term plan now had the necessary funding component.

She began to notice one of the more junior supervisors at the plant, a Mr. Ping, would often stare at her from a distance as she worked on the executive car or one of the staff vehicles. He was strange and creepy, and she found herself very uncomfortable in his presence. Given her proximity and work with the Chairman, coupled with Ping's relative junior status at the facility, she felt relatively safe. Nonetheless, Sparrow preferred not to be left alone with him.

Her role at the malting complex grew over time. In addition to her driving responsibilities, she was given a job accounting for spare parts in the maintenance group and was learning important skills in the quality control lab. She had no women friends at the plant. They all felt her advancement was the result of her incredible good looks and cozy relationship with the Chairman of the board. At first this tended to bother her, but later on she accepted the jealousy for what it was. She was going to use everything at her disposal to learn, advance, and conquer.

Sparrow paid close attention to her appearance. Her uniform was always clean and pressed. Her hair was always washed and styled. She applied makeup sparingly. She always greeted fellow workers and the supervisory staff formally. She chose a singular item to express her individuality—her white driving gloves. She had several pair. Made of linen, the gloves had a modest lacy pattern closing at the wrist giving them a particular feminine appearance. The gloves remained in the executive car when she was assigned other work. She had noted the Chairman staring as she would make a show of putting them on at the beginning of a trip or taking them off when they had reached their destination. Her gloves became a symbol of her feminism and class.

CHAPTER 5

On a spring day, she was instructed to pick up one of the Western investors at the Nanjing airport. She arrived at the international arrival hall with time to spare and held a small sign indicating the joint-venture malting complex. She expected to accompany an older gentlemen to the Xuan Wu hotel that evening and then to the malting offices the following morning. The young man, who approached her, was not at all what she had envisioned. He was likely ten years older than her, with reddish-brown hair, clear blue eyes, and a friendly smile that seemed to draw her in. With an athletic build, he carried himself with a degree of confidence. Within a few meters of her, he stopped to bow slightly and introduce himself in broken Mandarin as he handed her his business card. The card introduced him as Alex Cutter, with the Royal Bank of Scotland, serving as a financial consultant. She returned his welcome first in Mandarin followed by English. He was impressed and took a moment simply to stare at this beautiful Chinese woman with a coy smile. She went to help him with his carry-on bag, but he would have none of that. She felt a twinge of electricity as his hand released hers from the bag. They both paused as he held her gaze a little longer than before. Sparrow finally turned and motioned for him to follow to the waiting car.

Despite the effects of jet lag, Alex was immediately smitten with this young woman. Her petite hourglass frame, intelligent eyes, and dark hair swept back with two broaches were intoxicating. Her English-speaking skills surprised him. There was something about the way she carried herself that set her apart. The bearing she carried underscored confidence and class.

Sparrow seductively put her white driving gloves on. Alex attempted some conversation in his broken Mandarin from the back seat while Sparrow navigated the snarling Nanjing traffic. She did not respond as she professionally wove through the mass of humanity on motorbikes, on horse-drawn carts, on bicycles, and on foot. Occasionally they maneuvered around other state vehicles, which, to Alex, seemed to give their black government sedan deferential treatment. Alex noted the national flags waving from each front fender. Given the darkened windows, admirers could not decipher who was the VIP in the back seat.

Sparrow removed her driving gloves and assisted with his luggage as they walked side by side to the Xuan Wu reception desk. Paperwork had been already done, and she rode the elevator up with him to the executive floor and room 1890. She dropped off his bag at the entryway. Alex reached for her hand to deposit fifty renminbi, which she refused using her English skills.

"At the very least, please join me downstairs for a drink," Alex blurted out.

"Mr. Cutter, it remains in business hours, and I must return to the plant and my duties there. Let me know what time you would like to be picked up tomorrow morning."

"I must apologize; my internal clock is a bit screwed up since departing from Winnipeg yesterday. Seven-thirty tomorrow would be fine." Rather than just see her walk away, he added: "Should you be free after work for a drink, I would love to take a walk and see the local sights with you." He immediately recognized it came across more as a plea than a polite invitation. He looked down a bit sheepishly.

Sparrow was taken off guard. Tonight she did not have an appointment with the Chairman as he was on business in Beijing. She had no responsibilities after work at the plant, nor at the cabaret. She surprised herself saying, "I would love to show you some of the unique aspects of this old city."

Taken back by her response, Alex said, "That would be great. Does six-thirty sound OK?"

Showering later in his room, he could not believe his luck in getting a date with such a beautiful, intriguing young woman. He planned to use the Cutter charm for all it was worth tonight.

Waiting in the hotel lobby bar with windows facing the main drag, Alex nursed a Tiger beer. It was after their preassigned time when he saw her walking up the street toward the hotel. He spotted her among a large crowd waiting to cross the main fare road. She had changed. She wore a printed blue Burberry dress, silk sandals, and minimal jewelry. Tonight she wore her long hair up with a few stands falling around her earlobes. The juxtaposition of those workers in their drab gray clothes next to her finery was stunning.

They both ordered: a Campari and soda for her; another Tiger beer for him. They looked into each other's eyes. He struggled with his limited Mandarin. She teased him. They laughed and flirted. She got up abruptly and said in English it was time for the tour. He paid at the table and followed her out into the busy thoroughfare. They walked and talked. She showed him some of the city's well known sites. The majestic walled city—the longest walled city in the world held the Zhonghua Gate. They walked past the Mausoleum of the Ming Dynasty. He held her hand, and it seemed to be the most natural thing in the world. At eleven it was getting much cooler, and Alex offered his sport coat for her shoulders. They crossed the ornate Qinghai River Bridge, and he stopped and kissed her. The kiss he received held nothing back.

The walk back to the hotel seemed more like a dream. Without hesitation she joined him in room 1890. Initially they were both like awkward teenagers, but that quickly changed. Her tongue tasted like tangerine and fire. She lost her fingers in the back of his scalp. Alex caressed her neck and back, stoking her enthusiastic desire. His hand glided from the smooth of her stomach to the curve of her hip. Somehow they got into a rhythm. She was on top, straddling his manhood. He was caressing her hips and buttocks. He held her face with his thumbs tracing her cheekbones. They kissed with eyes wide open. His hand gently fell from her belly and touched and stroked that slight protrusion. Her moan could not have been faked—nor his. Her intense pleasure was literally unworldly. She kissed him lightly as they decoupled.

"I know so little about you," Alex whispered as he played with stands of her hair around her earlobes.

"And I know so little about you," she replied as she stretched. "There is little mystery to me. I come from a small rice farm far from the city but still in the county. Today, I have a job driving for the malting plant."

"My sense is there is much more to that story," Alex replied. "I want to learn everything about you." He kissed her again.

"I will return for your pick up at six-thirty," she said in English as she pushed away at his chest with both hands and smiled.

Alex was star-struck with this incredible young woman. Although becoming a driver of a joint-venture company vehicle was by no way a small job, it seemed below her talents. In fact, a female company driver was rare. Who really was this woman?

The cab ride back to her room at the cabaret took only fifteen minutes at this time of night. She thought about the present. This man from the West had touched her strangely. He had been hauntingly gentle. She felt safe when he held her. Given her perfect posture behind the wheel of the company sedan and her telltale white gloves, she doubted he would have guessed her evening occupation at the cabaret.

The tailored white satin gloves fit snugly on her slender fingers. The V-pattern at the wrist was trimmed with lace and small pearl buttons. The gloves held the image of privilege and class. They underscored a degree of self-assurance and purity of purpose.

Usually she focused her time on the future and what needed to be done. She planned. Every action had a longer-term reason to fit into a master plan. This tryst with this Western traveler was out of character for her.

CHAPTER 6

Sparrow would also spend time reliving the past. She often would take the bus back to Jiangsu County and the rocky hillside where her father was buried. She would bring flowers and sit alongside his marker and talk out loud as if her father was there. She would ask his advice on things. She would weep. She would recollect the good times they had shared when he had been a rising star in the Party and everything seemed possible for them both.

She grieved the mother she hardly knew. She had died in an automobile crash. The black and white photograph of her was wrinkled with time, but Sparrow pulled it out frequently. Her mother had been a beautiful woman. Statuesque, with almost a regal bearing, her mother at thirty something years old was stunning. The smile in the picture held untold secrets and the limitless possibilities now open to both Chinese men and women as the new openness spread across the country. Her mother's eyes in the photo spoke of an intelligence and curiosity that was cut short by her untimely passing.

As a young girl, Sparrow worshipped her father. He would spend hours reading to her and answering her many questions. He was always patient. Looking back at those simpler times, Sparrow would reflect on his intellect as well as his playfulness. She loved him dearly. As she grew older, the quality she most admired was his integrity.

Years later Alex Cutter would think of Sparrow often. His life since his internship with the bank had taken many turns. He had completed his undergraduate work at Delaware in two and a half years—earning a 3.95 grade point average. He played varsity lacrosse and tennis. He dated infrequently, preferring to concentrate on his studies. He enlisted in the military. Special Forces had taught him how to kill efficiently and how to interrogate. He became an expert in martial arts, weapons, and counterterrorism.

In Afghanistan his team had been ambushed by a force three times their size. His heroism that night had earned him his first bronze star. He did a second tour—this time engaged in the Gulf War. He had seen first-hand the wicked devastation of mustard gas on the Kurds civilian population. In his last year in the service, he concentrated on security issues, prior to his honorable discharge.

His intellect, curiosity, and foreign experience landed him at Oxford. He completed his MBA among the ivy and upper crust of English society. He also had a fling with a fellow graduate student. She was studious and challenged him intellectually. She wore glasses, which did not detract from her extraordinary figure. They made love the very first time on a single bed in a local hospital where she worked part-time. They amicably split up when she chose to enter medical school and he had been accepted to Yale Law School.

Alex met his soon-to-be wife while at Yale on the tennis court. Susan was cute and athletic. She was a bit silly and to a certain extent frivolous. She was live-for-the-moment. Alex was a serious planner. She had many friends. Alex was a bit of a loner. Alex had a good serve. She had a wicked backhand.

Susan was an undergrad at Yale and six years junior to Alex. She loved the fact that she was dating a law-school student but did not care for the many late nights he studied. Susan (she never went by Sue) was an only child. Her parents had separated when she was a teen. She had learned to use her sexuality to her best advantage, including a brief relationship with an English teacher fifteen years her senior. Beneath the veneer of her confident persona and perpetual tan, Susan was very insecure. She exhibited pathological narcissism. She had problems with empathy and sincere intimacy. Alex didn't recognize these traits as he typically saw her once on the weekends and over midterm breaks.

At first they dated other people at the Ivy League school. They became more or less exclusive by the second semester. Alex was drawn to her playfulness, her self-assuredness, and her good looks.

They married after a brief courtship and moved to San Francisco. Alex started his security business and began to travel around the world as it grew. His clientele included the US military, the Saudi government, several hedge fund managers, and multiple international banks.

Susan spent most of her time at the country club when Alex was away. She played mixed doubles at a high level. Her partner was an attractive man many years her junior. The guy was a professional model and a tennis instructor with plenty of free time to spare. Their affair was virtually public knowledge at the club. Alex was completely unaware.

Alex self-managed his own investments. After a rigorous review, he had invested $200,000 in an Internet start-up called NetAppLink traded on the Hong Kong Stock Exchange. In three months his initial investment had more than doubled. He purchased additional shares. In another seven months, his stake was worth well north of $1.3 million. In two overnight trades, he sold all his shares, reinvesting much of the profit in his own company's growth.

Her pregnancy caused her to miss the club's tennis championship; however she and Alex were there to welcome their daughter, Alexia, to the world. In Alexia's fifth year, their only child exhibited tremendous curiosity and language skills. She was also ambidextrous. Alex felt guilty spending so much time on business travel as his precious daughter seemed to be growing up overnight. Susan had little interest in her daughter. She enrolled her in day care six days a week. The hired nanny became the surrogate mother for young Alexia as her mother worked on her tan and her tennis serve.

CHAPTER 7

Jerry Primrose sat alone in the nonsmoking economy car on the last leg of his two-and-a-half-hour train journey. He looked uncomfortable, and he felt uncomfortable. Dressed in a rather bright-yellow golf shirt, a bit too tight for his expanding midsection, with a brown Mickey Mouse insignia, his wrinkled brown Bermuda shorts, and new Nike with white socks that sported two thin yellow stripes, he felt utterly ridiculous. Coupled with an aging 35 mm camera hanging from his neck, he would not be mistaken for a local. He lit off the train in Nord-Brussels—not a convenient stop—but he did what management wanted. He hailed a taxi to his hotel off Boulevard Du Regent—a block from the sleazy video peep-show establishments.

Jerry would much prefer working alone in his loft apartment in the Hague—just himself and his powerful computer. He had left a California start-up dot-com business in late 1997. He served nine months at another e-commerce business only to be shown the door when it went belly-up in August 1998. Now as a freelance programmer with a chip on his shoulder and the promise of finally receiving the recognition for his considerable expertise, he looked forward to the face-to-face meeting with Herr Reins.

As instructed, he did not tip the cabbie, carried his luggage to the run-down hotel, paid for one night in cash, and took the studio room assigned. He had time before the expected meeting and quickly disposed of his costume. Recovering the boxed dry cleaning from his worn luggage, he changed into the clothes he was more comfortable with—a deep-blue cashmere pullover, tan slacks, and Ferragamo loafers. The shoes had cost

22

more than he had previously made in a month of freelancing for a woman's lingerie website. Frustrated with further instructions not to boot up his PC while on this assignment, he walked downstairs and out into the chilly Belgian mist in search of a Diet Coke and pommes frites with extra mayo. Returning to his room, which smelled of stale cigarettes and strong coffee, he pulled down the bed, pulled off the expensive shoes and crashed as his head hit the mushy pillow.

The next morning, Jerry shaved and readied himself for the long day ahead. He was not scheduled to meet Herr Reins until seven that evening. After a strong morning coffee and flaky chocolate croissant, he walked past the St. Gudula Cathedral to the famous Manneken Pis along the narrow lanes of the historic city center. The statue of the little boy taking a pee seemed to draw a large tourist crowd. Later in the afternoon, he made his way to the Musée d'Ixelles, the former slaughterhouse now housing great nineteenth- and twentieth-century Belgian art. He found himself lingering at a collection of Flemish masters adjacent to an interesting collection of fin de siècle posters. He finished exploring the museum at 4:30 p.m. and stopped for a strong coffee in a pub kitty-corner from the famous museum. Rather than catch himself in a rush later, he elected to take a rather expensive cab ride back to his hotel and mentally prepare for tonight's important meeting that could well change his life.

Albert Fenner received the long-distance call in a bank of decrepit phone booths just opposite the bus station. He did not say hello, he did not speak, and she knew he was on the line given the labored breathing she had learned to recognize. After the cryptic report was received, there was a lengthy silence—then he simply said, "Phase one complete," and the phone line went dead. Albert Fenner shuffled, actually limped, from the public phone booth located just a block away from the Grand Palace square in Brussels. Dressed in a tattered light topcoat, blue jeans, and well-worn scruffy shoes, he appeared as a local pensioner living perhaps on the very edge of the poverty line. Those who venture a glimpse in his direction would look away expecting the older man to ask for a handout. Most pedestrians simply ignored the broken man. He entered the public urinal and chose the last stall on the right. Just then, a young man was leaving the stall. He was heavily scarred from juvenile acne and wore a brass ring in one nostril. He bumped into Albert as he left without apology. Albert locked the door and stripped. The young man's satchel yielded clothes fit for a different persona. Leaving from a back emergency exit, Mr. Fenner cast a significantly different shadow as he crossed the famous square—a forest green topcoat outlined in the finest leather trim, dark woolen slacks with a measured crease, and black leather shoes shined to the point they made their own light. A walking cane completed the outfit with a silver etched crown and a classic Munich style gentlemen's hat complete with an understated feather plume. He walked without a limp of any kind, the walking stick more a symbol of past aristocratic blood. Mr. Fenner had once again morphed into Herr Reins.

He entered the boisterous La Brouette (the Wheelbarrow) tavern on the Grand Palace square. Greeted by the headwaiter as Herr Reins, he was escorted to the second level overlooking the busy promenade of both tourists and residents below him. In perfect Flemish, he ordered a Duvel and *croquettes aux crevettes*. After his first taste of the Belgian beer, he relaxed and peered again through the mild distortion of the old small panes of glass onto the square. Phase one, which would finance the overall strategy, was complete and on schedule.

CHAPTER 8

Jerry Primrose walked through the Grand Palace square past 13 Rue des Bouchers and the impressive Aux Armes de Bruxelles and to the La Brouette restaurant. Herr Reins had insisted they meet at table three early Sunday evening at 1800 hours. The maître d's eyes disapproved of him as he entered the restaurant through the old revolving doors, but at the mention of table three, he snapped to attention with an approving smile.

Herr Reins sat alone, perfect posture with clear gray eyes taking in all activity from his back table. He motioned for Jerry to join him with a casual hand gesture. Chantal, their exclusive waitress for the evening delivered a '95 Chateau Patache d'aux with two polished glasses. Jerry reached for his glass of wine, but Herr Reins placed his cold hand on Jerry's wrist and shook his head ever so slightly. "Please do not get too comfortable as our business will not take but a moment," he stated using the Flemish idiom. "Our organization has successfully completed phase one of the project, and your contributions to date have been recognized by management. Your required sum has been deposited per instructions with a tidy bonus, if you will. More importantly, we will require your expertise moving forward. I request you to not return to the Hague apartment, as your building has unfortunately completely been destroyed by fire. Your software and computer will be available custom cleared at the Cape Town airport. Your fee will certainly more than cover replacement of your personal belongings and those two pesky cats. Find your ticket and fifty thousand South African Rand in the same lock box used previously." Jerry began to ask a question as his mind was working overtime but was immediately cut off. "Mr. Primrose, all the details will be provided in South Africa by a Mr. Romano Jenker when you arrive next Wednesday—have a safe journey. That is all." And with that the maître d' appeared and pulled his chair back and bowed respectively. Jerry understood the dismissal. His mind was racing in many directions, returning to the lump sum in Switzerland. Those Swiss francs would make him forget the two cats. Hell, the one never really got the litter-box thing anyway.

With Mr. Primrose dismissed, Herr Reins sipped the '95 vintage with pleasure. Chantal arrived with his *waterzooi de volaille*. The creamed chicken was magnificent at this establishment. He would call for his car for the short trip to the private hanger, but the crew could wait—a '95 Patache should never be rushed.

The private Citation II climbed to thirty-six thousand feet, and Herr Reins removed his shoes and relaxed with a brandy in hand. The flight from Brussels to Bangkok would allow him plenty of time to review the success of phase one and to contemplate various iterations to consider for phase two. Phase one had gone off flawlessly considering the complexity involved. Phase one was all about funding. They had successfully been able to crawl their way into several of the most secure electronic trading sites on the planet. The key was not to be greedy. Get in and get out, and leave no electronic fingerprint. Having the ability to pause key global market platforms such as the London Metal Exchange, the Chicago Mercantile Exchange (CME), and the New York Metals Exchange (NYMEX) gave the syndicated group unfettered access to market depth on both the bid and ask side. Last Tuesday, their brief proprietary access to those key markets for just a few minutes allowed the group to position short-term trades netting them US$22.6 million. The pause in the three key global markets was later blamed on dysfunctional back-up systems unable to take the necessary corrective action given the brief but nonetheless highly disruptive solar flare. The fat Primrose had proven a key technical component in the ruse. Herr Reins did not care for the overweight techie but was pleased with his results.

As the Citation cruised over the Black Sea on its route over Lahore, Pakistan, and then further south to Bangkok, Reins motioned for the flight attendant to refresh his drink. He pushed aside the dossier on the desk in front of him. He had pretty much memorized the background information for the information-technology professional he was visiting for the first time in Thailand. The attendant returned with the amber liquid in cut crystal. The tall Russian girl was meticulously coiffed and wearing a smart uniform. Herr Reins was pleased. He preferred everything around him to exude class.

Without a word to her superior, the flight girl poured. Reins watched as she returned to the galley with a seductive gait. Now staring out his window, he allowed himself to reflect on how far he had come in this life. As a boy, he had been given to his birth mother's sister and her husband, who lived on a decrepit farmstead on the border of Germany and Poland. There was little love between the substitute parents and the young boy, and even less love between the husband and wife. Cheap Polish vodka more often than not led to a beating of the boy by his slovenly second father. His substitute mother never intervened. As the boy matured and grew stronger, the animosity grew. One late evening, the drunken sub-father entered the small bedroom the boy had above the barn with his strap at his side. The boy-man, now nineteen years old, expected the violent sub-father this particular evening. As the man entered his bedroom, his cussing loud and stammering, he tripped on the cord at ankle height. The young Reins straddled his back in an instant. Another cord expertly bound the hands. Still another cord secured the ankles together. A sponge, which had been soaking in lye, was shoved in his mouth and secured with tape surrounding his head and neck. A sobering panic was evidenced in the eyes of his near-father. Reins turned up the volume of his transistor radio. The small room was filled with a Polish folksong. The first two cuts severed the Achilles heels and the loud snap of each nearly drowned out the music playing. Next he used the blade to enter the ear canal and his then-father screamed his voice only to be muffled by the sponge. The next several minutes involved various cuts and slashes to various body parts.

Now years later, Reins could not recall them all. The wooden floor they were on became slippery with blood and excrement. Reins continued the torture but with little forethought. When the man had passed out, Reins continued the revenge surgery.

Later that same night, Reins cornered his surrogate mother. He used a rag soaked in lye to cover her nose and mouth. His mother was found in the barn by a neighbor weeks later. She was still hanging from a cord around her chubby neck. The crows had made a mess of her face. The neighbor had called local authorities. The stench from the surrogate father's body caused even the coroner to puke.

The young Reins had made his way to Ukraine working for two years in the wheat fields as a hired hand. He spent all his limited free time reading and becoming an expert on human behavior. What followed was an accelerated growth curve working for an organized-crime syndicate operating out of Minsk, the capital of Belarus. Reins began as an enforcer, but the *pakhan*, or "boss," recognized raw talent and elevated him quickly in the organization. Reins spent time in both illegal drugs and prostitution and grew both business units exponentially. In five years he was handpicked to work in their political unit. He was as smart as he was smooth. The syndicate rewarded him.

He was transferred to the United States and an offshoot of the Odessa Mafia. Again he thrived. After ten years he moved back to Europe. He was well established and respected. His peer group in the organization could not find a weakness they could exploit for their own gain. Reins did not drink to excess, he did not use drugs, he did not have a mistress, and, as far as anyone could tell, he did not steal from the organization. One trait, familiar with anyone who knew him, was his vindictiveness. Those who crossed him were met by a vicious counterattack. This would include their wives, their courtesans, their families, and even their close associates.

His home was in southern Germany. Actually it was a twelfth-century castle, completely remodeled with the exception of the dungeon and the moat. The dungeon contained a unique oubliette, or forgotten chamber. This fifteen-foot vertical shaft was large enough only for one individual to stand in. It was constructed in such a way that the prisoner could not crouch, kneel, or sit down. The pit was so narrow the individual could not turn around. After the prisoner was lowered into the shaft and reached the bottom, the lowering rope was released back up and the trap door closed. The prisoner was forced to stand in the completely dark chamber, his muffled screams absorbed by the thick stone walls. Herr Reins had used this several times for captured foes. On a few occasions, he had heard his staff complain about recovering the bodies.

Reins fancied himself as an art collector, and as such his home was filled with original paintings and sculpture. He also collected ancient writings, which filled his private library floor to ceiling. The library was a self-contained space with temperature and humidity control to protect the rare books and manuscripts he had collected over the years.

A bump in the air brought him back to the present. He must have dozed off. The brandy glass had been removed.

"Sir, we are descending through ten thousand feet, and I will have you on the ground in less than ten minutes," the captain said over the speakers. "I hope you've had a good flight, Herr Reins."

"Be sure to have a limousine on the tarmac to pick me up, Captain," Reins instructed via the intercom system. "I have a very tight schedule."

"Yes sir, Herr Reins; it has been prearranged, but I will double-check as we roll to the hangar," Captain Keith Rodgers replied. "Is there anything else?"

"Have the plane fueled and ready for departure in the early morning. I want to be in Hong Kong by dinnertime. Keith, get us out of here before the normal commercial rush. I may have one passenger joining us on the next leg."

"You got it, sir."

"Keith, can you do something about this humidity?"

"No, sir, but I will have the limo driver max out the AC," the captain said with a degree of lightness to his voice.

Herr Reins's limo sped off to his meeting with another brilliant IT practitioner at an obscure closed US air base northwest of the city.

The limousine made the trip in forty minutes to the decrepit airfield. Herr Reins entered the front office of a hangar, which had a single light on over the door. He was met by three security personnel dressed in camouflage, each carrying an Israeli Uzi. These were big men, and there was a no-nonsense way about them. They frisked him politely but also very thoroughly. He noted several more men of equal size and composure on the perimeter of the ancient hangar. He was escorted through the door and entered a cavernous space.

"Good early morning to you, Herr Reins," the small Indonesian man said in perfect English as he walked toward him. "I trust you've had a good journey." Charlie Leong formally bowed with his comment.

"I have. Thank you for meeting me on such short notice," replied Reins. Despite having studied the dossier on this man, he was taken aback by how small this guy was. He wasn't short, rather he was miniature. Could it possibly be a distortion given the relatively large room they were meeting in with twenty-foot ceilings? No, it was not. This guy was tiny. They shook hands a bit awkwardly. "As you know, you have been highly recommended to us."

"Thank you, Herr Reins. You must have only solicited my close friends for your review," he replied jokingly.

"No, that was not the case," Reins offered in a very businesslike fashion. "I do, however, want to hear your story. Why did you leave a multinational company such as NetAppLink?

Charlie Leong paused before his thoughtful response. "You are correct to question my decision to leave. I had plum assignments in Australia, India, and China. After eight years, I became a vice-president of the data storage division. After ten years, I was promoted to a corporate officer's position with NetAppLink. I was chosen to give the keynote address at the shareholders last meeting. My last year's bonus was in the seven figures." Leong paused to allow that fact to speak for itself. "Two months ago, I stumbled on some serious discrepancies in the audited Data Fabric

Division. I brought my findings to the platform lead after thorough analysis. I expected a pat-on-the-back and likely further recognition. Rather than respond to my allegations, he ushered me into the chairman's office. There it became clear that they were also fully aware of the financial discrepancies; however given the pending stock split and interest from a US buyer to acquire the entire company, the timing was not right. As a company officer myself, I explained my legal and moral obligation to expose what was a meaningful discrepancy. They both then laughed nervously. Bottom line—I was given a severance package for my silence, which I could not refuse. I doubt that detail was in your dossier of me."

"All right. I will require some detailed confirmation of all this, which I can dial into at a later time. I appreciate your candor," Reins said again in his businesslike fashion. "I am here today to offer you a unique opportunity."

"I'm listening, Herr Reins," Leong said. "I know you did not travel this far without good reason."

"I need to break into the IT platform of the Standing Committee of the Politburo, specifically targeting one individual. I need to do this without detection, and I need to do it by week after next."

"As I am sure you are aware, there are nine members on that committee, and they are the most powerful men in China," was the initial reaction from Leong. "These men control the six key systems within the People's Republic, namely the military, party affairs, all organizational affairs, politics and legal affairs, propaganda and education, and finance and economics. Information technology falls within the finance and economics bucket. That bucket is controlled by Mr. Xin.

"That is exactly why we need the best for this assignment, and we believe you are the best."

"As I said, we are targeting one key individual on the Standing Committee of the Politburo, a Mr. Xin. Ultimately the Shanghai exchange reports to his office. Our organization has proprietary access to key markets in the United States and England now. The Shanghai market will be a key component to our broader strategy moving forward. If you can get us access for just a few minutes, undetected, it will be very worth your while." Herr Reins stopped pacing and sat opposite Leong. "Our timetable is tight, and frankly we need to know if you are game for this assignment or not. I am prepared to offer you three million US dollars for the job."

"Herr Reins, there are likely less than half a dozen experts in the world with the expertise to hack into the Chinese platform and remain undetected. Most of those would require some degree of collaboration with other IT professionals, and I would wager your consortium would prefer to keep numbers of participants to a minimum—am I right?"

"Correct."

"I will take the assignment under these absolute unabridged conditions:

1. The fee will be six million US dollar equivalents. It will be split into six various currencies at prevailing exchange rates and wired to my accounts on the day of the successful break-in.
2. I work alone.
3. Upon conclusion of the assignment, I share the code with your team and retain the right to hold same for my own purposes at a later date.
4. These terms are nonnegotiable."

"These are tough conditions, my new friend," Herr Reins said. "I accept them on behalf of our group with the understanding this will be concluded in the next fourteen days."

"Done," said Leong as he produced a bottle of VSOP Cognac from his bag. "Let's drink to this new partnership."

Out of courtesy, Herr Reins lifted a glass, tipped it toward Leong, and swallowed the nectar in one gulp. "I will leave you with our dossier of Mr. Xin and everything we know technically about the exchange."

"Thank you, sir. I will have two of my security detail follow you back to the airfield. This is not the safest neighborhood."

With their business concluded the two men, from very different worlds, shook hands and went separate ways.

Herr Reins returned to his limo and instructed the driver to return directly to their aircraft. He reflected on his meeting with Leong. The dossier on the experienced IT professional seemed accurate. The small man from Indonesia possessed the skill set they needed. His fee was high, but Reins figured they would recoup that with several proprietary swaps between the Asian and European markets. Back at the airstrip, Herr Reins strapped himself into his seat and told the pilots there would not be an additional passenger tonight. Within a few minutes, the private plane had reached forty thousand feet and its cruising speed back to the capital of Belgium.

CHAPTER 9

Mr. Leong left the hangar with two of his bodyguards and driver. He arrived at his downtown hotel in less than an hour. He logged into his remote supercomputer, which resided in Jakarta. As his various passcodes navigated through security, Leong called down to the concierge desk to order three pots of strong black coffee, six bananas, and several chocolate bars. He expected it to be a long night. The PC in front of him raced through the multiple security walls. The black and white screen rapidly scrolled through zeros and ones page after page. Finally the telltale little bell sounded assuring him of his proprietary access. The work was tedious in front of the black and white screen, as he fully expected. More coffee and more chocolate bars kept him engaged. By nightfall his screen became the only source of light in his suite. He rubbed his eyes and continued.

At 4:00 a.m. local time, he had successfully breached the information technology security on the politburo server. As he had planned, the virus he had planted was recognized by the politburo system. The Chinese system put everything on hold and addressed the virus. This took only several minutes. During that diversion, Mr. Leong had downloaded and copied the relevant files of Mr. Xin.

As he switched to tea, Leong's sharp analytical mind caught an unexpected consequence in the captured data. Mr. Xin was putting together a file on a Mr. Mao Ling. Ling was known in Nanjing as the Chairman, as he served on multiple joint-venture businesses. The dossier was extremely damaging. It detailed the renminbi he was siphoning from each of these joint-venture companies for personal gain. It was clear Mr. Xin planned to use this incriminating evidence against the Chairman very soon. In the People's Republic, such an act was punishable by death. Reading between the lines, Leong recognized that Secretary Xin had previously been quite a supporter of the Chairman's career. It would become necessary for Mr. Xin to distance himself from the perpetrator prior to releasing the criminal evidence.

Exhaustion caught up with Leong. He needed to rest. His last thought before crashing into a nearly hypnotic sleep was estimating the value of this information across an array of potentially interested parties. He slept.

CHAPTER 10

The trip from Brussels to Amsterdam's Schiphol airport was efficient on the fast train. Jerry Primrose showered and changed in the first-class KLM lounge. He chose dark gabardine slacks, an off-white silk turtleneck, and black slip-ons for the journey ahead. He selected an isolated table adjacent to the darkened windows overlooking the tarmac. The waiter brought him still water, Maker's Mark bourbon neat, and a plate of cold salmon. Unconsciously his thumb would scratch the black leather-woven money belt holding the South African rand.

The twelve-hour flight to Cape Town was interrupted, as he requested, four hours into the trip for his preordered lobster steak. "Pardon the interruption, Mr. Primrose. What would you care to drink with your dinner this evening?" The KLM flight attendant, attractive in a sexy librarian way, reached over the empty seat next to him to catch the overhead light. Her high heels accentuated firm calves, and the lines of her legs against the dark blue skirt led to the wave of hourglass hips. Her white blouse was unbuttoned at the top to reveal perfectly shaped breasts. Her eyes were emerald green with reddish hair pinned back with the exception of two strands that hung across her forehead.

"I will have the Heidsieck Brut Reserve Rose, thank you."

Primrose turned slightly to observe the man one seat back across the aisle. The man wore a white robe and a *shimagle* covering his neck and most of his head's features. He stared forward in a trancelike state. Primrose noted his deep-set eyes, sharp nose, and perfectly manicured nails. The man was still as stone. He appeared to be in the exact same position when

Primrose had rotated his seat back for his earlier siesta. The Brut champagne arrived. He glanced back at his first-class terrorist. The man gave him the creeps. Then returning to his plate, he enjoyed the lobster steak with the spicy Moroccan accompaniment.

Upon arrival, Primrose met his driver outside customs. The drive to Aqua-Sian took them by some of the worst of Soweto. The Mercedes S-550 glided pass the twelve-foot discolored corrugated steel fence holding over thirty thousand colored inhabitants in conditions not fit for cattle. He could not help but feel the uneasiness in the air. The juxtaposition of the haves and have-nots could not be more pronounced. He reached forward, tapped the driver, and said, "Let's be quick about it." The luxury sedan accelerated and Primrose closed his eyes.

Forty minutes later brought them to the heavily armed gates of the seaside private community of Aqua-Sian. Security fences were double spaced—each fourteen feet high and topped with coils of razor wire. Pit bulls roamed between the well- lite fenced perimeters. Upon clearing two security checkpoints, he reached the door of his temporary apartment. The initial impression was of a luxury safari camp. The floor was teak with a herringbone pattern. Woven rugs of tightly knit red, yellow, and brush straw were interspersed with wild game skins. A gas-fired pit was offset from the center of the room. The pit was semi surrounded by straw-colored couches with various oversized pillows of various animal skins. A collection of Masi warrior spears hung from the back wall. Opposite the seating area was a heavily wooded bar—English pub style. The crowning glory of the room was the floor to ceiling windows holding back the spray of the Indian Ocean.

Two young girls lounged on the couches facing the firelight. With skin of ebony, the first girl's dark hair hung like a mane to her lower back. Her fine features were accentuated by bright eyes with pupils as dark as eternity. Her silk outfit clung to every enticing curve. She smiled with ivory teeth outlined by full lips. The second girl was Eastern European, perhaps Russian. Her blond short hair framed an angel face, but her hardened eyes betrayed any such innocence. Her polyester one-piece outfit fit her body as if another skin.

The Eastern European girl proved to be anything but demure. The darker girl was certainly open to any of Jerry's suggestions. The night played out—chocolate and vanilla. Given Jerry's instructions, the two women began to kiss and fondle one another. They undressed the other. Each stretched catlike on the plush ivory rug in the middle of the great room. Each light stroke of their fingers was followed by a nibble to the neck, the stomach, and the warm nest between their legs. Jerry watched from the couch as the women brought the other to climax. Their images cast shadows on the ceiling as their hips found a rhythm. Jerry motioned for them to join him. Chocolate kissed him on the mouth as Vanilla removed his trousers and underpants. She stroked his manhood and flicked her tongue on the underside of the inflamed penis. The girls removed his shirt and eased him on his back on the now moist shag rug. Chocolate straddled him as Vanilla guided him inside her. Chocolate rocked back and forth with her arms held high. Jerry's hands instinctively cupped her massive breasts. New positions were found and fully explored. The fireplace was but embers when they had found themselves wanting nothing more.

Jerry dismissed the women. Jet lag, a bit of alcohol, and the companionship finally caught up with him. He forced himself under the spray of the oversized shower, dried off, and found a sports drink in the icebox. Initially he had the overhead lights on to read a fictional novel, but that quickly succumbed to a heavenly slumber.

CHAPTER 11

Primrose sat comfortably alone on the veranda, sipping a dark roasted coffee with a dollop of heavy cream, just as the sun came peaking over the Indian Ocean. Words spoken by his born-again father many years ago came back to taunt him. "If any harm follows you, you shall give life for a life, eye for an eye, tooth for tooth, hand for hand, foot for foot, burn for burn, and wound for wound." Primrose remembered it from Exodus. His father began to quote scripture after his release from San Quinton. He remembered him returning home to Oakland, California. It was late spring and a welcoming afternoon rain danced on their metal roof. His father stood just outside the front screen door, hair plastered to his broad forehead, holding a green plastic bag with all his belongings. Primrose saw the pathetic figure and closed down his Macintosh. The old man shuffled in and fell into the faux leather chair. "Bring me a beer, Pim." That was as sentimental as he could be. He had served hard time for his role in a botched robbery where a security guard had lost his right eye and would never walk properly again. Primrose, a teen at the time, returned with the beer to find his father snoring peacefully in the chair. His old man did not respect the young Pim, given his focus on computers, rather his infatuation with technology. Pim had not played football; he had scorned sports in general and was seen by his father as weak. Primrose snapped open the beer and retreated to the back porch. No, he was not a tough guy. But he was anything but weak. He could destroy men through cyberspace using only a keyboard and his mathematical mind.

The thought of his father upset him as he walked barefoot across the teak flooring past the master bedroom to the office. The view here was spectacular overlooking the rock island three hundred meters offshore. Typing in a series of passwords followed by banking codes, he locked into his primary Zurich account. As expected, the new account total had been improved by 15,300,000 South African rand converted to 1,530,000 Swiss francs. Satisfied with the transaction, he closed down, took a final sip of his coffee, and padded back to the master bedroom. The dream was in vivid Technicolor. He was reaching for something and both arms seemed to be growing longer and longer. Then he was in a dark pit with just a pinhole of light high above. Then he was riding a dragon, his legs wrapped around its horny neck. Coming up quickly from behind was another dragon—this one carried the first-class terrorist he had seen on the Cape Town flight. The terrorist was mouthing something he could not understand. The second dragon shot past him in a blur, and now he could make out the scream—"nothing is what it seems, you fool."

Primrose awoke suddenly; his sweat soaked T-shirt clung to his torso and his breathing seemed restricted. He swung his legs to the near side of the bed and got up to splash his face. As he cooled down, he looked up into the mirror. His thinning hair, droopy eyelids covering red-rimmed dull-green eyes, and rather chubby cheeks were quite normal. Nothing to be concerned about—it was only a dream. It was time to get to work. He grabbed two croissants and another cup of Joe and retreated to the office and the powerful computer left for him there.

By late morning his mobile rang, and it was the expected Mr. Jenker on line.

"Good morning, Mr. Primrose. I hope your journey was uneventful and you have found your current accommodations satisfactory."

"Everything has been fine; thank you." Primrose formally responded. "What do you have in mind?"

"I have not been told anything and have been waiting for your call."

"Let's meet for an early lunch at Mama Africa on Long Street. I will send a car for you at eleven. We can discuss business there," Mr. Jenker said with a rather thick South African accent.

The car turned out to be a limousine. It became obvious the black driver had been instructed not to visit with the European on this trip. They passed the outskirts of another Soweto on the east side of the highway. Primrose saw ribbed rusted tin enclosures as far as the eye could see running right to the foot of Table Mountain. Rocks and worn tires held down the tin roofs of most of the homes. Remarkably, most shacks were linked to a mismatch of electric poles and wiring. Naked children were taking a bath in an orange plastic tub. Black tarps seemed to be the repair item of choice. Black fifty-gallon drums were being used as stoves and raw garbage littered the gullies adjacent to the dusty walking paths. Primrose turned away. Just at that time, four dark men carrying bats and wooden sticks approached their vehicle as it slowed for a pedestrian. Without hesitation the driver accelerated, nicking the woman in the crosswalk and leaving the assailants in their review mirrors.

Primrose met Romano Jenker in the darkened lobby of Mama Africa's restaurant. He was shorter than Primrose expected for some odd reason. Midforties, tan slacks, and a jacket covering an open neck white shirt with his ear plastered to his mobile. They awkwardly shook hands as Jenker concluded his call. They were led to a discreet table in the rear of the establishment.

"Good to finally meet you, Mr. Primrose. I have heard you are quite good at what you do. Before we get to our business, let's look at the menu."

They both ordered: lamb curry for Jenker and ostrich steak for Primrose. Black coffee was ordered for each. The waiter retreated.

Primrose began the conversation. "We will be working closely together over the next few weeks, so please call me Jerry."

Jenker's phone rang, and he ignored it. "Fine, and you should call me Romano. I am pleased to be working with such a professional."

The formalities completed, Romano reached into his inner jacket pocket and produced a leather portfolio containing both his passport on one side pocket and a flash drive wedged in the other. He passed the standard drive across the table. "Here is what we have so far. It's not much but should give you a head start." Primrose was stoic. He expected much more detail. He remained quiet and reserved and stared at his counterpart across the table.

The waiter brought the strong coffee and retreated to the kitchen. Romano took his first sip, and Jerry noticed a slight grin forming. "We need you to hack into the personal computer of one of China's leading political figures. Do it without being noticed and leaving no electronic footprint. We need it in less than two weeks. And, I might add, the stakes are extremely high." Romano paused as he took another sip. "The man we are targeting is named Mr. Mao Ling, and he is often referred to as the Chairman, given he sits on a number of joint-venture boards."

Of course Jerry expected this to be a cybercrime of some sort, but to pry past the security of the People's Republic of China was another thing entirely. Jerry put down his coffee cup in order to avoid his shaking hand exposing his trepidation.

The waiter returned with their lunch, refilled their coffee, and discreetly left the men to their business.

Jerry gathered himself. "The time frame will be difficult, but you certainly already recognized that. Allow me to review the thumb drive this afternoon. There can be no distractions from here forward. I will need a discreet Chinese interpreter."

"Done."

"I will need an interpreter who is technically savvy."

"Done."

"I will need access to some junior guy in their system who has even the most limited link to the periphery of their platform."

"Done."

"I will need more protected space on the cloud than I witnessed this morning."

"Done."

"I will need a thorough dossier on the individual we are targeting. Their business dealings, their families, their education, their travel, their mistresses, their banking, and their frailties."

"Done."

"All right; let's finish here with a chocolate desert, and then get me back to Aqua-Sian ASAP. I have a lot of work to do. I will get back to you later today with any further technical inputs I may need."

"Jerry, I am impressed. You are certainly the right guy for the job. I will cover all the ancillary details so you can concentrate on your work."

CHAPTER 12

Jerry opened the thumb drive he was given at the lunch meeting.

> Mr. Mao Ling, (Chairman), Age 49; Graduate Wuhan University 1994
> Graduate school: People's Military Academy 1996
> Retired Major, People's Army at age 44
> Member of the Communist Party, reporting directly to Executive Director Infrastructure, People's Court, Beijing, the Politburo
> He serves as chairman or voting director on the following ten joint-venture companies: Nanjing, Wuhan, and Tianjin. He is often referred to simply as the Chairman.

The Chairman's board résumé was impressive:

a) Great Wall Malting/Jiangxi—Nanjing
b) ABI Malting—Wuhan
c) General Electric NCC—Nanjing
d) White Cedar Semiconductor/Nanjing People's Office—Nanjing
e) Toyota/PICC—Wuhan
f) Harley Davidson & Nanjing Motors—Tianjin
g) Heavenly Hill/PRC Distillers—Nanjing
h) Bank of China/Morgan Stanley—Nanjing
i) Shandong Ltd./Bear Stearns—Nanjing
j) Provincial Engineering/Atlas of Atlanta Engineering—Nanjing

Married, one daughter, (Lu Sin);
Courtesan Miss Lin (known as Sparrow)
Primary residence: 29 Chan Han, Apt. 3 Nanjing, PRC
Personal computer—Hewlett Packard Model 3E-1600
Last known password: 3skWALL1362 #
Secondary residence: 14 Sundown, Beijing, PRC
Guanxi—Strong personal relationship with Mr. Xin of the Standing Committee of the Politburo.
Strengths: Party loyalty, intelligence, English-, French-, and Japanese-language skill set, Organizational skills, well-traveled, grasp of Western business practices. A superb mah-jongg player.
Weaknesses: Alcohol, young women, computer expertise, greed.

Jerry studied the dossier and began to draft his list of questions. The more he studied, the better he felt about the project. The fact the Party recognized Mao Ling's poor computer knowledge may prove to be the inside track to gaining access to his account. Jerry had witnessed other executives in other domains who dismissed personal computer safeguards. By 1700 hours the next afternoon, Jerry received his requested translator, who also was familiar with the central platform for the government server. They both ordered tea and began the detailed work. Jerry was impressed with his translator's expertise on the PRC system. Jerry learned this young guy had been passed over for promotion on numerous occasions when he worked at Central Information in Beijing. It seems the key supervisor there had a preference for either young or willing women or for his own relatives despite limited technical ability. The translator and PC expert was fired from his junior post after a heated disagreement with the supervisor on a security issue. Nonetheless, this disgruntled ex-employee was perfectly suited to the task. Given his direct experience with the platform, they created several algorithms exploring possible entry points into the massive Chinese government information system. They both worked side by side for the first fourteen hours on that first day. The following day it was another fourteen-hour marathon session together. Jerry became more and more enamored with the guy's intuition and expertise. On the third day, Jerry had them work through dinnertime. He surprised the translator by shutting off his powerful computer and requesting he do likewise. They retreated to the main living area. The two young girls from Jerry's first night at Aqua-Sian were lounging near the floor to ceiling windows overlooking the sea. Jerry nodded to his new assistant, referencing for him to make a choice. The young translator and PC expert chose the Russian blonde. Jerry sat next to the dark beauty and tapped the lights to their dim setting as Diana Kroll filled the room with a soft ballad.

Afterward the translator joined Jerry, in their workspace upstairs, as they continued to hack into the personal account of Mr. Mao Ling, the Chairman.

It was well past midnight when one minor success yielded to another. Their excitement grew with each building block falling into place as they deconstructed the security code. By 4:00 a.m. they had broached the platform's security and the personal ID used by Mr. Ling. This is all they needed. They found they could log into his personal account while he was online without his knowledge. They put their tea aside, and Jerry went to the bar to grab two beers. The translator and PC expert had already downloaded recent data from the personal PC to the data cloud space they had previously created before he returned with the beverages. Glasses clinked, and Jerry was already thinking about how he would spend his windfall gain. Both men eventually collapsed on the great room couches after their third beer.

The following afternoon, Romano Jenker reviewed the work with Jerry. He could not have been more pleased. They analyzed the official board documents from the ten joint-venture companies on which Mao Ling served as either a board member or chairman. Comparing that data with electronic bank transfers to Mr. Ling's (Chairman) offshore account revealed enough inconsistencies even a junior-league sleuth could figure out. The guy was a crook and not in a let's-skim-a bit-off-for-me sort of way.

The guy was big league. In just twenty-six transactions, they calculated he had defrauded the People's Republic of China of at least RMB 8,569,000, which was in excess of $1.2 million.

"Jerry, I knew you were the right guy for the job," Romano complimented.

"It was both a challenge and a pleasure," Jerry replied as he took another sip of his Coca Cola.

"I will have your open-return tickets to Europe delivered here by ten tomorrow morning. In the meantime, relax and enjoy the view," Romano Jenker said with a smile.

Romano left with the memory sticks that contained everything he needed. Jerry tossed out the remaining Coke in his glass and walked to the bar. He found one bottle of 1996 Heidsieck Brut Reserve and called for the Russian girl. Life could be a bitch.

CHAPTER 13

Romano had more than what he needed with the content of the memory sticks. Direct evidence existed of the Chairman stealing funds due to the federal government, and it was uncontroversial. The Chairman's appetite for the good life was catching up to him. Romano packaged the key elements of the electronic sting in an executive recap for the Standing Committee of the Politburo. Romano expected to be well compensated for his work. He was flying to Beijing tomorrow to personally meet with Mr. Xin, a senior member of the elite politburo controlling everything related to finance and economics in the country.

Romano thought of Mao's famous quotation from years ago: "The Party must always control the gun; the gun must never control the Party." Romano's flight to Beijing was delayed as the pilot skirted a line of severe thunderstorms.

The next morning Romano met with the diminutive Mr. Xin, who was wearing a Western-style suit. His office was Spartan and kept cool, and they exchanged pleasantries as tea was poured for them. When the assistant left the room, Romano produced the memory sticks and placed them next to Xin's steaming cup. "You will not need more than what is captured on these," he said as he tilted his head in a bow.

Mr. Xin's small hand encircled the memory sticks and placed them in an inside suit pocket. He sat stoically as his guest outlined the details of the Chairman's deception. The crimes ranged from accounting irregularities to tax fraud to cronyism. Mr. Xin did not ask any clarifying questions, which surprised Romano. When Romano had finished his expose,

Mr. Xin thanked him and had him escorted to a senior assistant's office down the hall. The assistant bowed deeply, offered tea, and got down to the business of transferring funds to Romano's offshore account.

Secretary Xin had more than enough evidence to have the Chairman arrested and most likely executed for crimes against the state. Nonetheless, Mr. Xin worried about appearances. He had hosted multiple banquets in Beijing and Shanghai with the Chairman as a featured guest. Any linkage to the inappropriate business with the Chairman must be avoided. The triad was the tool he could use to make this problem go away. He made the call and was promised the problem would be taken care of. The quasi-official relationship, between the senior leadership of the PRC government with the senior leaders of the well-organized triad, was not recognized by the West. One side enjoyed the power and prestige of leading 1.3 billion people. The other side enjoyed the fruits money could buy if they agreed to work in the shadows.

CHAPTER 14

Predawn over the eastern foothills of Nanjing spilled like an egg broken over the side of a cast-iron skillet. The gray-blue clouds filtered the oncoming morning as if to withhold a secret. Mr. Mao Ling was often referred to as the Chairman. He was always satisfied and rather calm after each tryst with Sparrow. He was taller at six feet than your typical Chinese. His face was as round as a pizza-pie dish. His eyes were two gray slits in the fleshy dough. Today he would wear his shiny gray Western-style suit. His nails were dirty and dress shoes always a bit scuffed.

Mr. Mao's driver would pick him up precisely at seven under the portico of his apartment complex. The new driver, Miss Lin (Sparrow), showed no emotion as she glided the state-owned automobile with darkened windows to his curb. She wore her customary white gloves and a state-supplied uniform that simply could not hide her attractive frame. Easily fifteen years his junior with no Party status, he found her captivating. When this was all over, there would be time for Miss Lin—perhaps as an escort to the City of Dreams Casino in beautiful Macau. His mid-level government position, with responsibility for employment figures, gave him the perfect cover. The government role was envied by his old classmates from Jiangsu University as their roles fell somewhere between traffic cop and accountant.

The Chairman's political connections had landed him a prestigious role in the People's Republic of China. He was given an apartment in central Nanjing with five rooms and heating that often worked. His career had flat lined briefly when two benefactors were caught engaged in *wubi*, which could be loosely translated as "cooking the books" for a joint-venture manufacturing company in Tianjin. One was jailed until his case would be heard from the magistrate in two years. The senior man was executed for tax fraud against the state. The Chairman was successful in distancing himself from the fray. After that fiasco, his career had taken off. He became Chairman of the board for several joint-venture companies and a voting director on several others. He reported directly to a senior man within the politburo. The success of each of these Western-led joint-venture companies translated into significant tax revenues for the party. In each company the Communist Party held between 49 percent ownership all the way down to just one percent of the shares. Nonetheless, the Chairman exerted what he liked to call "local oversight" in each company. The powers that be in Beijing were pleased.

Mao's inclinations were aligned with activities not fully supported by his midlevel salary. He enjoyed mao-tai, sexy young women, gambling, and American jazz. An internship during his university years in Baton Rouge, Louisiana, gave him the bug for the unique music. In order to afford the luxuries, he began to leverage his English-speaking skills and government connections to maximize value for the Nanjing Triad. He considered this simply a business accommodation—not criminal, although the triad was recognized as the Chinese mob. He was only supplying a service between the wealthy Western companies having joint ventures with the county government and those same companies who wanted everything commercial and political to go smoothly. The sophisticated mob activities focused on prostitution, money laundering, and extortion of foreign joint-venture companies located in the new enterprise-free zones. Mr. Mao Ling's expertise was the later.

The 1995 gray Toyota Camry edged through the crowded main drag of Jiangsu city, Miss Lin (Sparrow) dodging the countless bicycles, pedestrians, and the occasional motorbike. The meeting had been hastily arranged. Mr. Mao, who also served as Chairman of the malting company, was annoyed as he was scheduled to depart early the next morning for Hong Kong.

The car swung through a loop in the road and eased to a stop at the side entrance of the Xuan Wu Hotel. A very short man in a drab brown oversized suit rushed to the door escorting the Chairman through the lobby. Mr. Ping, a junior executive from the malt plant, joined in the poorly lit lobby, which smelled of broiled fish and garlic vegetables. An old unattractive woman escorted the men to the second level, depositing them in a nearly dark meeting room. The Chairman shivered in the unheated room sitting opposite the younger Mr. Ping. The attendant brought steaming green tea in large glasses with ceramic tops and left the room. The Chairman studied his young protégé from the malting plant. He was rather peculiar with his black Coke-bottle thick glasses with milky eyes detached behind. He wore a dark suit with his long jet-black hair swept straight back, which outlined his narrow skull and hollow cheeks. He spoke at first quietly with deference toward the senior man, but as he told the tale, the voice lowered an octave building with confidence.

Mr. Ping thanked the Chairman for his valuable time, apologizing for the meeting being called on short notice and in subpar surroundings. He continued as his eyes held the older gentleman's.

"Mr. Chairman, it regrets me to bring forward the proven facts for your thoughtful consideration."

"Get to the point, Mr. Ping; I am a very busy man."

"Mr. Chairman, there are those you trust who have betrayed that trust and placed one of your more profitable businesses at great risk." To underscore his point, Mr. Ping paused to lift the ceramic top from his tea, the steam causing his glasses to fog over. He reached for the white pressed pocket square and cleaned his glasses, as his voice became sharp as fractured glass. "Your treasurer and controller have stolen your money, dishonored your leadership, and schemed to overthrow you as head of the company."

The Chairman stared at Mr. Ping. This Mr. Ping was never one of his favorites. A graduate of Wuhan University, he was recommended by his cousin in Beijing. The unspoken accommodation being a good position for Ping would result in ease of securing export malt permits, worth hundreds of thousands of renminbi. The Chairman watched Ping clean his glasses. Ping's eyes darted around the darkened room as if to locate an exit hole. "This is discouraging news, Mr. Ping, having serious consequences. What proof do you bring?"

Mr. Ping reached into his briefcase to produce a green-bound document. Using two hands, he lowered his head and passed the tome to the Chairman.

In the dim light, the Chairman studied the document over the next twenty minutes without saying a word. "This is all I need for now," he said, rolling the papers into the tube and abruptly getting up from his chair. "My heart is heavy; my trip tomorrow morning will be cancelled. Meet me at the plant offices twelve hours from now. Not a word of this to anyone. Do you understand?"

"Yes, Mr. Chairman, as you wish," Ping said with a slight grin on his face.

CHAPTER 15

Mr. Shu, the malting complex treasurer, and his wife lay atop their single blanket on this cool, not yet cold, early November evening and drifted off to sleep. The upcoming New Year would provide for a nice cash bonus and much earned time off from keeping the books at the malt plant. Much later, awakened by muffled voices and a scraping sound at his apartment door, he reached for his glasses and moved slowly to the door, his arthritic ankles refusing to bend. The dim green fluorescent clock registers 2:55 a.m. On hearing his name whispered by a familiar voice, he opened the door. Mr. Xie's large head and body virtually blocked all the limited light from the simple bare bulb fifteen meters down the hallway. Mr. Xie, his controller at the plant, mumbled something he could not understand. Rubbing the sleep from his eyes, he stepped into the hallway and closed the door to allow his wife to sleep. Readjusting his glasses, he looked up to his large friend for some explanation. As he did, strong arms wrestled and locked his behind and a knee came from behind to rest in the small of his back. A third man stepped from the shadows, smaller, younger with greasy black hair. The beating begins. First a blow to his left rib cage, but a reflexive turn produces a glancing blow. The young man followed with four quick blows to his midsection, which left him gasping for breath. The next several moments became a blur. The man behind thrashed his head against the cement wall. The humid air around him evaporated and the lack of oxygen squeezed his head in a vice grip. Eyeglasses cut his nose and upper cheek and the world turned upside down. The small man was swinging again and all his blows connected solidly, the final one puncturing his left eardrum. Clear fluid mixed with crimson streams from his scalp. The man behind released him—a ragdoll on the cold hallway. The smaller man retreated, then spun, and kicked hard just below his left ear, jerking him violently. The two triad thugs retreated down the hallway shadows. Mr. Xie stooped on one knee and whispered in his good ear, "You must grant me this one *renging* (favor). Do not discuss our accounting considerations with our Chairman." Wheezing as he stood up, Mr. Xie mumbled, "I am sorry, my friend, but things are spinning out of control—silence your tongue."

Mr. Shu lay on the cold cement, the dry heaves jerking his chin from a pool of blood. Mrs. Shu cautiously opened the door to see her husband crushed against the wall in a fetal position. She rushed to cradle his head. A series of rapid-fire questions: "Who were those men? Where are you hurt? What trouble have you brought upon our family? Were those government men? Where are your glasses? What can I get you? Please, please let's get you back in the apartment."

Mr. Shu heard little from his wife and the complete deafness in one ear and severe headache disorientated him. One thing was very clear and he would remember—"silence your tongue."

Mr. Shu was overweight. As the state's representative on three separate joint-venture boards, Shu had little incentive to engage in a healthy lifestyle. He drank too much, smoked too much, and loved the banquet circuit associated with his government job. The attack had left both him and his wife shaken. She had asked repeatedly what he knew that could bring such violence to their home. He had shaken his head as if to say he had no idea, with the bandage pressed tightly against his damaged ear. But Mr. Shu understood completely. The next morning, he must see Mr. Mao Ling, the Chairman.

Mr. Xie's stomach was contracting, and he was having difficulty breathing between the dry heaves in this filthy back ally. He never dreamed the late-night meeting with Mr. Shu would turn violent. He had expected the two triad businessmen to warn of the pending audit—get your books in order and so on. It was known, Mr. Ping, their superior at the plant, tended to move some of his travel and entertainment budget to direct manufacturing. Not a big deal—a warning perhaps. Now it had escalated. Boy, he wished he could catch his breath. What a mess. Mr. Shu would have to remain silent.

Mr. Shu and Mr. Xie stood before the Chairman's desk. Both controller and treasurer were ashen faced and haunted. They looked guilty. The Chairman patted the rolled green document on his desk without a word. Mr. Xie was first to speak. "Mr. Chairman, we both come to—" He was silenced by Mr. Shu tapping his arm.

With downcast eyes, Shu simply said, "We have dishonored you, Mr. Chairman." Both men's shoulders slumped as if their bones were weighing them down, standing side-by-side, awaiting the executor's sword.

"But why?" the Chairman asked, with genuine concern in his voice. "I have given you impressive positions, company cars, nice apartments, and expense accounts. You have dishonored me, dishonored the Party, and brought dishonor to your family names."

Mr. Xie attempted to interrupt. "Our tax strategies may have been aggressive and—"

"Be quiet, you country fool. Lay down your company badges and your credit cards. You are nothing to me now." With that he motioned for two security guards to enter his office. "Remove these traitors from company property—they are not allowed to stop at their former offices; they are not allowed to speak with anyone. Get the swine out of my sight."

CHAPTER 16

The Chairman was a proud man. He traced his Han ancestry back to 1355. His uncle Zhu Yuanzhang had defeated the Mongols in northern China and established his rule in Nanjing. As his private car rolled out of the factory entrance, he was contemplating the necessary story to placate his handlers in Beijing. He sounded tired on the car phone. "The two top financial guys are gone. I will require you here immediately to clean up this tax mess. I am headed to the Party's headquarters to clean up the political damage either caused or yet to be caused."

As the car sped along the freeway, he thought more of his elaborate family heritage. He claimed to have a blood relative in the court of Taiping Tianguo, which ruled the Heavenly Capital of Nanjing in 1864. These ruling elite predated the Chinese communist movement. Its leaders claimed divine inspiration and preached of both a personal salvation and a theocratic collectivism. The Chairman smiled to himself. This past blend of utopian Confucianism and Old Testament Christianity focused the masses on extermination of demons and social harmony. Keep the masses fed and busy, he mused, not unlike today. Today Nanjing was home to over nine million people. The enterprise-free zones that ringed the city had encouraged significant Western investment. All Western investors needed were connections, or *guanxi*, which the Chairman could provide for a fee.

His Beijing handlers would nod with appreciation when told of the swift terminations. He was above the fray. His hands remained clean. He could be trusted. Now he had to rush to another joint-venture meeting in Tianjin in the north of China. He was not overly pleased to promote Mr.

Ping as deputy general manager, but he had little time to do otherwise. Besides the move was temporary until he could evaluate a list of qualified candidates in a month or two. He nodded farewell to Ping and rushed off.

Ping watched as the Chairman was taken to the airport in the company limo, driven by the captivating Miss Lin. He lit up a cigarette and sat back to review his latest good fortune. He was now in charge of the largest malting plant in the country—it may be officially temporary for now—but he would see that change. The country's largest brewers would be securing their malt supply from him. Ping reflected on his rivals back in Hubei Province. He wished they could see him now. He had come so far since growing up in a rural region of Hubei. His family belonged to the Hui Chinese and was looked down upon by the majority Hans. His family spoke Jin-yu Chinese rather than the typical Mandarin. His father had a difficult job in one of the many coal mines. Ping watched his father and cringed on the likelihood of following him to the mines after his schooling had completed. Ping's father came home from work every day filthy from head to toe with the black grime. Typically he would drink strong beer and harass Ping for being such a bookworm. Frustrated by his lot in life, his father would beat Ping occasionally with a stick.

Ping's mother, being Hui-Chinese, took work wherever she could find it. Hospital laundry and short stints at the city sanitation department were most prominent. She never interfered when Ping was being disciplined with the stick. In many ways she ignored him.

Ping was smart but not overly so. He learned to speak Mandarin to better fit in. He grew his hair much longer than his peers in order to hide a birthmark on the back of his neck. He studied fairly well, but resorting to cheating was preferred. He was not particularly large or muscular, but he was mean and very clever. Throughout his early schooling, he lied, cheated, and intimidated others. He charmed instructors. When at all possible, he would blame others, and when situations called for adulation, he would take full credit. He sprung traps for other students and traps for the younger teachers. He found a way to cheat on entrance exams, which found him in Wuhan studying mechanical engineering. Even over the New Year break at school, he never left school to visit his parents. Somehow he made it through the curriculum and landed a lower-mid manager's position at the joint-venture malting plant in Nanjing.

Now, through a series of incredible circumstances, he found himself as the acting general manager of the malting complex, which included sizable barley receiving silos, world-class manufacturing, an energy complex driven by coal and malt sprouts (a by-product of the malting process), and a finished product-packaging plant. He had well over four hundred employees, some of whom were single women looking to get ahead or at least get a better assignment in the company.

CHAPTER 17

Mr. Ping sat smugly in his new heated office inhaling his cigarette with a wet rattle. With Mr. Xie and Mr. Shu having left in disgrace, he had moved into the much-larger office space at the malting plant. The Chairman had left the site in a hurry, but just as he departed, he gave Ping the title of deputy general manager—a huge promotion. What should be his first order of business?

Ping called a staff meeting for all first shift plant supervisors, office staff, and laboratory workers. It was a large group so he held it in the cafeteria. The large room smelled of fish and grain dust. After everyone was seated, Ping stood in front of the salaried group cleaning his glasses. He kept cleaning them until everyone had settled down and the side conversations died away.

Sweeping his dark hair back with both hands, Ping stared back at the crowded room through his thick glasses. Most in the room did not know Mr. Ping or what his role was in the company. Some had seen him walking around the facility. Some women in the office thought he was a bit creepy.

"My name is Mr. Ping. The Chairman was just here and has appointed me deputy GM of the malting complex." Ping paused there and let the news sink in. Immediately there was a murmur across the crowded room. Ping understood theatre and allowed the sidebar whispering to continue for a moment.

"Mr. Xie and Mr. Shu are no longer employed here," he stated flatly. Again there was a buzz around the room. These two guys had been very senior in the company. They were referred to as "moneymen" by just about everyone. "A few more changes are necessary for our continued success." Now you could have heard a pin drop in the crowded room. "There are a few individuals among us who have not truly committed to our goals." With that prelude, Ping selected individuals to come forward and face the main group. He had three from the laboratory; two plant supervisors, one from security, and one from the transportation group come forward. When all were properly assembled, Ping stated, "These fellow workers are clearly not committed to our communal success and are released of their duties effective immediately. Security, I want these people escorted off the site."

This was unprecedented. Once selected to be employed by a joint-venture company, the individual was assured a great wage and spectacular benefits. There was another buzz across the crowded room. Many were thinking—could Mr. Ping do this? Did he have that kind of authority? Apparently he did. Ping's stature and importance were solidified in that brief moment.

"Please return to your duties." Ping smiled and returned to his heated office. Nothing like letting the masses understand whom to fear.

As dusk settled over the Nanjing factory walls, Ping's face was hidden as if by a black cloak. "Call for my car and Miss Lin the driver," Ping demanded his assistant.

Miss Lin (Sparrow) and the company's black SUV arrived minutes later at the steps of the four-floor brick headquarters. Ping climbed in the back and barked the destination as Hotel Ian. He studied her from his roost in the luxury leather-trimmed rear seat. Miss Lin, with her perfect posture, her perfect figure, and those sexy white silk gloves with the lace trim, now reported to him. Ping lit another cigarette and stared out the darkened windows to the Nanjing facade of the many family businesses lining the Boulevard Hankou. The students were rushing between classes on the other side of the street. Ping thought back on his University days filled with long political discussions late into the night, full ashtrays and empty Tsingtao bottles.

Miss Lin pulled under the hotel's portico. Bellmen rushed to open the back door. Before disembarking, Ping turned to Miss Lin and said she should join him upstairs in the Wild Man lounge after parking. He smiled to himself. Greed and fear—Ping understood both far better than most. Tonight would be a special night as the new deputy general manager of the multinational joint-venture company. He requested a back table on the second level overlooking the expansive bar and dance floor. She arrived shortly thereafter with white gloves held in one hand as she entered the club. Her skirt swung in perfect rhythm with her confident stride. He caught her eye, and she slid next to him in the red booth.

The two triad thugs approached the newly appointed deputy general manager. In a highly deferential manner, the smaller man addressed Mr. Ping. "The financial management personnel at the malt house will cause no further problems. We expect no further adverse influence from either man. Upon returning to their apartments today, they found all their belongings on the curb. Their bank accounts have been drawn down to nothing. They will never find work in this city." The small thug confidently slapped his black gloves against his thigh and with the nod of his head motioned for his partner to withdraw with him.

Mr. Ping smoothed back his greasy hair with both hands. Pleased with himself, his devious plan, and the unexpected promotion, he turns to Sparrow. "Here is a key for my room upstairs. Remove your clothes and wear only your white gloves. I will be along shortly."

Ping ordered another mao-tai, sipping the strong sorghum-based beverage and enjoying its overpowering fragrance. Two rather tall Nanjing ladies sat on both sides of him, their eyes forward to the dance floor and their hands gently resting on his thighs. Ping dismissed the courtesans and walked confidently to his room. Miss Lin sat on the corner of the bed with only the requisite white gloves. "Come here, my dear; I think you know what I would like."

A hard rain began to fall and the wind whipped the moisture against the darkened windowpane. Miss Lin felt her tears cross her cheeks as she once again bent her head for the task at hand. Thoughts of her late father filled her head, yet her performance was worthy of a Hollywood Oscar.

With the Chairman in Beijing on business for the next few weeks and no appointed general manager in sight, Ping was the senior executive on site. He planned to take full advantage of that fact. He would replace the two financial guys with men of his own. He would use whatever means necessary to clean up all past due debts from small brewers. He planned to intimidate the European joint venture just down the street from the plant into either a marketing partnership or an outright sale. He knew the Chairman received a monthly envelope from accounting—he would find out what that amount typically had been. He would double that bribe, and the envelope would come from his office. Ping would use his influence to lower their current cost of barge freight on the Yangzi River and do likewise for their over-the-road freight for outbound finished goods. Upon the Chairman's return, Ping would appear as an executive they could ill afford to lose. Each evening, Ping would call for the driver Sparrow to take him to the Wild Bunch, and after several drinks he would require her to join him upstairs. Ping was a small, mean man. He required Sparrow to perform outlandish sexual treats for his sick entertainment. Afterward he would have her drive him home to his wife and daughter in the hills to the southeast of the city. Typically he would have her come into his apartment and have two briefcases overflowing with paperwork for her to take back to his office. He made a point to demean her in front of his wife and any neighbors still awake at that hour. Sparrow's resentment grew with each passing night and a plan began to form.

CHAPTER 18

Jerry Primrose woke early before the sun danced across the Indian Ocean. He had money that needed to be laundered for Herr Reins. He used the proprietary encryptions to log in and comfortably placed the earpiece. There would be no need for the earpiece, but he was old school. He preferred to actually hear the clicks and electronic buzz as ones and zeroes screeched across cyberspace.

Primrose used his proprietary algorithms to connect with the Faisal Bank branch in Lahore, Pakistan. Even he was surprised at the ease to circumvent the electronic security. Once in, he focused on the big prize: access to the commercial real-estate accounts at the Dubai Islamic Bank Pakistan. As he expected, security was sophisticated but no hill for a climber. Three hours later he had cracked into the First Islamic Bank. In the light of Allah's commands, Islamic finance was purported to create a fair economic system. Riba (interest) was strictly prohibited in all its forms and kinds. Primrose, however, knew of one potential loophole. His phantom account would surrender Saudi oil field bogus leases in exchange for rupees, which immediately would be converted to UAE dirham over the Internet and subsequently to gold bullion held in Frankfurt, Germany, under the name Herr Reins. Given all the preset accounts and passwords, the Islamabad bank preformed the services in a matter of minutes, and the subsequent transactions occurred in milliseconds without any human intervention whatsoever. Herr Reins would be pleased. Primrose turned off his computer. His unique skill set would be amply rewarded with the completion of phase two.

His Dutch flight banked over the Indian Ocean. Abu-Zarqawi recognized Seal Island as the flight descended over False Bay on its path to Cape Town International. The Al-Qaida operative returned his stare to the back of the European's head two rows up. The overweight Caucasian disgusted him. He must have consumed all of three meals and enough liquor to make most men unsteady. Abu adjusted his *shimagle*, which cast a shadow across his features as the first-class passengers disembarked.

Customs were perfunctory given his exceptionally convincing documentation. The nondescript automobile picked him up just outside baggage. He and the driver did not exchange words. Seventy minutes later he had checked in at the posh hotel overlooking the harbor. He had always wished to be called into Al-Qaida's service as an international operative, one that struck at the heart of Western heathen society. However, given his grade-point average at the University of Islamabad and his curious nature, he was selected early on as a moneyman for the cause. This trip to South Africa, his sixth in so many months, was similar to the others. Over the next several days, he would be moving funds within multiple accounts to cleanse them of any connection with the royal families and various sympathetic governments, prior to an electronic exchange to the small, regional Faisal Bank in Lahore, Pakistan. He hoped another successful mission like this would elevate his stature in the hierarchy back in Islamabad.

Herr Reins made the introductions through a cryptic message board they both were instructed to use while in Cape Town. Jerry Primrose happened to catch it first. He was to meet Abu-Zarqawi this evening at 1900 hours in the lobby of the Cape Grace hotel on West Quay. Primrose was familiar with the boutique hotel and it's richly appointed lobby and main floor bar. He clicked on accept. Across town, Zarqawi was deciphering the same e-message and double clicking to confirm receipt of the message and his acceptance of the rendezvous.

The two men, from different parts of the world, would be meeting for the first time. Zarqawi adjusted his gray and white shimagle as he waited for Mr. Primrose in the waterfront hotel lobby with a view of the revolving front entrance. Zarqawi thought he recognized the overweight European, as the single man in his midthirties strode across the thick carpeting past the check-in desk and directly toward him.

As he rose from his lobby chair, the European extended his hand, saying, "You must be the banker Herr Reins has told me so much about."

Abu-Zarqawi shook the man's hand welcoming him to South Africa and indicated for the Westerner to take a seat opposite him at a small table. Immediately a hotel staff member appeared with glasses and a pot of steaming tea.

"No, thanks," Primrose said to the wait staff. "Make mine a Maker's Mark neat. Thank you."

Primrose studied the other man—younger than he would have thought and shorter too. The rag on his head and shoulders was of a certain cut that may have suggested royalty and the robe traditional for the Pakistan region. They waited for his drink to arrive and then clicked glasses before their first sip. "I understand you recently arrived at the Cape," offered Primrose as an icebreaker.

"I just arrived this morning actually. I normally stay across town. This is my first time at this hotel."

"I am not familiar with it either. Please call me Jerry. May I call you Abu?"

"Yes, you may," was the formal response from the Pakistani.

"I have an international client who wishes to remain anonymous. He has excess US securities, Canadian dollars, and German marks, which he would like to exchange for UAE dirham and Pakistani rupee. We believed, given your expertise in this area, you may have principles that may naturally wish to offset this forex opportunity," Jerry said as he took another sip of the fire-water.

"You may have come to the right source, Mr. Primrose."

"No, no. Call me Jerry. May I add this transaction would come with associated fees, which would all fall to your side of the ledger?

"What grand total amount are we talking here?" enquired the short young man from Pakistan.

"It should fall in the range of thirty-five to thirty-eight million US dollar equivalents, I should think," Primrose speculated as he doodled on his cocktail napkin.

"I can give you a firm exchange-rate quote, including all fees by tomorrow morning, if that fits with you."

"Perfect; here is my direct mobile line in South Africa," Jerry said as he passed a business card to the visitor.

"Let's enjoy the lamb here; I've heard it is spectacular."

After dinner the young man from Pakistan returned to his hotel room, logged on, and sent an encrypted message to his lead contact in Lahore. "My principal in South Africa wants to convert securities and cash in US dollars and German marks to Pakistani rupee. Coupled with a rich fee structure, we should net nearly one million dollars with the transaction. I will complete the necessary paperwork at my end. Please notify our leader of this windfall profit." Abu-Zarqawi closed his computer and smiled. He could do more for their cause than any single fighter with a PK-47.

CHAPTER 19

The Chairman's appetite for the good life was never satiated. He continued to siphon off money from each of the ten boards he served on. The CFOs of each firm recognized this as a cost of doing business. For the first time, he was getting some minor pushback from the chief financial officer of the malting company. He was told a Mr. Alex Cutter, who also served on the board of directors, was enquiring further than would be normal on some questionable line items on the quarterly financials. The Chairman did not need this sort of scrutiny. He would deal with this nuisance in due time.

Sinatra's soft melody playing in the background seemed odd to Candy Medford in Brussels's Drug Opera pub, located in the city center. A bit touristy, she thought, but looking around the dimly lit establishment, she realized it was simply a very local watering hole. She sat back nursing a Duval in one of the back booths. A simple tap on her right shoulder froze her. Without looking up, she first could feel Herr Reins's hot garlic breath on her ear. She sat looking straightforward and not at him, her index finger circling the beer glass.

"Phase one has successfully concluded. Moving forward to phase two will require you to collect a tourist-class ticket in box four eighty at the usual location. Your initial destination will be Chicago. Dress as a tourist. Go to the Chicago Mercantile Exchange visitor balcony on October third."

Candy Medford was a professional assassin. The blonde did not look the part. At five foot six and a half, Candy could easily be mistaken for a schoolmarm, albeit an attractive one. Too short for being an international glamor model, she nonetheless turned young men's heads as she walked by on the weekends in Tel Aviv, wearing skimpy flowered shorts and a simple tank top.

She had completed Mossad's airborne training at an early age and graduated at the top of her class. Given her uncle's influence, she was given an exemption to apply for acceptance in the Israeli special-forces training program. Candy was accepted. The grueling expectations weeded out all but the top 15 percent of her class. She was the only female. Upon completion of the ninety-day training, she served six years on a counterterrorism team.

The team had received international recognition during her last year in uniform. An ISIS four-man team had hijacked an Israeli commercial airliner and taken it to the Entebbe Airport in Uganda. Many commentators would later draw similarities to the raid on Entebbe in 1976. In this case, the Israeli jet had 216 passengers, including one supreme-court judge and two legislators from the Knesset, their legislative branch of the government. Candy had volunteered to approach the terrorists dressed as a civilian and appear as the go-between for the Israeli government. Her backup was the balance of her team strategically placed on the terminals rooftop and nearby hangers. Each had their scope trained on the aircraft. Candy had climbed the stairs to the front compartment and waited on the top platform for the ISIS spokesperson. Two of the terrorists emerged from the front-cabin doorway with one hostage being pushed forward. Both ironically carried Israeli Uzis.

In one fluid motion, Candy grabbed the neckline of the hostage's dress and violently pushed back and to the side. This motion caused the one terrorist, who sported a whispery beard, to lose his balance and trip backward. Simultaneously, she released the combat blade from its sheath on her forearm, which sprung to her right hand. The serrated knife cut cleanly through the second terrorist's throat. He dropped his weapon and both hands went to his gaping wound. *Pop-pop-pop*, the sound of snipers' shots rang into the cockpit, killing the hooded terrorist leader. Candy had moved in a step closer to wispy-beard-man but her knife thrust was blocked by the up-thrust of his machine gun. More sniper fire could be heard all around her. She countered with a head butt and kick to the spleen. The young terrorist fell, and she thrust the blade home just above the collarbone. The last hijacker was seen from the sniper's viewpoint as racing down the center aisle toward the back of the plane. Two Israeli marksmen would later take credit for the shot that brought him down as they lead him through the passenger windows. No hostages were injured; she and her team were national heroes.

Upon her distinguished honorable discharge from the service, Candy had inherited a sizable amount from her one uncle and settled into a comfortable life in Tel Aviv. She became an accomplished assassin, capable of discreetly eliminating those unwanted. Her carefree lifestyle was her best camouflage from authorities.

She worked for herself and was available to the highest bidder. Herr Reins had used her before and contacted her directly for this assignment. He leaned in closer and gave the verbal instructions.

"When the grain markets open, look for a blond man in a purple smock with a badge reading MHA. From the floor of the exchange, he will glance up to you in the visitors' gallery. Should he signal with an open hand, you will proceed to Nanjing, China, or should he signal with a closed fist, you will proceed to Singapore. Await further instructions in either case via our chat-room thirty-three on e-CAY."

Upon securing further electronic instructions, Candy found herself three days later dressed in simply cut tan slacks, a light green blouse, and scuffed black flats. She added white-rimmed eyeglasses and hair pulled into a severe ponytail. To complete the ruse, she added the mouthpiece, which gave both a grayish cast and overbite, hiding her perfect white smile behind someone who lived hard and dirty. Her smudged mascara was applied as if by a blind courtesan. The eight-hour flight to Chicago was on time. She stretched her back and legs in the aisle way in the back of the plane as passengers in the front exited. A smelly man behind her pressed forward with his pelvis on her buttocks. He leaned forward to whisper in her ear. She took a step forward and ignored him. This coach-class travel had to stop.

Candy shed the facade after checking into the Four Seasons Hotel, only blocks from the CME building. The concierge arranged for a light lunch of fruit, canapés, a dark-chocolate bar and sparkling mineral water delivered to her suite. Candy decrypted the message that was left on the silver lunch tray, giving her more detailed instructions for tomorrow's rendezvous at the CME. Comfortable with the necessary details for tomorrow's visitors-gallery session, she called down to the in-house spa and reserved a two-hour facial and massage.

The Four Seasons does a wonderful job with their spa treatments. Candy sipped water spiked with melon in the relaxation room after her session. She wore the hotel's cashmere robe and assigned footwear. A young male attendant approached to refill her glass. Candy crossed her legs and looked the attendant straight in the eyes.

"Thank you, but I am fine with the hydration taken and do not require more. I do, however, have a nagging ache in my lower back that seems to have gotten a bit worse."

"Shall we have one of our therapists come out when they are freed up? I am sure they will find the time to address the issue while you are still here." The attendant, most likely mid-to-late twenties, retained eye contact with her. He was in incredible physical shape with piercing blue eyes and a shag of longish hair falling over his right eye. He said no more. He held the water pitcher and stared back at her.

"That will not be necessary," Candy said without blinking.

The attendant mentally measured this older woman as a ten. She had auburn hair cascading down across shoulders, which could have been drawn by a classic Renaissance painter. A petite nose split to emerald eyes, high cheekbones, and a strong chin. Her shape was hourglass perfection. A small reddish birthmark just above her left eye was partially hidden by her bangs. This slight imperfection had the impact of underscoring her overall beauty. Her accent was difficult to place—European boarding school mixed with a southern US drawl. She moved with an easiness that comes with extreme confidence.

"My shift is completed in the next twenty minutes; perhaps I could be of some service immediately thereafter." The attendant stared back at her and for the first time grinned in an "aw shucks" kind of way. "I am not a certified technician, but I have learned on the job and may be of some personal assistance," he said with a degree of confidence in his voice.

"That would be splendid. I appreciate the gesture. I am staying in room four-three-seven-zero. Shall we say in twenty to twenty-five minutes?"

"I will bring a few of our lotions that dispense a measure of heat that I am sure you will like," he said while maintaining direct eye contact.

"Great. I will expect you then prior to the dinner hour."

"It may be easier if you kept just the robe on," he said rather matter-of-factly.

"I'd planned to," she said as she gathered up her reading materials and headed for the spa's exit.

The sex was satisfying. She found what the locker room attendant lacked in creativity, he made up for in stamina. Twenty minutes later she tipped him as if she was still in the spa, and he took that as a signal to leave her room.

CHAPTER 20

The signal from the floor of the commodity-mercantile exchange was an open-hand gesture. Candy was on a flight to Nanjing via Shanghai the next afternoon. She once again flew coach class and revisited her tourist persona. She was picked up at the airport by one of the Chairman's cars and whisked off to the Xuan hotel downtown Nanjing. Candy found it curious the driver was a woman, which was not normal for state vehicles. Also curious were the formal white gloves worn by the attractive competent driver.

Later that same evening, Candy Medford was met by the Chairman in the executive lounge on the twenty-sixth floor of her hotel. They found a discreet table off to the side.

"Ms. Medford, I am pleased you were able to make the trip on such short notice," the Chairman said rather formally using his English-speaking skills. "I understand you have made initial contact with our Mr. Alex Cutter."

"I have, sir. We shared a drink at an airport lounge."

"What were your first impressions, if I may ask?" asked the Chairman as he motioned for the waiter.

Smiling a bit, Candy Medford responded, "He was an egotistical jerk, if I may be so blunt."

Giving their drink orders to the waiter and then motioning him away, the Chairman smiled back. "He is self-confident, I'll give you that. You must know Mr. Cutter and his company have invested rather heavily in Nanjing, and he has been a friend of the Party since selecting Nanjing for their factory nearly nine years ago. I have sat on their board since its inception."

"I am sure Mr. Cutter is a good businessman. That notwithstanding, what would you like done?" she asked in a very businesslike tone as the waiter brought their drinks.

"It's quite simple, my dear. I want Mr. Cutter killed," he stated rather flatly and took a sip of his beverage. "I have no restrictions to how or where. I do have one restriction, and that it is to be done within the next fortnight. "

Candy began, "That should not be—"

"Pardon me, I was not finished," the Chairman cut her off. "This is a highly professional dangerous man we are talking about, and speaking frankly, I did not expect a woman to get this assignment when I spoke with Herr Reins."

Candy was seething inside but was professional enough not to let it show. She listened to the Chairman's litany of characteristics he would have chosen for the assassin. When he had clearly finished, she spoke with complete deference overlaid with a subtle confidence.

"I am sure the Chairman recalls the successful mission at the offshore oil rig in the Yellow Sea less than a year ago," she said without losing eye contact.

"Of course, I do. It was important to remove the Danish engineer who challenged my requirements. I recall the tragic accident, which did not impede our joint-venture negotiations at the time. It was well planned and executed," the Chairman said as he placed his drink back down.

"My mission." She paused. "And it was completed solo."

"Impressive certainly," he replied. "I was not aware you had silenced one of our international critiques. Well done."

The Chairman shifted in his seat and leaned forward across the small cocktail table. "Cutter is no intellectual; he is a lethal weapon, and he proved it once again in Ireland."

"Certainly you recall the triad leader with a strangle hold on Upper Mongolia's mineral deposits."

"Yes and the circle of security he had around him at all times," the Chairman responded as he again leaned back in his chair.

"Another solo mission, and by the way, I froze my ass off," she said, switching to English.

"Impressive indeed for such a young woman," the Chairman complimented her in a meaningful way. "I believe you can handle Mr. Cutter. If it appears to be an accident, all the better. Don't let anything get in your way."

"I can assure you, Mr. Chairman; Mr. Cutter will not be an irritant any longer." With that, she nodded in deference to the Chairman and left.

The Chairman watched her distinctive sway as she departed and motioned for the check. The evening was still early. He called his security chief and arranged for a woman masseuse/companion to meet him in his suite in thirty minutes.

CHAPTER 21

The nonstop first-class ticket on Singapore Airlines would deposit Sparrow in San Francisco for a much-anticipated meeting with her mentor from years ago.

Upon clearing customs and entering the welcome hall, she recognized him instantly. From a side angle, she noted his natural curls of reddish brown hair, turning gray now at the temples. The athletic frame remained, though almost two decades had separated them. He turned, and she caught his clear blue eyes and reassuring smile. He wore faded black jeans, work boots, and a heavy brown bulky sweater with a wide collar covering a pale-blue work shirt.

Her high heels clicked against the tile floor in a rhythmic cadence as she approached him. The cadence quickened with just ten meters separating them. Sparrow threw her arms around his neck hugging him more as a lover than one who had mentored her as a young woman.

Alex Cutter had not personally witnessed the transformation of lovely girl to stunning woman until now. They had been separated by more than nine years. Her jet-black long hair was held back with a stylish red headband. Her girlish figure had been replaced with a woman's hourglass shape. High cheekbones, perfect complexion, and startlingly dark eyes completed the picture, which he wished to freeze frame in his memory.

Cutter hugged her back but not nearly as passionately. "Alex, oh Alex, I am so happy to see you," she said, if slightly out of breath. "You look great."

He brushed a strand of hair from her face and looked deep into her dark pools. "Sparrow, you have certainly grown up. I am so glad you are here. Let me grab your bags," Alex said without the enthusiasm he had expected. His wife and daughter were waiting for him across town right now, expecting him home early from work on this Friday to take them to Muir Woods and the family picnic they had planned.

"I've booked you a room at the Fairmount downtown. I hope that is all right."

"Alex, take me anywhere. I just want to be alone with you," she replied. "I am so happy to be here."

Alex Cutter drove them to the Fairmount and escorted her to the room on the executive floor that he had previously booked. He closed the door behind them, and Sparrow had her arms around his neck again. This time they kissed each other as intimately as humanly possible.

Then Sparrow reached for his hand to lead him to the bedroom off to their right. She could see the Golden Gate Bridge through the floor to ceiling windows. But after just a few steps, he stopped her. She looked up at him confused.

"Sparrow, I cannot be with you just now," he said with his eyes focused elsewhere. He released his hand from hers.

"What do you mean?"

"When we had first talked, you had planned to fly in on Sunday. Unfortunately you've arrived earlier, and I have a commitment. Actually, I have a family commitment." There he had said it. He had no idea what her true reaction might be. Anger, disgust, surprise, or even understanding— Alex had no clear idea.

Sparrow stood alone in the cavernous hallway. Her head was lowered and shaking a bit. "Alex, you are one son of a bitch," she said rather softly. He attempted to close the gap between them to hold her, and she threw up her hands and arms in protest. "Get the hell out, Alex. Get out now," she nearly screamed.

Alex retreated to the door and left the room key on the credenza. He left without a word of comfort.

Sparrow changed her flight and departed the next afternoon.

CHAPTER 22

"When you have more pasts then futures, you will understand," said the tall elderly Mr. Ingoorsal. "Everyone betrays everyone at some point." Donny Ingoorsal's litany was directed at his much younger protégé Billy Boyd.

The stoic Scandinavian Ingoorsal coughed up some phlegm and spit into the corner. Fifty years of smoking unfiltered Russian cigarettes had pretty much completed its mission. Billy ignored the filthy expression. Billy had grown up on the south side of Dublin and witnessed much worse. The older man loved the fact that Billy hung on his every word. This working-class Irish pub was preferred by both men if they had any business to discuss. It was boisterous, loud, and always overly crowded this time of night.

Billy Boyd was strong. This was not worked-out-hard-in-a-gym strong; this was street strong. Standing only five foot six and one hundred and sixty-five pounds, Billy could hold his own against men much taller and broader than he. Donny had witnessed numerous altercations in which Billy had taken down much-larger opponents. First off, Billy understood there was no such thing as a fair fight. Typically he would retreat from a brewing altercation rather than risk unnecessary injury. However, should a pending altercation be virtually unavoidable, he would always prove the aggressor and cast the first blow. None of Billy Boyd's fights lasted long. Not like in the movies with men crashing tables' over heads and standing toe-to-toe landing punches to the midsection and upper cuts to the jawline. No, Billy's battles were typically over in less than twenty seconds.

Using his elbow, Billy would catch his opponent just above the ear. The cranium is well protected on the frontal lobe and the back of the head has similar bone hard as armor. The side of the head is much less protected. The initial blow would bring immediate dizziness and nausea. The second blow would crash into the same spot, and his opponent would collapse as if a trapdoor had just been released.

Donny Ingoorsal tipped back his fourth Guinness and motioned with his nicotine-stained fingers for Billy to order another as well. The waitress caught the older man's gesture, but Billy waved her off as he sat across from his mentor.

"Billy, you look well. We haven't spoken for nearly half a year. Have you been busy?"

His red hair fell across his forehead and into his downcast eyes. He wore faded blue jeans, and a black T-shirt tucked in and covered with a slightly oversized well-worn black bombardier jacket. Slowly he raised his head from this near reverent position, tossing his longish red hair back with both hands, and looked his mentor directly in the eye. "I have kept busy enough, all with the renewed skirmishes with the British police and radicals in the north. There are plenty of side jobs that pay quite well."

Donny smiled and wiped the Guinness foam from his stubby whiskers with the back of his hand. "Billy, you are meant for great things. This next job will pay triple. It is a rather straightforward assignment. Follow a guy from the Glasgow airport on Sunday evening. He will most likely walk to his favorite restaurant, Assums, from his hotel. Even if it's raining, he will most likely walk. He is a bit of a health-nut. This should make things a bit easier."

"What do you want done to this healthy visitor to Ireland?"

"I want him killed. I want it to appear as a bungled robbery gone wrong," said Donny under his breath.

"Why does such a simple job pay so well?

"The targeted man is dangerous. He is older now but I still consider him extremely capable." Donny leaned back in his chair and began to open and close his customized lighter. "I am not concerned with any collateral damage. I have no restrictions. I just want this done. I have suggested the hit take place between the restaurant and the hotel. You are the professional; just see to it being done." Donny leaned forward and stopped clicking his lighter. "Billy, I really need you for this."

The waitress appeared, and Donny tapped his empty glass. She stared at Billy, and he ordered a Jameson. She left giving Billy a smile that even a schoolboy could interpret.

"The fee is good. Prior to the job, I will take one million South African rand deposited in my Cape Town account, plus one hundred thousand Irish pounds for spending money. Immediately upon conclusion, the balance of the fee will be deposited in US dollars in my Denver, Colorado, account.

The waitress returned with their drinks. She passed a matchbook to Billy and tapped the top of his hand. She winked knowingly at Ingoorsal. She left with a distinctive flip of her dark auburn hair.

"Done," Donny said as he reached for his fifth dark beer. "You are simply the best."

Billy drained the shot of Irish whiskey and picked up the matchbook. "Thanks for thinking of me, Donny. You won't be disappointed," Billy responded.

Billy left the pub and opened the matchbook: "Off at midnight—join me at the Brassiere across the street." A direct approach Billy mused. A smile crossed his lips. This would be a rather productive night all the way around.

Her name was Kristen. Her hair had the scent of jasmine and beer.

Donny Ingoorsal left the pub and dialed the proprietary number in Beijing. Despite the multiple time-zone changes, the call was picked up by the Chairman on the second ring. The Chairman listened intently. Once he was assured the Irish assassin was capable of the assignment, he thanked Ingoorsal and requested to be informed immediately upon Mr. Alex Cutter's demise.

In the Chairman's opinion, Alex had outlived his usefulness to him. In fact, Mr. Cutter could be viewed as a liability. His one company in Nanjing was making very good money, but some of his internal audit people were questioning some of the payments made to the Chairman as being extravagant. Cutter was also beginning to gain more favor in Beijing for his business acumen and, in a way, was overshadowing the Chairman. The clandestine trysts Alex Cutter had with Sparrow were the coup de grace for the Chairman's decision to have him eliminated. There would be no suspicion given this would be seen as a robbery gone badly with a Western businessman being at the wrong place at the wrong time in Ireland. The Chairman now had two professional assassins with their sights on Alex Cutter. Certainly one of them would prove successful. The attractive Candy Medford may have the edge given her feminine charms, but this Billy Boyd had a good résumé as well. In either case, the Chairman would be rid of Mr. Cutter in short order.

The corner restaurant catered to seaman, recovering drunks, and off-duty policemen. Billy sat across from his mentor watching him soak up egg yolk with the last of his Irish soda bread. Billy had no illusions of something for nothing. The big payday had to correspond to big risks. Having caught up with Donny Ingoorsal for breakfast, he reviewed the dossier of Mr. Alex Cutter.

Alex Joseph Cutter, Age 56, married, one daughter
Service Record: Special Forces, Distinguished Cross, One tour Afghanistan, One tour Gulf War
Purple Heart, Two Bronze Stars, Retired Military
Bachelor Degree: University of Delaware
Graduate Degree (MBA): Oxford, England
Law Degree: Yale
Current Occupation: Independent Security Consultant
Skills: Martial Arts, Weapons, Explosives, Counterterrorism, Corporate Security
Primary Residence: San Francisco, California
Secondary Residence: Oxford, England

"This individual is both smart and dangerous, Donny. I may have youth's step on him, but I will not underestimate this opponent."

"I am pleased to hear that, and it's what I expected from you. You're right, this is not a typical assignment in any way," Ingoorsal replied between slurps of hot coffee.

"I will portray a botched robbery only after securing the kill—period."

"I must agree with you, Billy, on that. Do you think you will need more guys?"

"No, that adds a measure of complexity I prefer to avoid. I can do this alone."

Their waitress came by to refill their coffee. She left with a particularly nice smile for Billy.

Ignoring the flirtatious staff, Billy leaned forward, tapping Ingoorsal on his forearm. "I will do this. I will do it quickly. I will choose the weapon, and it will be my decision on the timing."

"Of course, as you wish, Billy," a pleased Ingoorsal concluded.

CHAPTER 23

Next Billy learned the Assums restaurant was closed on Sunday evenings. Strike one. Next he learned the weather forecast for Sunday night was for heavy wet snow and wind, making a longer-range shot risky. Strike two. Later he would learn flight 1856 had been diverted from Glasgow to Cork due to weather. Strike three.

Upon disembarking at Cork, Alex Cutter secured a rental for the evening ride north to Glasgow. The mileage was just over 450 kilometers. Alex decided to dissect the distance and overnight at a bed-and-breakfast in Tipperary, just sixty-eight kilometers from the Cork airport. He rung ahead and booked the room. The relatively short driving distance was covered efficiently by the powerful Mercedes 550 Class rental sedan. Alex enjoyed a Guinness prior to his shepherd's pie and turned in quite early at the well-known bed-and-breakfast spot.

Miles to the north, Billy sat with Kristen in his nondescript rental car just a few short blocks from the Assums restaurant in central Glasgow. She was doing her very best to play the amorous partner with her hand on Billy's lap and her mouth on his neck as he casually looked around. Six fifteen stretched to eight fifteen with no sign of the potential victim. At ten o'clock, Billy decided to abort the planned attack and return to his place. Kristen remained in character, and Billy's evening was not a total bust.

Kristen had served with the Irish Army Rangers for three years after graduating from the military school at Curragh Camp, southwest of Dublin. She had been the only daughter of a large rural family. She grew up exceptionally poor. Her school instructors were quick to note her voracious appetite to learn, and her coaches were impressed with her natural athletic ability. She earned a full scholarship to the prestigious college. There was only one other female enrolled in the military's elite program. Both of them passed the rigorous program. Both of them warded off numerous unwanted male attentions and earned the respect of their unit.

Kristen and her female friend were deployed to Afghanistan in the late spring after graduation. Their special-forces team linked up with a German unit from the *Kommando Spezialkrafte*. The joint team was northwest of Kabul when they were attacked by a much-larger enemy force. Kristen's friend was killed by a single bullet severing her carotid artery. The unit suffered significant casualties, and Kristen was singled out for her heroism.

She returned to Dublin and retired from the service. The world had become a very dangerous place, and she had acquired a unique skill set much in demand by the private sector. She first met Donny Ingoorsal through a mutual friend in a smoky bar in a tough part of the city. The much-older man sipped his Guinness as he recited his unique background for her. Kristen moved her chair closer to his in order to hear over the raucous drunken crowd as the two-piece band began their third set.

Ingoorsal's face was a maze of creases, yet his blue eyes remained clear and calm. She was expecting a seaman's story. The scruffy old man surprised her. He had grown up in a small seaside town just outside of Gudvangen, Norway. His grandfather and father had been active in the resistance since the German invasion and occupation of April 9, 1940. The Wehrmacht had uncovered a plot by the resistance just prior to the war's end in May 1945. Both his father and grandfather were hanged in the village square for crimes against the state. Afterward a Wehrmacht officer raped his mother, while young Donny Ingoorsal was locked in the adjacent room. From that day forward, the young Ingoorsal would not trust the Allies, which could have saved them, or the Nazi pigs who took not only their property but also their heritage. For Ingoorsal the world was an unfair place. He would grow into adulthood caring only for himself.

The highest bidder could illicit his deadly services—no questions asked. He had never been a fisherman or a sailor. After nearly decapitating his mother's rapist, the young Ingoorsal escaped to the mountains and stayed with his bachelor uncle until he turned nineteen.

Alex left the bed-and-breakfast early, but only after a huge Irish breakfast of Donnelly sausages, bacon, black pudding, beans, and eggs. He grabbed a second tea for the road (very American of him). The skies were clear, and the road to Glasgow was wide open at this early hour. He made good time and checked into his hotel, just blocks from his favorite restaurant, Assums.

On a whim, Alex dialed Bridgette, a model he had met while she was working in New York a year ago. Surprised to catch her on the second mobile ring, he explained his brief business stay in the city and asked if she was free for dinner. After some rather obvious flirting back and forth, they agreed to meet at the restaurant at eight this evening. Alex donned his running gear and made way to Kelvingrove Park, passed the famous art gallery there, and ran along the river Kelvin. The day was picture perfect for late spring. He waved back to a small pack of Glaswegians running in the opposite direction. He was feeling particularity spry and decided to extend his run through the center of the University of Strathclyde before retreating to his hotel. The run had taken more than an hour and a half. Alex cooled down after a shower and sat on the bed in just his boxer shorts and pulled out the dossier for a Mr. Ping in Nanjing, China.

At 7:00 p.m. Alex finished dressing: gray linen slacks, dark loafers, and a black cashmere turtleneck with an extra heavy collar complemented by a camel colored sports coat. He was looking forward to sharing his favorite restaurant with Bridgette this evening. Scrolling through his phone he found this: Bridgette O'Malley, five foot eight, red hair, University of Glasgow, raised on a sheep farm in Limerick County in the southwest of the country, feisty, full of fun. Alex had added two asterisks to the reference.

Billy and Kristen arrived at the fashionable restaurant when it opened at 5:00 p.m. Billy tipped the maître d handsomely to be placed at an upstairs table with a clear view of the promenade below the establishment in both directions. He and Kristen simply ordered mineral water and one appetizer to share. Billy's eyes kept sweeping the view below. The food came, and the clock ticked past 6:00 p.m. Billy Boyd kept a close watch. At 6:45 p.m. he recognized his prey, two blocks away walking toward the restaurant from the east. The man looked confident. Billy had a clear view. The man he knew as Alex Cutter, late fifties, was right on schedule. Billy left the table with his light-black topcoat and was out the door. Alex was a block away and walking directly toward him. Billy's hand released the safety on the Glock in his right pocket.

Just then, from a cross street, one hundred meters away, a young woman rushed toward the target carrying an oversized portfolio briefcase of some kind. Billy picked up his pace and closed the gap between them to seventy-five meters. The woman threw her arms around the neck of Mr. Cutter, swinging the briefcase wildly and kissing him on the lips. Billy now was within fifty meters.

Alex kissed her back and laughed, surprised and elated with the welcome from Bridgette. As she spun him around in a complete 360-degree turn, his eye caught a young man accelerating toward them in almost a sprint. With little further thought, Alex simultaneously reached for his weapon in the small of this back and grabbed the briefcase in the other. The next few moments carried out in slow motion. The assailant was pulling out and firing a Glock pistol on the run while Alex tripped and threw the briefcase in front of Bridgette. Alex was crouched and firing his Walter PPQ (Police Pistol Quick Defense) at the assailant. The new trigger placement required only a .4-inch pull, allowing Alex to stay on target while firing rapidly. He pulled six times from the nine-millimeter magazine holding fifteen rounds. Billy's first shot was high, and his second penetrated the briefcase and grazed Bridgette's shoulder. Alex's first shot caught Billy in the upper shoulder twisting him around almost forty-five degrees; the second shot exploded his head—his long red hair flying in all directions. The next four body shots completed the massacre. The total of eight shots seemed to reverberate off the walls of the narrow cobblestone street. Pedestrians had scattered. One woman behind Alex was crying and holding her young son. Alex attended to Bridgette and replaced the Walter pistol in its holster in the middle of his back. Recognizing his date was not in critical condition, he lifted her and grabbed the damaged briefcase, waking calmly to the side street where he hailed a cab.

"Get us to Drumchapel Hospital," he told the cabbie.

"You are going to be all right," he assured Bridgette holding his blood-soaking handkerchief to her wounded shoulder. She simply smiled and said nothing, closing her eyes and allowing him to hold her close.

The young emergency-room staff was highly efficient. The single bullet had passed through Bridgette's soft tissue and missed the brachial artery. She was patched up, given antibiotic, and a mild sedative. Alex drove her back to her apartment and tucked her in. Alex stayed with her.

When Bridgette woke, she said with a smile, "That was rather cloak-and-dagger stuff back there."

"I apologize for us having to miss our dinner engagement but guarantee you we will redo once you are feeling up to it. Dr. Ripen says he expects you will have full recovery. The minor scar on your shoulder may become your signature for any swimwear shots," he said with a bit of a twinkle.

"Alex, I am still stunned. It all happened so fast. Who was that man? Are you OK?"

"I'm fine, thanks. I have spoken with the police. They recognize the shooter as a local hotshot. No criminal record, but someone who seems to have led a life far above his means. He would frequent several of the local pubs and was thought to be somewhat a ladies' man. They should have more info for us post-investigation. For now, I want you to rest, recover, and I will pick you up upon your release and get you home. Sorry for the extracurricular activity, and I still owe you a satisfactory dinner." Alex leaned down and kissed her first on the forehead and then deeply on the lips.

CHAPTER 24

The rendezvous was at Rathmines Library in the heart of Dublin. Ingoorsal arrived early and sober. He had shaved and was wearing an expensive tweed jacket over a wool turtleneck. The trousers were sharply creased and fell over new brown loafers. His hair was trimmed and fingernails polished. He trudged up the old wooden stairs to the top floor and found two seats in the furthest corner. He had purchased a newspaper and began to read and wait.

It was early and the library had just opened, and therefore there were few patrons around. He did not hear her coming up the old staircase. He dropped his paper simply because he sensed someone looking down at him. She was just a few meters away. The woman appeared hefty wearing a county smock that did well to hide her curvaceous figure. A wrap encircled her red hair and held it back from her face. Her black rain goulashes ran half way up her shapely calves. Now she wore thick eyeglasses and absolutely no makeup. "Good day, Mr. Ingoorsal," she about whispered.

"Good morning, Kristen; please have a seat," said Ingoorsal as he motioned to the empty chair next to him. "As you would expect, our employer is not pleased. I had warned Billy this was a dangerous man—even in his midfifties."

"Despite being surprised, the target reacted with catlike quickness," she said, keeping her voice just above a whisper. "From my vantage point in the restaurant, Billy had his weapon out early and fired the first shot. Alex Cutter's reaction was of a man expecting trouble, and his training kicked in. He was like a man half his age."

"Kristen, I received an encrypted message last night from China. Basically it said to wait for further instructions. I am not comfortable with that. I am suggesting we cash out now and go our separate ways." Ingoorsal paused and coughed into a gentlemen's handkerchief he had pulled from this jacket.

"I am surprised and pleased you came to this conclusion. I, too, have witnessed how dangerous this man can be."

"Good," Ingoorsal said and passed an envelope across the reading table to her. "I plan to travel east. I leave this afternoon. Your fee is enclosed."

Kristen did not open the envelope. These two had worked together for years, and she trusted him like the father she had never known. "Travel well," she said and tapped him on the top of his hand. She left the alcove first.

Kristen stepped into a coffee shop, the air thick with cigarette and cigar smoke. She pulled out the envelope Ingoorsal had given her. There were two items. As she expected, there was a bank receipt indicating her fee being deposited in her Irish account. She smiled as she opened the second item; an inexpensive greeting card, signed by Donny Ingoorsal. It simply said, "Have a safe journey." She snapped open her phone and called her personal banker. The instructions had been prearranged with passcodes, and she had 250,000 Irish pounds transferred to a local bank in the Bahamas. She would join the money by this time tomorrow afternoon.

Ingoorsal waited to allow her egress from the building. Later he filed down the creaky staircase to the main floor and left out of a side entrance. A private aircraft was waiting for him on an abandoned airstrip two hours' drive south of town. When Ingoorsal—the flights only passenger—arrived, the small plane took off bound for refueling in the Ukraine and then over the Ural Mountains with a final stop in Omak, just north of Kazakhstan.

Ingoorsal was enjoying Joseph Sitali vodka accompanied with Ercuis Transat caviar by his lake cabin the next evening. He pulled up the fur collar as the wind picked up and stared out at the whitecaps rolling in.

His companion, an older Russian lady with a hardened face, poured him another shot from the bottle encased in ice. Ingoorsal felt relatively safe here, yet his eyes continued to dart across the landscape for any danger. "Let's go back inside," he said in perfect Russian, including the southern dialect used in this remote outpost. She followed him to the luxury cabin carrying the vodka in gloved hands.

The Chairman learned of the botched assassination from an aid. They had underestimated Alex Cutter. The Chairman was not pleased with his Irish source, Mr. Ingoorsal. Although the man had delivered in the past for him, this key assignment was truly bungled. Perhaps the Scandinavian was getting too old. It would have been much cleaner to dispose of Alex Cutter while he was traveling in Ireland. The Chairman was prepared to wait until Cutter returned to mainland China. Perhaps he could use Sparrow as unsuspecting bait. He still had the charming Israeli, Candy Medford, to dispose of Alex Cutter.

Bridgette recovered from the ordeal rather quickly, and they found their way several days later to the Two Fat Ladies at the Buttery. The restaurant was classic Scottish from the tartan flooring to the heavy wooden paneling. They both started with the pear salad and then her with the Dover sole and him choosing the rack of lamb. Collectively they decided on a bottle of Louis Jadot Bonnes-Mares 2013. The rather complex pinot was ridiculously expensive at 630 euros a bottle.

As they sipped the first pour, Alex looked over the brim at his date. She was stunning this evening, wearing an off-the-shoulder cream-colored dress with her hair worn up. She was looking directly back at him. "Are you aware of what the French refer to as *terroir* when it comes to a fine wine such as this?"

"I'm not, Alex, but I have a sense you are going to educate me on it," Bridgette said as she put down her crystal glass.

"The French use that term referring to the almost mystical melding of soil, weather, climate, and topography necessary to create the fine balance this wine exhibits," he said as the sommelier poured them both a full glass and retreated from the table.

"Alex, I must tell you how terrified I was when that gunman approached us. Now that the adrenaline has completely worn off, I have to ask you about how you reacted. It was surreal. The event keeps rolling around in my head. Your quick reactions no doubt saved both of our lives. Do you always carry a weapon on a dinner date?"

"My old military training kicked in I guess," Alex said, trying to minimize his reaction to the lone gunman outside the Assums restaurant. "I am grateful you are OK. By the way, you look absolutely stunning this evening," he said in an attempt to deflect the conversation elsewhere.

"Thank you, but I need to ask about the pistol you were carrying that evening. Is that normal?"

"It's a fair question, Bridgette. Currently I am a security consultant for several international firms. Those firms are directly involved with significant import and export activities in ports across the globe. Many of those ports are controlled or influenced by some rather unsavory characters. I routinely carry a weapon as a result of those obligations; however I must confess that is the only time I have had to pull the gun from the holster. I am sure I was as scared as you at the time."

"Alex, you are so modest it kills me," Bridgette replied and smiled back at him. "Let's make this a special night with no gun-slinging, and I will stop interrogating you."

"Deal."

They lingered over their meal and coffee service thereafter. There was no hurry in either of them. As they left the restaurant, Alex placed his sport coat around Bridgette's shoulders and kissed her. After their second tryst of the night, Alex took her in his arms and held her. She purred and snuggled closer to the much-older man. She liked being held.

The sex had been spectacular for both of them. The second time was slower. They had laughed, and she had teased a bit. The kisses were longer. The touches were more like a gentle breeze against their damp skin. They both fell into a deep and restful sleep.

Alex left her apartment very early the next morning, leaving a note on her kitchen table, which promised to see her the next time he was in

Glasgow. He boarded his flight to SFO, got to his assigned seat in business class, and collapsed into a stupor type of sleep. Arriving in San Francisco early the following morning, he showered at the airport lounge and took a cab home.

CHAPTER 25

Mrs. Cutter was just leaving the house as his cab pulled into the drive. She trotted to his car as he was paying and gave him a welcome kiss on the cheek as she was on tiptoes.

"Was it a good business trip?"

"It was OK. I see you are out and about this morning. Care to join me for lunch later?"

"I can't darling; I'm meeting the girls for lunch at the club. Why don't you just rest, and we can catch up over dinner? I'll pick up some fresh fish on the way home."

"Sounds good to me. I'll plan to see you around three or four this afternoon. I'm going to take a nap," Alex responded and gave her a peck on the cheek.

"Sounds grand; I'll be home before four."

Alex retreated to his well-appointed study. He fired up the computer and read the encrypted message after it was decoded. The message was from his business associate Collins. Alex had served on the board of the joint-venture company in Nanjing referred to as White Cedar Semiconductor/Nanjing People's Office. Collins held a majority interest in the joint-venture company but used Alex as his eyes and ears on the board. Also on the board was Mr. Mao Ling, known locally as the Chairman. Collins wanted to know why anyone would be investigating the Chairman. He did not share in the communiqué the work he had done for Mr. Ping to secure the Chairman's e-mail account. He did mention Mr. Ping in the message but more as a reminder that he was serving as the temporary top post for the joint venture. Collins was thinking there may be a way to pit both men against each other and earn something from each.

Alex stared at the brief message. He was not particularly fond of either man. This was the first time the head of White Cedar Semiconductor had ever reached out to him privately. His initial impressions of Mr. Mao Ling (alias the Chairman) was of a midlevel government man being given the opportunity, by the handlers in Beijing, to act as their eyes and ears in a number of the ever growing joint ventures, given his English-speaking skills. Alex had always seen the Chairman more as a tool for Beijing to keep a reign on the joint-venture companies by keeping them informed on a timely basis. Perhaps Alex had underestimated him.

Alex thought about how little he knew about Mr. Ping, having met him just twice. First impressions were not particularly noteworthy. The deputy general manager of the large malting plant, he remembered, had unusually thick eyeglasses and greasy longish hair. Ping had always appeared very deferential in the presence of Western executives visiting the plant. Frankly, Mr. Ping was not that memorable other than his odd appearance.

Alex was prone to a quick response through the encrypted line saying he had no idea why anyone would be investigating the Chairman. On second thought, something didn't smell right about the innocent enquiry. First off it came through their secure encrypted e-mail account. Next, why did he mention Mr. Ping in the same communiqué? Was Mr. Collins really asking him to do some local reconnaissance? Alex decided there had to be more to this enquiry, and he was going to dig a little deeper before responding to Mr. Collins.

CHAPTER 26

At the same moment, on the other side of the world in the slums of Beijing, Lin was wakened by the Rolling Stones pleading for him to get off their cloud. The alarm music gave him pause as he rolled onto his back and stared at the ceiling fan. He allowed one more refrain from Keith and Mick. He looked out his sole window to the thick smog hanging over the capital city.

Lin peered through thick glasses at a single petri dish under greenish grow lights. This time it had worked. The H7N9 bird virus was successfully transferred from the Shandong Province duck and was expanding exponentially on the red agar medium on the standard-size petri dish.

Lin grinned and subconsciously nodded his head as he removed the protective gloves. The mysterious stranger he had met in the Shanghai beer garden had offered US$20,000 for three milliliters of the condensed viral suspension. This one petri dish held much more.

The unemployed biologist could not contain his excitement. Multiple trials had proven unsuccessful, and his limited resources stretched to the limit purchasing sick birds from rural animal doctors. The huge fee he would collect from the stranger would get him out this hovel. He could afford a motorbike. The devilish side of him would put aside a fraction to visit the brothel on the city's outskirts, which tended to accommodate midlevel officers in the Red Army and visiting businessmen.

The first crisp evening forewarned of the coming autumn. Lin tipped the collar of his threadbare coat and briskly walked to the rendezvous. He was a bit early. He was nervous. He had never really succeeded at anything. He had failed his initial university-entrance exams. He had lost his part-time job at the dairy last month. He was unsuccessful with the women on the production line at the toy manufacturer. Most nights found him alone in his two-room ground-floor apartment. A genuine loser...up until now.

As instructed, Lin was to deliver the deadly bird serum in a vial provided by the stranger. His armpits had become slippery and he had to convince himself to walk calmly to the southwest corner of the park. He would make this work—he must.

He recognized his contact approaching just as the sun was setting, and his contact appeared more as a silhouette. Nervously he palmed the slim vial that would change his life. The park was partially busy yet others seemed wrapped up in their own lives, and he felt invisible. Two older teenagers listening to their iPhones were trailing him.

The first blow came from behind. The kick expertly placed behind his left knee collapsed his frame down and forward. The second teenager caught him as he lurched forward. A crisp blow to his windpipe left him reeling. The vial was snatched from his weakened grip. A final blow to the eardrum left his world black.

The two teenagers relinquished the vial to their handler, a rather short man with thick glasses, who folded several thousand renminbi notes into their outstretched hands. The stranger placed the important vial into a protective black case. He stepped to the curb and slid into the back of a waiting black sedan with darkened windows.

Mr. Ping lightly tapped the black case in the back of the sedan. This deadly vial would further his ambitions in the Party. He reached forward, and his cold hand fell on the drivers shoulder. She did not react. Her white gloved hands were firmly on the steering wheel and eyes fixed on the dark road ahead. His hand moved to the nape of her neck and caressed her.

"Drive us to the Xuan Hotel. I still have some time for you my dear," Ping leered.

Sparrow accelerated the state car without a word to her tormentor. They arrived at the popular hotel thirty minutes later. Ping was actually giggling in the back seat. "Join me in the same room as last night, my dear, after you have parked." He said as his sticky hand reached from the back and caressed her cheek and neck.

Sparrow had plans for Mr. Ping, but tonight she was not fully prepared to execute her scheme just yet. Reluctantly she followed behind him through the ornate lobby. She could only imagine what sick and twisted roles she would be required to fulfill tonight. Each evening, with the Chairman still away on business, Ping had increasingly humiliated her in every way possible. Tonight would be no exception, as he giggled and unlocked the room.

The next morning, a triad representative picked up a sample of the deadly serum from Mr. Ping's office safe. Ping was expecting the pickup and stayed well away from the admin center—the stuff scared him to death. His assistant would manage the handoff and collect the fees.

Lin regained consciences a short time later. The sun had set, and it felt much colder. Unsteadily he got to his feet and made his way back to the apartment and his straw-filled mattress. He lay on his back, allowing the drugs he had swallowed to overcome the headache and nausea. He forced himself to get off the bed a short time later. The only source of light in his apartment came from the greenish glow of the growth light focused on the agar mediums. Even since his brief absence, the bird-virus strains had continued to multiply under the ideal conditions he had created.

Simply too excited to rest, Lin split the growing virus strain into several vials, all held at the correct temperature and pH.

Despite the sever earache, Lin's excitement was growing. To be attacked and robbed by the triad thugs suggested this viral concoction had true street value. He would approach his distant cousin who worked at the Nanjing malt house. His connections could prove very valuable.

Lin was not aware that his cousin, Mr. Shu, had lost his position at the Nanjing malt house when he got the call back. Shu was much more engaged and interested in talking with Lin.

"I believe I have a buyer for one of your vials, my cousin. If it should be as deadly as you say without leaving a trace, I may have buyers for your entire inventory," Shu said in a rather hushed tone over the telephone.

"I believe it is worth at least twenty thousand US dollars per vial," said Lin.

This seemed excessive to Mr. Shu, but he did not wish to discourage his younger cousin. "Give me the balance of this week to secure a buyer or buyers."

"OK," said Lin over the phone, his spirits lifted. He hung up the receiver and noticed his body aches and damaged ear felt better already.

"I have one buyer for all three of your vials," Shu exclaimed enthusiastically over the phone line. "It's through an intermediary, which I believe represents the triad. These are tough men. Should it not work as advertised, these principals will not hesitate to kill us."

"I completely understand, cousin. This implied guarantee is understood. This virus will kill any living thing in a matter of minutes," Lin promised. His excitement was building. "I can have the vials ready for you tonight. How are we being paid, may I ask?"

"Small Renminbi notes," Shu replied. "They will have a small mammal with them to test a small portion of the poison. Should that work as you say it will, we will both be fairly wealthy men by this time tomorrow." The triad intermediary brought with him to the preassigned transfer point a small rabbit. A small dot of the poison on a carrot had the poor victim convulsing almost immediately, and its breathing stopped a few moments later. Shu counted the renminbi in the dim light of the transfer point. The equivalent of US$60,000 was most certainly in the leather satchel. Lin and Shu were rich. Prior to the triad representative's departure, they were given an order for three more vials to be delivered in a week's time. Lin indicated that could be done, as he attempted to hide his excitement. Shu returned with his portion of the money to join his wife at her mother's house. Lin returned to his shabby apartment and checked on the small sample he had earlier cut out of the third vial. It was growing exponentially as he had hoped under the ideal conditions. He hid almost his entire share of the money under a loose floorboard and kept a few of the notes for his trip to the outskirts of town and the brothel he had heard so much about.

Lin sat in the parlor of the large house. A young girl in a very short dress brought him a mao-tai, the sorghum-based liquor, which quickly put him at ease. A much-older woman appeared and gave Lin the rules of the house. She concluded by outlining the cost for one girl and the cost for more than one girl. She collected the necessary amount and left.

Five girls came into the room and stood across from him. They all wore high heels and very provocative clothes. One by one they would introduce themselves and walk across the room to touch his forearm or brush their hand across his lap. Lin thought they were stellar. He had not been with a woman for over a year. Lin took another sip of his drink and motioned for the girl standing on the far left of the line-up to join him. The other girls disappeared. His choice walked up to him confidently and took his hand. He got up from the couch and followed her hand in hand down a narrow hallway. She stopped at the end of the hall and turned into a bedroom larger then Lin's whole apartment. She closed the door and led him to the bed. There she slowly removed his shirt and then his pants. Then she began a little slow striptease for him. Later, Lin would criticize himself for his awkwardness and hurry. Nonetheless, the cost for this little foray was minuscule compared to his fortune back home under the floorboard and the growing culture under his greenish bulb. Lin would most likely return to the brothel given his newfound wealth. Next time, he mused, he would have two of the girls invite him to one of the backrooms.

Ping took a vial of the bird virus from his office safe. With an eyedropper, he squeezed a few drops into a glass of mao-tai. Even though he was in control with the deadly virus, it made him extremely nervous. He had invited Mr. Xie back to the administration building within the industrial campus. Although he had fired the financial guy just a few days ago, he wanted to personally test the potency of the virus. He had sent word to

Mr. Xie to come in for a meeting after working hours. Perhaps there was a path to reinstating him. Xie jumped at the chance of potential reconciliation and arrived promptly at 1800 hours. Since the staff had left for home, he knocked softly on Ping's door.

"Please come in, Mr. Xie. I was expecting you."

Xie entered the deputy general manager's office and politely bowed. "Mr. Ping, thank you for making this meeting possible. I know you are a very busy man."

"Please have a seat." Ping gestured toward the table with the sorghum-based liquor. "I will come right to the point. I have had both our security and finance investigate the charges brought against you earlier this week. Their conclusion is the wrongdoing was squarely with your colleague, Mr. Shu. He was the principal behind the tax-fraud issue. Nonetheless, you were his supervisor and should have caught the error. That being said, the investigation clears your name, and I would like to offer your old job back to you."

Mr. Xie began to shake and weep at the same time. "Deputy General Manager, I cannot thank you enough for your thoroughness and consideration." He bowed his head in deference.

"Please, Mr. Xie, stop your weeping. I expect you back at work Monday morning."

"Thank you; thank you, Mr. Ping. You will not be disappointed in my work."

"OK then, let's celebrate your reinstatement. After all it is after business hours, and I have poured us both a mao-tai." With that, Ping reached for the tainted glass and handed it to Xie. Ping reached for his own glass and raised it high. "To your continued success, Mr. Xie."

After the first sip, Mr. Xie smiled and took another swallow draining the glass. Ping was about to pour another when Xie said, "This is crazy!" A yellow pool was gathering at the end of his trouser. Xie was embarrassed beyond belief. His bladder further relaxed and another flood of urine passed. He looked back up to Ping, but his mouth would not work, nor his hands, yet his mind was awake. A moment later his respiratory system shut down as he tipped over onto the floor.

Ping looked down at the man he had poisoned. It was closer to a clinical stare. This stuff worked, even in minuscule quantities. Ping noted time of death—less than three minutes upon ingestion. Ping waited twenty minutes for good order sake and then grabbed a walking stick and clubbed the dead man with it. Next was to call plant security. No one would look for toxin in the dead man. A fired employee had lost all control and attacked the man who had fired him earlier in the week. The brave acting general manager had struck the attacker in the head killing him. Security would do the rest. Ping put away the mao-tai bottle and called down for this driver, Sparrow, to pick him up in five minutes.

Across town, Lin was harvesting the next generation of the bird flu and carefully placing it in a travel vial. The triad representative would meet him and Mr. Shu at the same location they had transferred ownership the week before. The two cousins arrived at the spot early wanting to be sure there would be no complications. After their cursory look around, they both ordered tea from a street vendor and waited.

Their expected guest arrived in the cab of a sanitation truck. He had two partners with him. Lin and Shu put down their tea and gave each other furtive glances. The two extra men were large but stayed by the truck as the triad intermediary approached the bird-virus peddlers. This time the man had a small cat in his arms. The deadly serum droplet was placed in a bowl of milk. The predictable outcome came within two minutes. The triad middleman handed over a laundry bag. Lin and Shu nodded and began to walk away. The two large thugs followed from a distance. The trackers closed the distance between them. Lin and Shu began a half-run and turned down a side street. For big men, the triad pair moved well. The laundry bag was awkward and slowed them down. Lin and Shu moved left down a narrow street. Their pursuers closed the gap, and in a few short moments, the four men came to a halt and stared at each other. Shu looked scared. Lin began talking and begging for them both.

The larger of the two men stepped forward and took the laundry bag filled with cash. Shu readily gave it up. Without a word the two large men turned and left.

"We are in over our heads, Lin," Shu whispered. "I thought those men were going to kill us."

"Now that they know we can supply the deadly virus in a usable form, we remain useful," Lin replied. "Let's get back to my apartment and transfer the virus colonies to another more secure location." His cousin Shu looked like he was going to be sick.

A moment later, he was. Vomit spewed from him as he bent over. Shu wiped the spittle with his sleeve and said, "I cannot do this anymore; it is far too dangerous." A second bout of being sick left him speechless and bent over at the waist. He vomited all over his scruffy shoes.

"OK then, cousin; I will proceed solo," Mr. Lin said, as his nerves calmed. "Let's get you home."

Lin took care of his distant relative and then returned to his apartment. He carefully gathered up the virus, his hidden cash, and minimal personal belongings. He left the putrid apartment and checked into an upscale studio near the city center. He was optimistic. His future was the black molds on the pink growth cultures.

CHAPTER 27

The chosen rendezvous surprised Alex Cutter. The barrio, off the Gran Plaza in Monterrey, Mexico, was littered with garbage and empty of passersby. The sign hung crooked on the split black wooden door—*Carrelo* (closed). He tested the door, and it creaked open. His eyes were slow to adjust from the brilliant Monterrey sunlight to the dark hallway comprised of broken red tile and a half century of dust. The hallway's history, its charm, was long wasted on the earlier veneer of its youth.

It had been many years since his last contact with the Dragon. He had hoped and prayed everything would have been forgotten. Never forgiven but hopefully tucked in that remote place we all have to deposit undesirable memories, forgotten loves, frightening dreams, and lust.

With genuine deference, he approached the man known as the Dragon sitting across the tired room at a lone table. Even in the dim light, he recognized the sparking cuff links peaking from the dark suit coat. The Dragon sat in a shadow. He took a seat across from him. He did not shake his hand. In fact, they had never shaken hands. Years ago they had communicated via public phone booths at opposite ends of the People's Bridge in Nanjing.

"There is a glass of Montevina poured for you. I am convinced you will recognize the vintage."

Something was wrong. That was not the Dragon's voice. His was much more forceful and commanding. He remained in the shadow and said, "You must recognize my voice."

He did. One of the Dragon's senior lieutenants from so many years ago had reentered his life. Alex sipped the fine Mexican merlot, which tasted of sweet blackberries. "You are familiar, yes."

"The Dragon has sent me to settle a debt."

The simple statement was both clear and concise. Alex took another sip of the red nectar and listened as his feet began to sweat.

"The Dragon recalls the debt repaid in Nanjing, and I trust your Zurich account was amply rewarded. He also recalls the monthly stipend being cashed. The young woman known as Sparrow has recently been approached by the Guangzhou government authorities for information linking you, the Dragon, and the Nanjing mayor to events that may compromise people in high positions. There is no alternative. We want her killed by next Wednesday. Make it look like an accident. That is all." He adjusted the white cuffs of his dress shirt beneath the handmade black suit. He got up off his chair and left.

Alex sat stunned. His hand was shaking red wine from the brim of the glass. His mind was racing with questions. The Chairman, also referred to as the Dragon, did not allow for questions. Alex was paid for answers. They paid him well for solutions.

Alex finished the red wine. He sat there thinking of the intricate webs we all weave over the course of our lives. He had not needed to become involved with the Dragon or the Chairman as he was known to many in Nanjing. He was not in debt. He was not searching for excitement or fame or fortune. He was a highly successful Western businessman. Back when he had first met the Chairman, Alex was much younger and certainly naïve. Now he was forced into a matrix with no exit. He had never killed a noncombatant. He had killed the assassin Billy Boyd in Dublin. That was self-defense. He was not lily white. He had stolen and brokered sensitive business information to the highest bidder but was never directly or indirectly involved with violence. That seemed so unnecessary. You could cause such harm and pain with the click of a mouse or the hum of a copy machine—why resort to a blunt blow to the head or shot to the chest. He was confused. He was angry and disappointed with himself.

These circumstances he found himself in were from his own making. This sucked. He threw his empty wine glass at the wall. That didn't help; in fact it was sophomoric. Disgusted with himself, he retreated through the darkened hallway he had entered earlier.

As Alex walked back to his hotel, the Crown Plaza, the questions swirled in his head. How could he kill the young woman who had touched his heart so many years ago? Why was he chosen for a task much better suited for the triad killers? Could he refuse? How could he save Sparrow?

He passed a street beggar with her wares displayed on a dirty blue blanket. She sat with one child in a knapsack over her shoulder, her dark hair hiding the baby's face. Another child lay next to her sobbing. The handmade Mexican dolls were laid out in three neat rows. The fabric of the dolls' clothes far exceeded the rags on the filthy woman and her children. Alex bent down to place ten pesos in her filthy hand.

Her fingers closed around the coins. She tossed her hair back to look him in the eye. "Kill the Chinese woman," she said in perfect English.

He stepped away as she gathered up her dolls and children. Nothing is as it first appears. Shaken with the underscored message, he crossed the street to Casa Oaxaca Restaurante and ordered a Negra Modelo. He sat alone, stunned by the events of the past hour. He stared down into the dark beer, confused, angry, and scared.

As he sat alone starring at the foam on his beer, Alex began to formulate a plan. He would go to China, not to kill Sparrow, but to warn her. It could place him in grave danger, but in some strange twist, this mission of death began to clarify his thinking of what the future could be. What did he want out of life? A loveless marriage or bring up his daughter to understand true meaning in life? He wasn't a paid assassin. He wasn't someone's lackey. He was an accomplished businessman with a daughter he adored and a guilty conscience for not being there for her early on. He had the means to repurpose his life. Why wait any longer?

Alex finished his beer and walked back to the hotel. His rational mind began to outline all the necessary steps he would need to take in China. It would require steady nerves and a rather convincing acting job. The men he was dealing with could be ruthless. He had been told by the Chairman's senior lieutenant to eliminate the young woman who had touched his very soul. His plan was simple. Warn Sparrow, and start a new life with Alexia somewhere safe.

Alex arrived home in the north side of San Francisco late the next night. He went to his daughter's room and gave her a kiss. He tiptoed down the hall, shed his suit, and crawled into the king-size bed next to his wife. She stirred just a bit and then rolled over to face the wall still in a deep dream. He lay there in his own bed with eyes wide open, dreading the next steps.

The next morning he showered later than normal and came down to the breakfast nook.

"Honey, you're going to be late," she said as she handed Alex a black coffee and pecked him on the cheek.

"I know. Something weird came over the telex from our Beijing office on some customers pushing back on previous commitments. John has asked me to look into it personally as that geography reports to me now and given my exposure to business practices there when I served as an intern." He said hopefully, half-convincingly.

"OK," she said without much further thought. "Does that mean a trip then?"

"Unfortunately it does. I will leave on the late-afternoon direct flight. I expect this to take only two to three days. I will be back for the Hauser's garden party," he half-lied, turning his back to her and refilling his coffee.

"Do what you have to do darling. You know I have never questioned your business travel, and I don't plan to start now. By the way, did you remember I was going to Sacramento with the girls today?" she said, oblivious to his moral dilemma.

He gave her a kiss on the cheek and she turned to look him in the eye. He pulled her in close and kissed her. He hated to be so deceptive. Had she known he planned to travel to the other side of the world and warn a young woman of her death sentence, how would she react? "I knew you had that trip planned long ago; wow, time flies. If I remember right, you were going with Louise, is that right?" he dodged.

"Yes, Louise and two other girls from the club," she offered.

"Watch how much wine you have. I think Louise may be a party-girl," he added to detract from his pending international trip.

"You're impossible," she said as she lifted on tiptoes and gave him another peck on the cheek. She gathered her satchel and headed for the garage. "Have a safe trip, and don't bring back any diseases," she teased.

He called for the car service and went upstairs to pack. He hated lying to his wife. The limo picked him up, and he was at SFO nearly three hours before the direct flight to Shanghai.

CHAPTER 28

"Good evening, Mr. Cutter; welcome aboard," the lead flight attendant chirped with a smile. "May I get you something to drink?" she asked as he tossed his minimal luggage beneath the seat in front.

"Good evening; may I get a Heineken?"

"Of course, Mr. Cutter, and here is tonight's menu," the flight attendant said.

Cutter enjoyed his cold beer, asked only for the salad, skipped the dessert tray, and popped two sleeping pills with bottled water. He reclined with a sleeping mask and slept almost to destination.

He was met after customs by one of the Ping's lieutenants, who took his one carry-on bag and deposited him, after a three-and-half-hour car trip, to Nanjing's best hotel. There was a written message scrawled on hotel stationery.

> "Welcome back, Mr. Cutter. I have the subject's address and rough schedule for your review. Let's meet for breakfast at your hotels buffet at seven."—Ping"

Alex despised Ping when he had been an intern years ago. Something about the guy gave him the creeps. The slicked back hair, the leering eyes, and his secretive nature gave him pause. Alex was usually right about his first impressions.

They went through the buffet line, Ping heaping his plate full and Alex simply cherishing the fresh melon and weak tea. They sat by themselves in the very back of the room. Ping went at his food as if he had not eaten in a week. When nearly finished, he lifted his head from his plate and used both hands to run his fingers through his black mane and smiled a devilish grin.

"I have Sparrow's schedule at the club this evening," he smirked.

"I am not doing this at the Wild Bunch," Alex said emphatically.

"OK, Mr. Cutter. This is your call. I am here only to assist."

"Get me a reliable weapon that has been thoroughly tested, Mr. Ping. Can you do that?"

"I have a stolen police weapon from over a year ago, which has been thoroughly vetted. I have it with me in this satchel," Ping said as if he was delivering a birthday cake.

The reality of the task weighed on his shoulders. He could not focus on the rest of what Ping was saying. How could he deceive the Chairman and his minions, given his true intentions? Surely they knew a foreigner committing such a crime would be caught, prosecuted, and sent to a Chinese prison in Gansu Province. Could he warn Sparrow, retreat from China, and enjoy a normal life afterward? What was he really doing here? The confusion in his mind coupled with staring at this rotten human being sitting across from him built up to a crescendo. "Let's get out of here now," he said.

Ping passed the satchel to Alex in the hallway as they left. Ping kept walking across the street. Alex felt the weight of the weapon in the zipped bag. This was getting crazy. Was it worth the risk? He returned to his hotel room, took an ice-cold shower, and then examined the gun and the ammunition left in the satchel. Murder in China is not as commonplace as it seems to be in the United States. He had to make this deception work. He sat on a simple chair in the corner and thought of everything that could go wrong.

CHAPTER 29

C. J. Collins, founder of White Cedar Semiconductor Corp. in San Francisco, had just concluded the video conference with his counterparts in Shanghai, Mumbai, Saint Petersburg, and London. Like chess pieces on a global board, the group had maneuvered over the late 1990s to establish themselves as the go-to firm for information-technology firms. Going public post the market crash of 2008, White Cedar had perfectly caught the market updraft, and all senior executives had become very wealthy men. They had almost a religious loyalty toward C. J. Collins.

Chairman Collins retreated to his corner office with its floor to ceiling windows overlooking San Francisco Bay just as the western sun was catching the tops of the regatta's sails. He had told his private secretary, Miss Kate, to go ahead and leave early for the day. This further privacy allowed him to recheck the encrypted message on his private e-mail screen. His mood instantly soured. He had played in the devil's cauldron way back in the late 1990s when his then-small firm needed commercial traction. An important man had approached him in Shanghai looking for an entrepreneur to break the security code of a government official in Nanjing. The man was extremely persuasive and rather threatening as well. The cash payment of RMB 1.4 million at the job's conclusion would allow Collins to not just weather the storm but exponentially expand his company's reach.

He took the job. He didn't share with his employer the relative ease of hacking into a prescribed electronic platform. The work took only four days. Collins worked solo. His employer, a Mr. Ping from Nanjing, rewarded him with the equivalent of over US$212,700 in small renminbi notes.

That was in the past. He had not heard again from the notorious Mr. Ping. Collins was always aware his role back then had been illegal. The fact he had compromised a Chinese government electronic platform had made him extremely nervous. Collins condoned the effort in his own mind by arguing if the government official targeted was not doing something illegal on the government's site; nothing should come of the hack. He also felt invisible given the anonymity of the World Wide Web.

And now it had come back to bite him in the ass. The encrypted message was demanding his expertise once again in China's electronic world. The threat of noncompliance was also crystal clear. Ping would expose his previous treachery from the initial hack. This would be ever so tricky and extremely dangerous. In the seventeen years since the first assignment, cyber security had become significantly more sophisticated. Mr. Ping was treading on very thin ice. Collins was to hack into the personal cyber world of a senior man in Nanjing, known as the Chairman. This man was connected to senior political representatives of the Central Committee in Beijing. The Chairman held board positions on multiple joint-venture Western companies. He literally was the government's eyes and ears in the highly touted enterprise tax-free zones in Nanjing.

Collins was perspiring, and his stomach felt like it was carrying one huge stone. Mr. Ping owned him. The likelihood of the Chairman having his influence on these joint-venture companies was absolutely significant. Tax due to the federal government and tax due to the provincial government, not to mention audits of financial statements, would place the Chairman in a position of strength at each and every company. Messing around with this guy's personal e-mails and server could prove fatal.

Collins called home and said he expected to be at the office rather late and to go ahead and have dinner without him. He tapped out an electronic response to Mr. Ping.

"I have received your message. I will personally address the issue at hand over the next two weeks and provide you with the necessary electronic key to bypass the principal's cyber security. The risks are immense. The fee will be commensurate with the risk profile. Three tranches of one point five million renminbi will be transferred simultaneously to my banks in India, Russia, and the UK. Under separate cover, I will forward the necessary account numbers and access codes. The funds will be converted to Indian rupees, Russian rubles, and English pounds at the time of the transfer. This is nonnegotiable."

Ping, multiple time zones apart at the time, responded almost immediately. "Your terms are agreed to."

Collins could feel his heart beat rapidly in his chest. Had he taken on too much? He shifted back and forth in his seat facing the computer screen. This could mean a defining moment for the growth of his company and his personal net worth. He stared at his screen and the one line response, "Your terms are agreed to."

Collins had multiple requests for proprietary information prior to beginning his hacking. In every case Ping was able to secure them. Collins cleared his business schedule for the next week, claiming he needed the extra time to focus solely on a highly secretive acquisition. By the week's end, Collins delivered the ID and password of Chairman Mao Ling. He had also copied all records obtained on two thumb drives. Collins made himself a stiff Johnny Walker Black over ice and dialed into his offshore accounts. As promised, he stared back at RMB 4.5 million, which had been converted three ways into Indian rupees, Russian rubles, and English pounds. Upon checking the conversion math and finding it accurate, he made himself another scotch and planned for his return to business as normal next week.

CHAPTER 30

Years earlier, as she lay in bed in the predawn, Sparrow heard the faint whistle from the train five kilometers away, pulling steam coal from Gansu Province to the Nanjing powerhouse to ignite the many foreign joint ventures residing in the enterprise tax-free zone. Her head turned on the burlap pillow, and she caught a different sound just outside her door. A cigarette-cough followed by rapidly fired words, the southern dialect difficult to discern, another deep cough, and a brief scuffle. She thought she heard her father's calm voice. Then she heard a whoosh sound—something vicious cutting through the heavy humid air. A single blood-curdling scream was followed by absolute quiet. Her ears strained to pick up more. Then there were faint sounds of something being dragged to her doorframe. A smug, nervous laugh came from a male's voice as another man coughed up phlegm and spit. Her ears strained for more, but they were gone. She heard the squeal from their one lone pig penned in the backyard as it stirred from its slumber. She threw off her thin sheet and came cautiously to the door.

Her father lay in two pieces. His torso lay like a forgotten rag doll, his neck and head a few feet away, with the thick pool of blood that had mixed with the earth to form brown goo. Stuffed in his mouth was a note that read "Silence your tongue."

It had been twelve years ago, yet she recalled every detail as if the nightmare had happened this morning. The method of ultimate submission by the triad was well known in the Northern provinces. She never understood. Her father had been an accomplished midlevel manager and member of the Party prior to his steep fall from grace. Prior to all of this, her father was recognized at an early age for his intellectual curiosity. He was bumped several grades in school and had excelled at every level. Recommended by his teachers and after extensive testing, he was enrolled in the prestigious Beijing University. He excelled at math, and his career path in engineering was a natural. He had always shown an interest in politics, and, after receiving his engineering degree in three years, he completed a course study in political science. The Party had recognized this multitalented young man and placed him under a mentor in Nanjing. His first role was working in the Office for Commercialization of Technology at the University. There he worked for a Dr. Li Shu, an older gentleman with a sharp scientific mind and considerable patience for his subordinates. Given the sensitivity of the assignment, her father also reported to a key political boss downtown. Her father referred to him as the Chairman.

Over the course of a year and a half, her father had been promoted three times and had become a member of the Communist Party. Their life at home improved as well. They moved into a state-sponsored apartment on the good side of the river. They had modern kitchen appliances, and Sparrow had her own bedroom. She remembered on summer weekends he would take her to the lake to swim and picnic. She loved going to the circus and to the theatre. Her father never remarried and the limited free time he had was spent with Sparrow.

The assignments for her father grew in complexity and importance. He worked longer hours. Unknown to him, there were a number of his peer group jealous of his overnight success. The leader of this clandestine group was a young man named Ping. This guy was younger than her father by a good ten years, yet held strong ambitions. Ping was the antithesis of her father. Where her father was tall and fit and carried himself in a military posture, Ping was short and overweight with thick glasses and stringy long hair. Her father was well read and interested in the arts. Ping was more interested in porn and fucking. Her father attempted to view problems from multiple orientations. Ping reached a singular conclusion without consultation. Her father was smart. Ping was crafty.

Over the course of several months, Ping set a trap for her father. One of the new projects being considered by the politburo for commercialization was an advanced geothermal technology. This exciting proprietary technology would not only produce electricity at the lowest possible cost but had the potential to create high financial returns. This revolutionary technology far exceeded solar, wind, and legacy geothermal energy production. The politburo was understandably excited about the invention and was committed to keeping the intellectual property secret.

Ping would spin a web of lies, plant bogus clues and link her father to a plot that appeared to transfer the intellectual property of the project to the highest international bidder. None of this was true of course, but Ping had successfully planted the seed in senior leadership's collective mind-set. The actions taken by the politburo were swift, and once the ball started rolling downhill for her father, no one wanted to have any linkage with him.

Ping was successful. Her father was stripped of his prestigious job, Communist Party credentials, and state-owned apartment. Sparrow could see the shame in his eyes. All the trappings of success were gone as well. There would be no state limo to pick them up for banquets. There would no longer be access to special Party-only stores for luxury goods. Her father's previous colleagues in the Party would avoid both Sparrow and her father. Being ostracized from their community was the worst of it. Mr. Ping was gloating. He had won again.

Forced to move out of their Beijing apartment, Sparrow and her father settled on a small slice of rugged land in rural Jiangsu County. Her father, the intellectual, now spent his days tending the small fields of rice, vegetables, and winter wheat. They lived in a stone and wooden building attached to the small barn holding their one sow. Evening lighting was poor, but Sparrow would sit and finish her homework as her father read next to her. His temperament and resolve always left a lasting impression on Sparrow.

Her father had accepted his role as a peasant farmer with a degree of dignity. He became the simple farmer trying his best to raise his beloved daughter, Sparrow.

She had shoved her pathetic self-absorbed grief deep inside her soul and replaced it with the only thing available—retribution. The anger she had focused on slowly metastasized into a medieval suit of armor. Nothing could penetrate her invisible shield. Leaving her father's grave was one of the most difficult things she had ever done. She had learned everything the local school could provide, and she had been a sponge to learn what her father shared over each dinnertime discussion. Physically she had gone from an athletic good-looking teen to a curvaceous young woman with a fair degree of confidence. The train ride took her to Nanjing. She walked from the station to a club/brothel on the city's southwest side. It was called the Wild Bunch Cabaret. She had initially heard about it from some girl-friends, who had tended to romanticize the place.

CHAPTER 31

Candy Medford stood back in the immigration line watching as the efficient KLM attendant whisked Alex Cutter to the front of the line and through to the arrival hall. Her assignment had proven much easier than she first expected. The ignorant Mr. Cutter had spotted her in the KLM preboarding lounge, fumbling with travel documents and finally dropping a lipstick case and boarding pass at the reception desk. Alex had moved forward to retrieve them. The gallant approach was anticipated by her. There was a subsequent conversation, some flirting on her part, and then his offer to upgrade her from business to first class on this flight, given he had an additional voucher.

He must really be into himself, she thought to herself. He was easily her father's age. He flirted. She flirted. She gave him a kind of wistful look and wide-eyed wonder to his every story. She licked her lips as if a nervous habit; her ruse had worked.

He must see her as an attractive, modestly educated young woman, who was obviously unattached on this international trip. He could not have known she despised everything he represented and would have preferred to slit his femoral artery. Surprisingly, they got seats together, 2A and 2B. After a superb dinner and after-dinner drinks, she doused her reading light and lightly placed her hand on his thigh beneath the KLM wool blanket and fell asleep.

Upon arrival in Amsterdam, they exchanged cards and numbers. Candy hurried off to call her superior with news of the successful "chance meeting" and likely future rendezvous. The old man, Alex Cutter, had been smitten with her. She still despised him; however, he was kind of cute in an ageing movie-star sort of way.

Candy Medford checked into her downtown hotel, showered, and changed into jeans. Through an encrypted message, she advised her handlers that she had made contact with the subject. She rehydrated with some of the hotel's bottled water and lit off to stretch her legs in the city center.

The trip from Johannesburg to Amsterdam had gone smoothly enough. The few drinks before dinner, the altitude, and the coincidence of bumping into each other prior to departure led to casual nonthreatening conversation. Given her interest in geopolitical theory, photography, and golf, Alex found the conversation both flirtatious and satisfying. As the lights dimmed after the dinner service, her hand naturally rested on his thigh and remained there as she drifted off to sleep.

As they disembarked, he wished her good luck with her upcoming photo shoot for L'Oreal in Paris. Alex met his limo driver just outside customs and proceeded to the airport Hilton. Subsequent to checking into the executive floor, Alex fired up his machine to check his encrypted e-mail account. The message was third from the bottom on his current listing. "Further instructions will be given to you upon your arrival in Nanjing. Meet me at the Xuan Hotel." Alex made the necessary travel arrangements and was in the old capital city the following evening.

He was nursing a Heineken at the hotel's lobby bar when he saw one of Ping's minions approach him. They grabbed a small table in a corner alcove.

"We have learned from our customs sources that Sparrow just arrived in Shanghai. She is traveling under a different name and forged documents, but we are certain it is her," said Ping's lieutenant. "We do not have her exact coordinates but are working on it."

"Where is Ping?" Alex responded in a frustrated tone.

"Unfortunately he had another commitment that took precedent to this meeting," said Ping's lieutenant.

"That's bullshit. I have traveled from Monterrey, Mexico, to handle this delicate matter for him." Alex switched over to his broken Mandarin. "I am president and CEO of a successful international public company, and I will not be treated like some for-hire peasant. This is simply unacceptable," Alex said as he stared at his counterpart at the table.

Also switching to Mandarin, the lieutenant attempted to act more subservient. "Mr. Cutter, you are an important man and well respected in this country. Unfortunately Mr. Ping had to remain at the plant to address an industrial accident at the malt house; one of the workers fell from a silo to his death. The government is much more sensitive to deaths in the workplace at the joint-venture companies. Mr. Ping expects the visit by local authorities to be perfunctory but for good orders sake thought it best to manage the situation personally."

Switching back to his native tongue, Alex said, "I was unaware. It may just delay us a day."

The lobby-bar waitress returned with two more Heinekens, and the lieutenant paid and waved her off. "I have the most updated intelligence we have on Sparrow," he said, passing the memory stick to Alex.

"OK. That's all I had expected tonight. Inform Mr. Ping that I will be staying at the Sheraton. Have him meet me there over breakfast tomorrow," Alex instructed. With two more sips of his beer, he got up and left the table.

A proper nights rest was impossible given the jet lag and the uneasiness Alex felt in his gut. So many things could go wrong. He studied the memory stick's contents on his laptop. There was little new information for him, with the exception of Sparrow becoming the Chairman's courtesan of choice. Alex's handlers knew nothing of the intimacy shared with Sparrow during his early days as an intern. Alex paced the hotel room and opened the balcony door to receive some of the cooler night air. To fill time, he disassembled the Israeli semiautomatic handgun. Alex was familiar with the Jericho 941 and appreciated its simplicity and weight in his hand. The nine-by-nineteen-millimeter-caliber weapon was as deadly as it was easy to conceal. Alex cleaned the weapon for the third time and reassembled it expertly. He may need the weapon to forge his escape should things go wrong. By 4:00 a.m. local time, he lay down to rest for a couple of hours before meeting Ping.

The hotel's service rung his phone at 6:30 a.m., and he cursed as he picked up the receiver. "We will have your tea brought to the room in fifteen minutes, sir."

Ping was on time in the hotel's breakfast restaurant. His longish was hair slicked back as if he just came from the shower. He had a small plate of *hokken*, steamed buns filled with bean paste in front of him. Steam was rising from his personal ceramic teacup. "It's good to see you, my friend," he told Alex as he arrived at the table.

"I understand you had a tragic workplace accident to deal with last night."

"It's a large industrial complex, and we expect there to be unforeseen accidents. I hope it was explained to you last night why I could not meet with you. It was one worker out of four hundred fifty-five at the plant. We have a long list of applicants wanting to work for an international joint venture. We have the replacement worker on site for training this morning. As the senior executive on site, it was imperative to personally handle the government authorities looking out for worker safety. Let's just say the two investigators should have a memorable time at the Wild Bunch Cabaret with our company picking up their tab for the evening. Nothing much will come of their investigation except a long written report to appease their superiors."

A waitress poured Alex some tea. As she left the table, Alex leaned across the table directly toward Ping's face. "I want to be out of China in the next forty-eight hours. I require her coordinates. I want them now, Ping."

Ping took another bite and stared back. "She has entered our country illegally with forged documents. We should have much more detail for you later today. It's also in our best interests for this matter to be cleaned up, I assure you."

CHAPTER 32

The night before the Chairman was scheduled to return to Nanjing, Ping had designed another bizarre evening. His sexual sadism had escalated his arousal only in response to Sparrow's total humiliation. He began the experimental evening much earlier than normal. Sparrow remained the coy participant, at times whimpering, which she discovered he loved. He would make the most out of this last night with the enchanting Sparrow.

Afterward, Ping feeling every centimeter the dominant figure, lay back on the oversize pillows, and ordered Miss Lin (Sparrow) to the bathroom to gather up some lotion and to massage his callous feet. As requested, Sparrow fulfilled the exercise by humming a rural working song and gently rubbed her new master's calves and feet. Shortly his rhythmic breathing turned to a hissing snore. Sparrow left the bed and closed the yellow drapes. Her bag contained all that would be necessary: duct tape, cord, scalpel, and a red rubber ball. Expertly she tied off the cord to the bedpost and slid the premade lassos over each wrist. Making a V with her elbow, she crushed it against his temple, followed by a quick thrust to his throat. The lassos were tightened virtually at the identical time. The impact of both blows rendered Ping nearly unconscious and the natural reaction of gasping for his next breath. The cord tightened and the red ball was inserted in his open mouth, duct tape holding it in place.

Binding his ankles with the lassos took but another moment. Mr. Ping's eyes bugged out as panic kicked in. Sparrow left the bed and dressed, returning with her white cloves. Seductively she stroked his cheeks with them and then down his shallow chest to his privates. She left the gloves there.

The first cut was superficial and just below his left eye. The next, similar in depth, opened his left nostril. His panic reached a new level and now just whimpers could be heard. She turned to her bag, and in one final herculean motion, he attempted to pull at his wrist restraints.

The cord held. Sparrow began the cutting, deeper this time down his torso to just above his manhood. He almost swallowed the red ball. He thrashed back and forth the best he could. The next cut was rather like a circumcision and blood covered the bedclothes. She wiped the blade on one of her gloves.

He was getting weak with the blood loss and his movements remained pathetic to her. She slid off the bed and gathered up his wallet. Taking a RMB 1000 note, she laid out two coke lines and took both hits herself. The blood on the bed had formed a pool beneath the Y of his skinny legs.

Ping had many enemies. The local triad saw him as weak with limited connections. The Chairman saw him as simply a stopgap measure until he could promote one of his trusted lieutenants to the role of general manager. Those in Nanjing's government responsible for taxing the joint-venture companies were unclear of his true alliance. The important people, the ones who really counted in Beijing, saw Ping as unsophisticated and untested. They would have agreed with the Chairman to promptly select a GM and relegate Ping to a junior role he was more suited for. Now that Ping was gone, it made a transition that much easier.

Sparrow released Ping's body from the restraints and pulled the red ball from his mouth. She knew the triad code would require several of his fingers to be amputated as a lesson to others of personal greed. She began the cutting of the index and middle finger on one hand. She found it difficult, but she managed to complete the task and stuff them into his mouth. She threw her restraining cords and red ball into Ping's briefcase. She gathered up the bloody white gloves. She rummaged through his pocketbook and retrieved a fifty-renminbi note and stuffed it next to the amputated fingers in his mouth. She scrubbed and locked the room and left out the back alley with his briefcase. She knew the body would not be found for at least twenty-four hours—it was often when Ping had told subordinates to leave him alone as he enjoyed another sexual marathon with a paid partner.

Sparrow left Mr. Ping in a rather unattractive pose for the authorities. Castrated, with two of his fingers hanging from his lips and multiple deep cuts across his chest and inner thighs, Ping would initially be diagnosed a victim of the triad. Local authorities, particularly those taking bribes to look the other way for the high-class brothel, would not be encouraged to conduct a thorough criminal investigation. The victim had clearly been tortured while being restrained. Clearly two or three triad enforcers had delivered the message. Many would think Mr. Ping, not known yet by many influential people, had attempted to stiff the triad from their earned fee. No one would consider a petite courtesan as a viable suspect.

Sparrow took a cab to the Nanjing airport. She had purchased a second pair of white satin gloves at a high-end department store and changed into a business suit. As the cab fought the early rush hour, she stared out the window. The clouds peeled back like strips of gauze from the overcast sky revealing the burnt orange of the western sun. Somehow she took this as a positive sign. She tipped the cabbie and swung her shapely legs from the vehicle and walked with confidence to Tiger Airlines' first-class counter. She purchased a round-trip ticket to Hong Kong and settled into her soft seat in the front of the aircraft. The business suit did not detract from her shape and her makeup was done perfectly. Authorities at the airport simply glanced at her documentation and stole glances at the extremely polished and attractive woman. Airport security, dressed in their drab uniforms, all considered her multiple echelons above their class. Although officially in the People's Republic of China there were no classes, everyone knew where there was power. Sparrow emanated power and position. Perhaps she was married to someone in the politburo. Perhaps she was a senior member of the Party herself. No one could tell, but everyone who saw her recognized she was someone not to cross.

Sparrow ordered a light white wine after takeoff. One of her adversaries was gone. She felt absolutely no remorse. Why should she? She had been treated like a farm animal, and her father had been brutally murdered. Much of her young adulthood had been stolen from her. She passed on the snacks offered and got another white wine; then she drifted off to a peaceful sleep.

She awoke to the captain's announcement of pending arrival. Sparrow stared out her window to the incredible sight of Hong Kong lit up at night. She opened her briefcase with Ping's wallet, which contained RMB 40,000, well over US$5,000. She checked into the Four Seasons for the next five nights, paying cash in advance.

Sparrow kicked off her shoes in the entryway of her suite. She dialed downstairs for a bottle of '92 Barossa chardonnay and a half order of their caramel dessert to arrive an hour later. She enjoyed a bath and wrapped herself in a luxurious white robe just before room service arrived.

Curiosity caused her to turn on the TV station broadcast from Nanjing. Not to her surprise, there was nothing about a murder in an upscale brothel in a town of over nine million people. She clicked off the television and sat on her outdoor balcony overlooking the famous harbor. She had not felt this free for many, many years. She brought out the remainder of the wine from the minibar. Naked beneath the robe and with her painted toes resting on the balcony railing, she felt the shiver of the later evening, and she had never felt more alive.

Alex learned of Ping's torture and murder from two sources. Ping's lieutenant, the one he had shared a Heineken with just the other night, called with the news. Now the lieutenant, who was so brash and full of himself, was diminutive and scared. The second call came from the Chairman's entourage, which had just returned from a trade mission in Vietnam. This call had a distinctively different tone. An unwanted business partner had met his demise, and Chairman had absolutely nothing linking him to the event.

The absolute relief Alex felt was indescribable. No need to carry out the ruse of killing Sparrow and the subsequent risk of failure. No need to risk an investigation, which could lead to a dank cell in Upper Mongolia and perhaps his own execution. No further being owned by another person, like Mr. Ping. He felt light. He called home, left a message he would be home a day earlier, and contemplated the reasonableness of possibly seeing Sparrow one last time. Perhaps they could just have tea, catch up, and stare into each other's souls. Perhaps, he dreamed, there was the possibility of another tryst before his flight the following day. Alex shook his head in disbelief in how his world had changed in less than twenty-four hours. He called home a second time and caught the answering machine. He walked out into the misty, chilly Nanjing night. He found a café overlooking the polluted Yangzi and ordered a tea. He called his wife a third time, only to be routed to the answering machine.

The more he thought about it, the clearer it became. The loveless marriage he was pretending to ignore had to reach closure. His wife was far more interested in her Pilate class and tennis lessons. She had little to do with her daughter, and there were sitters at their home every week, giving her more time at the club. He loved his daughter and would fight for custody. He felt guilty for the time he had spent abroad on business, missing his daughter's birthdays and not being around for her little victories. He had made some serious mistakes in his life. He decided to make things right. His daughter gave him such joy. Up till now, he had been selfish, his career overshadowing everything else. He was committed to be a better father and a better man.

Sparrow had been a wonderful fling for him in the past, but she had moved on, and he certainly could not blame her. His expertise as a security specialist would find demand across the globe, and his solid reputation would provide more than enough satisfying work. He banged out an e-mail to his squash partner and attorney on the other side of the world. The message was straightforward. He would seek a reasonable divorce settlement but was willing to give up more than his share for outright custody of their daughter, Alexia.

He felt lighter already. His nemesis Ping was gone. His struggle to make his country-club wife happy would finally come to an end. He would give up on his foolish young man's fantasy with Sparrow and move on to adulthood. He would bring his daughter up with strong values and a worldly background. He dreamed of a cottage outside Auckland, New Zealand. He was enamored with the rugged countryside, its world-class transportation hub, and fine cuisine. He would work when it fit him. He would expose his daughter to the richness of the arts, of true friends, and of the pursuit of intellectual curiosity. He would expose her to the discipline of the martial arts. The more he dreamed, the more real it could all become.

Rather than wait another twelve hours for his booked flight home, Alex caught a cab to the Nanjing International Airport. He booked a one-way first class ticket on Tiger Airlines from Nanjing to Hong Kong, connecting to Thai airlines direct to Bangkok. He had only to wait an hour and forty-five minutes for departure. For the first time in many years, he felt he had clarity in his life.

CHAPTER 33

The connecting flight was on time. Alex took a limo directly to his favorite hotel in the world, the Oriental. The new clarity in his life coupled with a few drinks on the plane had him crashing for nearly twelve hours in his luxury suite. Midafternoon the following day had him taking the hotel's complimentary ferry to cross the Chao Phraya River. He sat behind a retired couple from Germany. They spoke in the Bavarian dialect, and he overheard something about lost luggage being finally recovered by the airlines. He checked his phone and the response from his old friend Nina was encouraging. She had promised to meet at the Royal Gardens.

The second ferry Alex caught took him in a southerly direction. In a few minutes, he spotted the domes of the Emerald Buddha housed in Wat Phra Kaew. The setting sun danced off the three gold plated domed temples giving the cityscape a surreal, exotic backdrop.

He stepped from the ferry onto a less than sturdy wooden dock shifting with the steady current of the Chao Phraya. Following Nina's directions, Alex walked east on Chetuphon Road until reaching the canal. Taking a left turn onto Rachini Road, he passed the Suan Saranrom Park with its old men playing dominos, young women pushing strollers, and boys darting in and out with a soccer ball. The scent of incense mixed with rotten garbage hung over the park. Another twenty minutes brought him to the northeast corner of Sanam Luang—the Royal Gardens.

Nina, his retired assistant, was seated on a bench with her back to him. She had allowed her hair to turn naturally gray, but the crinkles next to her eyes spoke of a life well lived and fulfilled.

"Nina, you look terrific," he said as he kissed her on the cheek. "Retirement seems to have worked well for you."

"Alex, you rascal, it's good to see you as well. I figured it's been close to twelve years now. Are you still working sixty hours a week?"

"Not anything close to that anymore." Alex laughed. "How is your husband? Antonio, right?

"We are both fine, thanks for asking. Tony retired just a year ago and now volunteers at the orphanage. I told him you were coming, but he was committed to assist at our church today. He was adamant to invite you to our home for dinner, however."

"That is very kind, and I accept."

"What brings you to our corner of the world, Alex?

"I have filed for divorce and expect to receive full custody of our daughter. Upon clearing all the necessary legal hurtles relating to it, I would like to erase my past and start new—similar to what you and Tony accomplished upon your retirement."

"I assume you have the necessary funding."

"Yes."

"You are prepared to walk completely away from your past associates, board seats, and public accolades?"

"Absolutely, and now is a good time given my daughter's age. I assumed you and Tony could help. I do not expect this to be done gratis—I will gladly pay market rate to disappear."

"Alex, we would be pleased to assist." With that brief exchange, she got up, took his hand, and walked through the park.

A great many details were worked out over the course of the following days. Not unexpectedly, Tony and his wife were experts at creating an ironclad dossier with supporting documentation for a new life. Forged documents with official stamps were but a fraction of the detail they covered with him. By the end of the second week, Alex Cutter had been found on the airplane's manifest, which had tragically gone down in the South China Sea. There were no survivors according to the China Post. His new persona was gleaned partially from a real man, about his age and build, and partially from the creative minds of Nina and her talented husband.

CHAPTER 34

She had been extremely patient since her father's murder. She had learned how both Mr. Ping and the Chairman were involved in her father's death. The Chairman's political influence had crushed her father's career. Ping's diabolical web of lies and influence with the triad had killed him. No longer would Mr. Ping place his sweaty hands on her. No longer would she be surrounded by the stench of his breath or devious sex games.

She had arrived in Hong Kong to meet the Chairman, who was due back from a trade mission in Vietnam. She knew he would be full of himself and horny. This morning she dressed comfortably for the Hong Kong humidity and wore flats. She walked to a boat shuttle to Kowloon. There she found the three pharmacies she knew would have most of her necessary supplies. One important component, high-grade cocaine, was not available over the counter, but she had handsomely tipped the hotel concierge with a whispered request, and two grams of the white powder miraculously appeared when she returned to the front desk for her room key.

Normally the Chairman would have doubled his security detail after learning of the hideous way Mr. Ping had died. The Chairman's sources had provided him a report that pointed the blame on Mr. Ping himself. Apparently Ping had employed the services of an offtake of the triad in rural Jiangsu County. Most likely, the report concluded, Ping had attempted to cheat the rural triad cell and paid a steep price. Ping was clearly over his head and lacked the guidance and protection of the Party and national triad. The Chairman would address the open management position at the malt plant upon his return to the city.

Given his history with Sparrow, he did not believe extra security was at all warranted. He would, however, increase security for his trip home to Nanjing. He instructed his lead security officer. The next two days in Hong Kong with Sparrow would relieve all the tension from the Vietnamese business trip. He instructed his security detail to get rooms around the corner from his luxury digs. They could have this first night off after getting him checked into his hotel. He would ring them if it became necessary.

Sparrow called down and ordered a late lunch to be delivered when the Chairman had checked in. Four lines of cocaine were laid out on a glass table in the living room of the suite. Sparrow double-checked her mental checklist. She spent time on her hair and slipped into the powder blue nightgown she knew was his favorite. It was show time.

A muted marmalade tone filled the penthouse bedroom as the sun lost its battle with the western horizon. Drapes were open to floor to ceiling windows, which drew upon the island of Kowloon and the early neon of Hong Kong. Even the jaded traveler recognized the unique beauty of the harbor as dusk settled. New lights peppered the coastline casting long shadows across the blue-gray water. The room remained artificially cool, as he liked. The room-service table was littered with remnants of the Beijing Duck and the caramel desert she had enjoyed only once before. The surround sound played "Take Five," the late Dave Brubeck track with the woeful sax on a low-volume setting.

For the third time since their arrival midafternoon, her hips and buttocks bucked against his manhood. The slap-slap of human skin was simply the backdrop for her whimpers, which the Dragon expected and preferred during intercourse. At the act's conclusion, he lay facing away from her. His left leg bent as he held the monogramed Mandarin Hotel pillow between his thighs. Soon his rhythmic breathing changed to rhythmic snoring.

Sparrow swung her shapely legs to the side of the bed. Her toes disappeared in the nap of the ivory carpet. Silently she made her way to the luxury bathroom and her overnight bag.

Returning to the soft jazz and rhythmic snoring, she rolled a HK$1,000 denominated bill and laid out four lines of cocaine on the glass table holding the remains of the duck dinner and caramel desert. She dipped her delicate index finger into the caramel sauce and touched her lips. The rubber surgical gloves snapped on with perfect fit. She climbed back onto the king-size bed and without hesitation plugged the suppository up his anus as she gently kissed his back. He stirred, mumbled, and returned to sleep.

She slipped again from the bedcovers. This would not take long. The suppository casing made of dissolvable corn-based dextrose would disgorge the cocktail of steroids, cocaine, and ricin. The certain result would come in three or four minutes. Initially the victim would awake with a sudden start, a pounding of the eardrums followed by the sensation of an elephant sitting on his chest-cavity, his heart compressed into his backbone. Given the difficulty to catch a single breath, the victim would not call out. Internal bleeding and severe damage to liver and kidneys would add to the severe pain. She stood at the foot of the bed and coolly watched as his eyes went from startled to utter panic. Late in the fourth minute, his convulsing body gave up and his eyes remained fixed on the ceiling. She reached for the Hong Kong currency and dipped into the cocaine line blowing some into his silent nostrils. She took a small hit herself.

It was important to work quickly and have emergency personnel on site. Time of death would be relatively easy to determine. She called down to the concierge, a Mr. Wing. She had flashed the elderly Mr. Wing her trademark smile as she took the arm of the Dragon upon check-in. He would not have forgotten her.

The call was answered on the second ring. "Something is terribly wrong," Sparrow screeched in perfect English. "Come quickly! Is there a doctor in the hotel? Oh my God! Hurry—room 2016." She paused as if to catch her breath. "My companion has stopped breathing! Oh my God; oh my God."

Sparrow now cut the surgical gloves in small pieces, disposing the fragments down the toilet and some off the balcony in the light night breeze. Naked would not work, so she changed into the powder-blue nightgown she had bought for the trip and waited for the authorities. She thought back to the days of using a hypodermic needle placed between the toes to avoid obvious injection marks on the victim. The suppository worked much better and left no trace.

The young hotel security officer arrived first at the double doors to the suite, and she cried and pointed to the master bedroom. She remained at the door, and within several minutes, a disheveled older man with white hair and a small black bag introduced himself as a physician. Sparrow followed him into the bedroom.

More authorities followed and there was a degree of confusion and anxiety in the room. It was obvious the tryst had included cocaine. The initial conclusion held by all in the room was that a rather older man was having sex with a rather stunning younger woman, and he must have experienced a massive heart attack. The Chairman's lead security man was summoned.

Sparrow's theatrical training coupled with her beauty kept the Hong Kong police and hotel security at bay. They all seemed more engaged to make her comfortable, console her, and change her to another suite on a lower floor. The police would ask a few more questions after she had been relocated. As she gathered up her overnight bag and slipped on a hotel cashmere robe, she left the suite just as the police photographer began his work.

Thankful but not surprised by her efficiency, Sparrow settled into her new room. She would make herself available for further questioning over the next several days. She called down to room service and requested a half order of Singapore noodles and a full order of the caramel sauce desert.

While waiting for the room service, Sparrow logged on to her computer. First she tapped into the Chairman's account in the Bahamas. Selecting the proper password and passcodes, she transferred all but $50,000 into her New York account. The offshore bank did not question the amount or destination of the funds. Several clicks later, she had $9 million at her disposal.

Detective Wu was punctual. He was also young and unattached. He knocked on her suite door precisely at 9:00 a.m. the next day to continue questioning the witness. Sparrow let him in. She was wearing just the classic full-length plush robe with the hotel's insignia.

"Please, Detective, come in, and make yourself comfortable. Tea or coffee?"

"Tea would be fine. You enjoy an incredible view of the harbor. Would you mind if I snapped a photo?"

"Please do, Detective. Cream?"

"No, thank you, Miss...?"

"Please call me Sparrow." She sat next to the floor to ceiling windows and crossed her shapely legs. The white robe rode up to her midthigh. "Please sit, and make yourself comfortable. Would you care for something with your tea?"

"The tea is fine; I had an early breakfast." Taking the seat across from her, he was mesmerized by the stunning young woman. A rich Oriental rug of brown and yellows separated them. "I know this may be a very difficult time for you, and thank you for agreeing to our appointment this morning. I have just several questions in order to properly wrap up our investigation." Wu pulled a small red notebook from his suit pocket.

"Detective, I am pleased to help in any way I might. It's all been a nightmare as I am sure you can appreciate."

"I recognized you have not employed counsel today. Are you OK to proceed?" he asked as he attempted to focus on her face.

"Mr. Wu, I have absolutely no reason to have legal assistance. Please proceed and ask away."

"Thank you, Miss Sparrow. I will make this as quick and efficient as possible." Staring at her composed face, he began with "Was your companion on any heart medication?"

"Not that I know of."

"This may be difficult, but was your companion taking any erectile-dysfunction medication?"

Sparrow laughed openly and readjusted her sitting posture. "It was our third round of intimacy, Detective, since we had checked in. He was a man with an insatiable carnal appetite. None of this was out of character."

"Miss Sparrow, again pardon my directness, but your companion was a rather influential and powerful man in China, yet there was no sign of extraordinary security either in the room or in the lobby downstairs."

"Mr. Wu, my companion preferred discreetness. Certainly his personal assistant was fully aware of his itinerary as were his bodyguards. Allow me to text you their contacts for good order sake." Sparrow pulled out her phone and tapped away.

"Miss Sparrow, thank you for your openness in this difficult manner. Those questions conclude my business here today. We should have our results on any toxins in the bloodstream later this afternoon. Upon clearing those through our lab, I will release you from any further restrictions our department may have placed on you. Again, thank you for your patience this morning." Wu placed his teacup on the saucer and bowed as he left the room.

At 1500 hours, later that day, Mr. Wu called and left a message for Sparrow: "All our testing is complete. The death certificate lists cardiac arrest as the sole cause. Thank you again for your considerate cooperation. You are free to leave. Travel safely."

Sparrow called down to room service and ordered a light dinner of prawns, Singapore noodles, and half order of the caramel dessert. A chilled bottle of 1992 Barossa chardonnay completed the minimalist order.

She read herself to sleep. The Dragon, also known as the Chairman, was no longer a threat. The Chairman's associates, however, could present a future problem should they link her to the stolen funds. She would have to deal with it in due time. That issue could wait.

As she laid down her novel, she dreamed of her freedom from the Chairman and Ping and the cabaret whorehouse. She now had the means to do whatever she wished.

CHAPTER 35

Alex Cutter was still in Bangkok getting his new documentation to match his new identity when he received the e-mail confirming the untimely death of the Chairman. The Chairman's head of security had confirmed the fatal heart attack. Alex felt lighter still.

Herr Reins followed up with Mr. Leong. He was pleased with his success on breaking into the politburo's IT system and Secretary Xin's private e-mail server giving Reins access to the Shanghai market. Reins confirmed payment to Leong for work completed. He made a new request to have Leong share the technical data with Primrose. Leong had agreed but for an additional monetary consideration, which Herr Reins immediately agreed to.

Herr Reins, at his opulent office in Brussels, was posted of the Chairman's apparent heart attack via call from the Chairman's security detail. He did not grieve but rather coldly evaluated his business options going forward. Prior to all this, he and the Chairman had examined multiple contingencies to their plan to hack into the Shanghai equity market and create an informational pause, which they could leverage against proprietary information on other international exchanges. They had never contemplated a partner's death. Herr Reins's man, Primrose, had successfully laundered their initial investment capital through the Faisal Bank, Lahore, and they were positioned to capitalize on the pause at the Shanghai equity market. Herr Reins was certain he had covered all the bases. Almost as an afterthought, Reins sent an encrypted note to Candy Medford. It said simply "Abort mission." Killing Alex Cutter was no longer necessary. Cutter had nothing to do with their scamming the equity markets.

Candy stared at the message on her computer to "abort mission." She was fine with the clear instruction. She was paid well in either case. She called the hotel spa and made a massage appointment and confirmed her ticket back to Europe the following day.

Herr Reins made another call. He instructed Primrose to pause the Shanghai market on Thursday precisely for two minutes. The pause should come with ten minutes remaining in the trading session. Primrose confirmed the instructions of the pause while still on the phone with his boss. Primrose also confirmed the funds cleansed through the Faisal Bank of Lahore, Pakistan, were available for wire transfers. These funds were distributed electronically to the various trading accounts Herr Reins controlled under different names. Prior to the prearranged pause, Reins would place heavy sell orders across a broad range of equities in the other market exchanges as well as the Shanghai exchange. He also placed heavy sell orders across the curve of both the aluminum and copper markets. Thursday's global equity and metals markets opened as usual. Late in the session, traders noted both the influx of extremely heavy sell orders in the equity and metals markets and the temporary closing of the Shanghai market "due to technical difficulties." Local day traders in each of the exchanges unloaded their positions and unknowingly tipped the scales in Herr Reins's direction. Within one minute and fifty-eight seconds of the pause, Herr Reins reversed all his short positions and placed at-the-market buy orders across every exchange. Future markets violently reacted to the prescribed volatility. Reins made a small fortune, with over 90 percent of his trades reaping huge profits. Before exchange regulators could grapple with the violent market moves, the market seemed to settle itself prior to the daily trading close of business, and the Shanghai market was back in business. Regulators dismissed the violent market volatility as simply an unusual volume of sell orders reaching the market at once, followed by an inordinate amount of buy orders as bargain hunters reentered the market place.

Herr Reins estimated his profits after commissions at the equivalent of 4.65 million deutsche marks. He was pleased. He had executed a similar strategy on the foreign exchange markets. Given the extreme depth of those markets, his profits were not nearly as steep, but they more than paid for Mr. Leong's fee.

At the politburo's central office in Beijing, Mr. Xin learned of the Chairman's demise. The need to neutralize the Chairman had taken a more natural course, and he could not be more pleased. His triad contacts, who had secured a deadly bird virus, could now be told to stand down. He had also learned of Mr. Ping's horrific death. Having never to have met Mr. Ping, the intelligence of his death came from his second tier of agents. Apparently, this Mr. Ping was a temporary general manager of the large malting complex in Nanjing. From Mr. Xin's perspective, this all worked out very well. Mr. Xin was now in the position to nominate and secure his own handpicked representative to hold board positions on the ten joint-venture companies previously held by the egotistical Chairman. Mr. Xin surprised his staff as he left the office early for a contemplative stroll in the park to enjoy the spring blossoms. C. J. Collins learned of Ping's death from a Chinese colleague managing the security platform for several of the Western joint-venture companies. This same contact shared the news of the Chairman's fatal heart attack. Collins could not be more relieved. His connections to unscrupulous parties in the People's Republic of China were severed, and he could move on with his life, never to look over his shoulder again.

Mr. Lin, through his cousin Mr. Shu, learned of the awful death of Mr. Xie. Lin immediately recognized the deadly symptoms described as coming from the virulent bird serum. Why the triad would murder an unemployed financial guy was a mystery. His cousin, Mr. Shu, was distraught. Lin attempted to comfort his cousin to no avail. His cousin also shared the location Mr. Xie had been found dead. This was at the massive malting complex, near the office of the temporary manager Mr. Ping. There were also rumors of Ping's untimely death in a whorehouse. Lin became increasingly nervous. He decided to sell a third of the remaining bird flu serum to his triad contact and disappear into Wuxi, the university town to the southeast of Nanjing.

CHAPTER 36

Sparrow woke early as was her custom. She slipped from the covers and into a black leopard print one-piece swimsuit. After forty minutes of laps in the hotel pool, she ordered one egg, whole wheat toast, and orange juice. The limousine deposited her at the airport; the driver's assistant followed her into the hall with her luggage. Check in was smooth and effortless. Sparrow finished one glass of sparkling water in the first-class lounge and heard her flight was boarding for New York. Slipping into seat 2A, she removed her high heels, ordered a sparkling water, and began to read the *New York Times*. After a light lunch and quick nap, she was disembarking at JFK. The prearranged limo deposited her at the Four Seasons Hotel. Given the text she had received while at the airport, she expected a visitor any time after 1400 hours.

Given his penchant for punctuality, he called her room from the hotel lobby and advised he had the prepared documentation with him. Sparrow advised she would join him in the lobby bar in just a few minutes.

As she entered the dimly lit cocktail lounge, Mr. Chang motioned for her to join him at a back table. She was impressed. Chang, the rather scruffy young man she had known in Nanjing ten years prior, had morphed into a sophisticated New Yorker. His black hair was trimmed and facial hair removed; a dark three-piece suit highlighted with a burgundy pocket square completed the metamorphosis. He smiled as Sparrow made her way to his table. She wore a simple white linen dress drawn in at the waist with off-white sandals. Her hair was a bit damp from a shower. She looked completely rested, content, and in command. She looked terrific.

Sparrow ordered a sparkling water and noted Chang had done the same. The back of the room smelled of expensive cigars and teak. A jazz track played from overhead speakers, and they were the only patrons in the lounge at this early hour.

"You have certainly matured since we last met in Singapore," Chang opened as he took a sip. "I trust your trip was smooth and uneventful."

Sparrow crossed her legs and simply stared at her friend for a full count of five. "Chang, you have pleasantly surprised me," she said as she moved her hand across her cheek and chin. "And your classic facial hair?"

"Gone—as are the eyeglasses and hearing aid," he said, truly pleased with himself. "And I must say you look terrific." Chang motioned for their waiter to return and ordered a small plate of herring. Taking another sip of water, Chang tapped on the manila envelope he had on the table. "It's all here as you requested. A new identity—US passport, an American Express Platinum Card, a New York driver's license, VISA card, membership card to the New York Symphony Orchestra, and even a library card from Queens. You are now Evian Bloomberg Gang. Your husband passed away from an aggressive lung cancer six months ago. You have inherited a rather comfortable sum, but nothing extraordinary. You have a Mr. Wiebold from the Wells Fargo branch on Long Island manage your portfolio. He has not met you but has had frequent communications via wire and phone messages. Though you did not request same, I have included four hundred dollars cash in small bills for good orders sake."

Sparrow smiled. She waited until the waiter had left the fish appetizer between them. "Chang, once again you have impressed me. You have been in the United States less than twelve years, and yet you understand how to get important things done."

"Thank you, Ms. Gang," he said, smiling broadly as he passed the fish plate to her.

Sparrow accepted the offering with perfectly manicured hands. "Your fee will be deposited in the Cayman account prior to close of business today. Thank you, Chang. I have always been able to count on you."

Chang dipped his head in deference to her, took one piece of the delicate appetizer, and finished his water. As he got up to leave the table, he gently touched the back of her hand, adjusted his suit jacket, and left her alone at the small cocktail table.

Sparrow, or as she would be known in New York, Madam Gang, deposited the manila folder in her oversize purse and left the lounge. She would spend the next few hours memorizing her new persona and call Mr. Weibold for an appointment and his advice whether to retain her sizable spread position. She had purchased renminbi in the market against selling of the US dollar. She had already come to her own conclusion but thought a bit of direct dialogue with the financial advisor would be excellent practice as the new Madam Gang.

Madam Gang (Sparrow) left the portico of the Four Seasons in a yellow cab the next morning. She met Mr. Weibold in his offices precisely at 9:00 a.m. After the perfunctory introductions, she laid out a proposed agenda for the meeting. First off was his recommendation on how to manage her foreign-exchange position. Weibold coughed and proceeded to ramble on about market dynamics and market momentum. Madam Gang (Sparrow) listened intently to the weak thesis. When he finished, Sparrow left her seat and began to pace around the conference room, maintaining eye contact with him.

"Let's see. The most recent market activity over the past three days may suggest our strategy is flawed. Have you considered a Condor hedge strategy or collar-option strategy to protect the profits we have in the current position? Let's pull up a price spread graph on the nearby exchange option months."

Weibold was scrambling to find the necessary information on his computer. Who was this principal that seemed to know more than he did? "I'll have it for you in a minute," he said.

She rattled off more financial jargon, half of which Weibold was unfamiliar with. He pulled a graph to the overhead screen. She pulled a black marker from the conference table and began to mark up the illustration on the screen. Weibold was out of his element. Wealthy customers always listened to him—this customer was giving a tutorial. After drawing her various technical support and resistant lines on the price chart, she drew back and said, "OK, I would instruct you to liquidate one-third of the position and place that in my cash account. Let's reverse our bull-spread and execute a deferred bracket strategy on the balance."

Before Weibold could articulate a response, she had collected her coat and was headed to the door. "Thanks again for your time, Mr. Weibold. I will look for that deposit tomorrow."

The additional cash deposit would adequately fund her new lifestyle for the next eighteen months.

CHAPTER 37

Having dispensed with her foreign exchange advisor, Sparrow returned to the Four Seasons' lobby and a light lunch of prawns and egg-drop soup. As she was finishing her lunch in an alcove overlooking the blooming garden, she was approached by a scruffy looking older gentleman with horrible shoes.

"Pardon me, madam, but I was asked to deliver this," he said in perfect English with a slight Scottish twist. "I was instructed to leave it in your hands and not allow the concierge to handle it," said the scruffy stranger.

"Thank you, kind sir" was Madam Gang's polite response. As she reached for her handbag in order to offer a tip of some kind, she saw the man begin to retreat from her table.

"I was paid handsomely to deliver the package. There is no need for further compensation." And with those few words, he was gone.

Sparrow opened the neatly wrapped package. In it she found a wrapped CD and a handwritten note. The note was scribbled on cheap yellow paper.

By the time you read this, you must feel safe. The Chairman and Mr. Ping are no longer threats...

The Chinese people thank you for your courage. The Chairman and Ping were vermin...no philosophical foundation, no meaning to their pitiful lives, untrustworthy.

No scruples. You have managed through some difficult situations, and your unique skill set is well appreciated...

Before we continue may I suggest you view the enclosed CD. We will remain in contact.

The note was written in an ancient Chinese script seldom used today, and it was not signed.

Sparrow folded the note and placed the CD in her handbag. Her head was spinning—who could have known? Who would even suspect her involvement in the deaths of the Chairman and Ping? Her feeling of well-being evaporated with the notes contents. She signed her lunch bill and retreated to her suite.

Throwing the handbag on the bed, she reached for the CD. She fumbled with it a bit as it was snapped in a plastic sheath. She popped it in. the screen initially was scratchy with no volume. Then she heard the voice of a young woman and the screen lit up in high-definition. The young woman, likely in early thirties was holding a white towel tied at her bosom with another towel wrapped around her just-shampooed head. She was giggling, as if she was a little drunk.

"Alex, please don't tease me anymore," said the model look-alike. She took off the headscarf and shook her long mane.

Next she heard Alex Cutter, off camera. "Bridgette, don't rush it. I have some fantastic hashish you'll find will enhance what the night promises."

The camera panned to the living room of some expensive suite. Several lines of the drug were on a glass table. Bridgette joined Alex in the massive room. Alex was shirtless and wearing just silk pajama trousers. Bridgette went to kiss him, and as her arms encircled his neck, the loose knot of the towel gave way, dropping to the floor. She heard them both laugh. Alex kissed her in a meaningful way. Sparrow almost had to look away. They sat on the couch and did the drugs. A '60s music CD played in the background. They both sat back with their eyes closed. Moments later Alex was preforming oral sex on her as she moaned in sync with the tunes being played. Sparrow looked away again, and when she returned to the screen, Alex's head remained between the outstretched legs. Minutes later he stood over her as she performed oral sex on his throbbing manhood. The coitus afterward had Bridgette screaming loud enough to drown out the refrain from the Stones.

Sparrow turned off the television screen. She was stunned. She was hurt beyond words. Then she got extremely angry. Her mentor, the love of her life, was fucking someone less than a month after her trip to San Francisco.

The suite phone rang. To her it seemed too shrill. She stared at the phone as if it was a foreign object. On the fourth ring, she picked it up.

"My guess is you have already viewed the video." There was a pause on the other end. "I suspect you had no idea," said the Voice.

Sparrow calmed herself with an inner resolve learned many years ago. "I have viewed the video," she stated with little emotion.

"A week later, Mr. Cutter, in this video, returned home to San Francisco and his wife and daughter."

The words hung like spittle in the corner of an old person's mouth. For Sparrow, the oxygen seemed to have left the room. Initially she remained quiet. The stronger side of Sparrow stood up from the couch and began pacing the floor. "What did you say? She whispered in the phone.

"Mr. Cutter's wife of eight years and eight year old daughter—"

"That son of a bitch." Sparrow raised her voice for the first time in the conversation. "With whom am I speaking?" She enquired rather formally.

"I represent strong voices in the politburo and the triad," said the Voice. "I can appreciate your response. We believe you can help us, and we can make any shadows from your past disappear forever."

"I will need more than that," Sparrow said. "My father was murdered by the triad."

"We know that," said the Voice calmly. "It was a locally handled situation without its own pitfalls. You will be given the names of those responsible, or if you wish, I can manage that from my end, including any senior people involved. It was an unfortunate circumstance, and we are prepared to make it right," the Voice calmly explained. "For us, in the bigger picture, is the necessity to silence Mr. Alex Cutter."

"Enough of this cloak-and-dagger stuff," Sparrow said raising her voice as bit.

"I agree. Let's say dinner at your hotel tonight at twenty hundred hours?"

Stunned once again, Sparrow replied, "How will you recognize me?"

Chuckling a bit, the Voice declared, "My dear, we have followed you since you were a little girl doing so well academically at that rural school-house in Jiangsu County. Do not be afraid; we are on the same side." The voice hung up the phone.

Sparrow dressed in black slacks with a wild leopard print Louis Vuitton silk blouse complemented by a simple gold cross necklace. Her black stacked-heel boots were the perfect accessory. Her purse contained a stiletto. She wore her hair up with a few loose strands looping around her ears. She arrived in the hotel's fine restaurant early by design and was shown a reserved table in a private room far in the rear of the establishment. A small intimate bar was set up in the room, and she helped herself to a Campari and soda. After her second sip, she heard a soft knock on the glass doors.

He was not what she had expected. He was in his early forties and a classic heritage blend of Chinese, Thai, and southern European. He was smiling and holding a small package, waiting for her to open the door. She did and caught just a whiff of his cologne as he handed her the package and headed to the bar. She placed the package on the dining table and observed him from behind. He was trim and muscular. His dark hair longer than any government man she had seen in the People's Republic of China. He wore dark slacks, an open neck creamy yellowish-peach shirt, and unbuttoned white jacket. He turned to her after making his drink of whiskey on the rocks, raising his glass in a little toast type gesture.

She sipped her aperitif and waited for him to pull out her chair at the table.

Upon settling into his seat across from her, he said, "It was good of you to join me. By the way, you look terrific tonight. Our photos of you simply do not do justice to your natural beauty," the Voice said complimenting her.

"Who are you? Why have I been selected? Who do you represent?" Sparrow had more questions but elected to pause and sip her drink and wait for answers.

"I am more of a senior intermediary between the power of the central government on one hand and the ruthlessness of the triad," he replied now switching to Cantonese. "It's best if you did not know my name." The voice stirred his drink and stared into her dark eyes. "Let's first address the brutal murder of your father. I have the names and contact information of the two local triad members who directly tortured and killed your father and the name and location of the senior triad man who ordered the kill. You may handle that in any manner that you find acceptable. We will not interfere in any way." The voice got up from the table to refresh his cocktail.

Also switching to Cantonese, Sparrow began to talk to the back of his head. "Why would you facilitate retribution on members of your own team?"

Returning to the table with his fresh drink, the Voice replied. "The men I have referenced are rogue, rural, and have no *guanxi*. They have no one above them to offer protection. They hold no special place in the triad hierarchy. They are garbage to the government."

Just then, with a quiet knock on the glass doors, a waiter appeared with an appetizer beautifully arranged on a bed of lotus flowers. He bowed respectively as he left the room.

"May I get your name?" Sparrow tried again.

Passing the appetizer tray, he said, "That is not necessary nor is it a good idea."

Letting that pass for now, Sparrow continued. "How can the politburo excuse the death of the Chairman?"

"The good Chairman," he continued in Cantonese, "was stealing from the Party. He was not merely skimming from the top, but rather lining his own pockets with renminbi that should have made its way to Beijing. He was a greedy man. He was a lustful man. His peers abandoned him several years ago. Your actions were actually viewed as being of great assistance."

The private waiter returned with lobster and multiple side dishes. He poured a chilled Furmint Tokaji. The snappy white drink held aromas of apple and straw leading to grapefruit flavors and a crisp finish.

After her first sip, the Voice returned to English asking, "How do you like the Hungarian wine?"

"I have never had this before. I think it's divine," she replied also returning to English.

They both enjoyed the meal without further dialogue, each evaluating the other in the candlelit room. Sparrow turned to the small package. "May I?"

"Certainly."

The wrapping was expensive and expertly done. Sparrow took her time opening it. "They are beautiful," she said as she lifted the earrings from the cotton pad. The jade from Nanjing and been placed artfully in gold. She tried them on, turned, and smiled at the mysterious man. He returned the smile. "Thank you."

After the waiter had cleared and offered coffee or tea, they left their chairs and stood at the windows, watching as a storm blew waves of rain against the panes.

"You have given me a tsunami of information, and, as you can guess, I am still digesting it. Your offer to assist me in bringing closure to my father's death is greatly appreciated. Your request to act as an assassin on behalf of the government and the triad remains for me confusing and truly scary."

"I can understand your conflicting emotions," said the Voice as he stared out into the storm. "In order to show a matter of good faith, I will have the necessary information on the men directly involved with your father's death and their superior to you by night's end. Allow me to share our latest intelligence concerning Mr. Alex Cutter as well. I should add one final consideration."

"What's that?"

"Upon your successful mission to eliminate Cutter, the firm will deposit one million US dollars into your account upon confirmation of the kill. There will be no serious investigation into his death. In addition, your killing business in Jiangsu County will receive similar lack of judicial interest."

"Who is the firm?" she asked.

"Let's say it is a consortium of senior men with direct links to both the politburo and the triad. These are men who despise publicity. These are men who have a greater vision for China than merely one or two generations. These are men of purpose."

"And should I decline?"

"That would be a terrible mistake. This operation can proceed without you. We have operatives with the necessary skill set. Having you complete the task is preferred and leaves no trace to Beijing or the triad. Please think it over, and give me your decision over breakfast tomorrow. Thank you for joining me this evening." With that, the Voice set his teacup aside and opened the double glass doors with a nod for Sparrow to precede him.

Sparrow spent a fitful night in her suite. The possibility of revenge was certainly a hook for her. The memories of the night she found her father in two pieces stayed with her always. She shook. She left the king-size bed and splashed water on her face in the luxurious bathroom. She looked at the reflection in the mirror and made the decision. Rather than wait for morning, she rang the Voice.

He answered on the second ring. "Well, hello, Ms. Sparrow. This call was not unexpected. Your history suggests a woman of action."

"I will kill Mr. Cutter for you. I will require a detailed updated dossier on Alex Cutter. I will require a cleansed weapon. I will need new travel docs and a full expense account. I will also require the necessary information on the triad thugs in Jiangsu County."

"I will have all of that for you at breakfast, in, let's see, only five hours from now."

Sparrow hung up the phone and found her muscles relax and with that her mind. She lay down right on the couch and was fast asleep. The next morning's sun welcomed her in the same position with her neck a little sore. She stretched for fifteen minutes, took a warm shower, and dressed for the breakfast meeting. This morning she chose a summerlike smock with white pumps and minimal jewelry. There was no reason to appear as an assassin in the lobby of the Four Seasons.

After their breakfast exchange, Sparrow had her necessary travel documents and travel stipend of RMB 7,000. She was packed and headed for the airport. By design she did not take a direct route. Their intelligence suggested Alex Cutter would be in China the following week. This would allow Sparrow to deal both with Cutter and the triad thugs who had murdered her father. She flew first from New York's JFK field to Portland, Oregon, then on to Melbourne. She spent one night in Australia before heading for Singapore and another night's rest. Tiger Airlines completed the trip depositing her in Shanghai the following evening.

Her flawless documents and cool mannerisms allowed her to circumvent any custom delays along the way. After a wonderful meal of duck and noodles, Sparrow rested comfortably for nine dreamless hours in the luxury Shanghai hotel. Waking refreshed, she took the elevator to the rooftop pool and swam for thirty minutes. She enjoyed a light breakfast of warm sticky buns, one egg, and black coffee.

CHAPTER 38

Her driver arrived under the hotel portico on time at 9:00 a.m. She got in the rear of the automobile and snapped open her iPad. Her driver, Mr. Tan, could be trusted. Prior to Sparrow's arrival at the joint-venture malt complex, Mr. Tan had been the number one driver. She had replaced him in terms of driving responsibilities concerning the general manager, other executives and of course the Chairman. Tan was demoted, and since Sparrow was on the scene, he was pretty much relegated to running errands and delivering documentation to the Yangzi River port. Mr. Tan took the demotion in stride. He was sixty-two years old and did not want to bring any undue attention to himself, which may jeopardize his role at the plant. Unusual for his counterparts, Mr. Tan and his wife had two children: one girl, now a woman forty years old with her own family, and one retarded boy, who remained home with them. Tan was a quiet man. In deference to his masters, he would not only bow but would bow deeply. His face was nearly always expressionless. Prior to becoming a driver, he had worked at the adjacent joint-venture company, which processed chemicals. During that stint in his career, he had suffered serious burns to his hands and left side of his face. When Sparrow had been selected to be the executive driver, he took no exception. She was not only a stunning woman but also a highly competent driver. Sparrow had recognized how difficult it must have been for Mr. Tan to relinquish his number one driver role to her. Despite his reticence and their age differences, she befriended him. Overtime a bond formed between them, more like a father-daughter relationship. She visited their home and was welcomed by both his wife and their genetically damaged son. Sparrow would always bring gifts—typically sweet treats for the boy and flowers for his wife. She always would leave a box of food staples just inside their front door before departing. Over dinner at their modest home, they would discuss politics and family matters. Sparrow learned of Mr. Tan's unique background. He served in the PLA, People's Liberation Army, until he was thirty-four. She learned he achieved the rank chief sergeant class during the Sino-Vietnamese War of 1979. In hushed tones, he had shared with her his disregard for the Chairman. When his daughter was thirty, she had worked in the malt complex's administration building. During that time, the Chairman had taken advantage of her. He declined to offer any details. He also shared with her his disgust for the local triad—both their laziness and shakedown tactics. Sparrow grew very close to this family. She would read to the retarded boy as she stroked his hair, always wondering if he understood the text. Her touch seemed to calm him. Sparrow's relationship to Mr. Tan's wife was like a loving stepmother she could trust and confide in. No one at work had any idea of the unique relationship Sparrow had with the Tan family. Since Sparrow's father's death, this was the only family she had.

On rare occasions at work when Sparrow was engaged in other driving responsibilities, Tan would be instructed to pick up various VIPs. Alex Cutter had been driven by Mr. Tan on several occasions. He drove usually to-and-from the airport during board meetings and a few times to restaurants and then back to the Xuan Wu, the preferred company hotel. Mr. Cutter always made Tan comfortable, enquiring about his family and his health. Cutter's Mandarin was horrible, but it showed him respect.

She and Mr. Tan did not speak as he turned the car to the west and the expressway to Nanjing. Three hours later the car dropped her off at a small hotel on the northern outskirts of the city. She paid cash rather than use a credit card and chose a room in the newly renovated Asian Tower. Her driver had left behind a small carry-on case. She unzipped the bag once in her suite; it contained an Austrian Glock 17, second generation, nine-by-nineteen-millimeter caliber, with twenty rounds of ammunition, a silencer, a holster, two black uniforms, an eleven inch Shadow

Ops Combat blade, several thousand renminbi notes neatly packed and secured by old rubber bands, and an ID card with her recent photo, which indicated she was a member of the elite People's Liberation Army, Special Operations Force. Her unit was dubbed the Sea Dragons, which wore all black uniforms. They had first gained public notoriety with their handling of Somali pirates in 2008. Many details on her security badge and documentation indicated classified, which would be enough for most officials to back off.

The next morning her same driver had returned under the hotel's portico with a dark government sedan. The windows were tinted, which did not allow interested parties to see the inhabitants. To complete the ruse, PRC flags inserted in the front fenders told any observer this was a VIP vehicle. Sparrow got into the sedan's back seat with her new carry-on bag.

She wore the elite all black uniform of the Sea Dragons. The gun was holstered at the hip. The blade attached under her left forearm in a leather sheath. She wore dark sunglasses, and her hair was pulled back in a severe ponytail. Despite her petite stature, she looked extremely menacing. Her driver stopped outside the storefront where the suspected triad thugs who had killed her father typically hung out at during the afternoon. The shop was typical for Nanjing. The proprietor sat behind a desk, and behind him was a wall of various concoctions to cure ailments ranging from liver damage to the common cold. There was a prominent advertisement for a natural erectile-dysfunction remedy. One old man was at the counter enquiring about a urinary infection. The proprietor was listening as he worked his ancient mortar and pestle. Sitting at a table across the room were the two triad thugs playing a dice game.

Sparrow pulled her Glock, dropped to one knee, and shot both men once in each knee—pop-pop-pop-pop. The sound was deafening in the small shop. Both men screamed in pain and reached for their weapons. The distance between Sparrow and the thugs was less than four meters. She shot both men in the upper inner thigh—pop-pop. She had not missed the femoral artery. Blood spurted out of the gashing wounds with each heartbeat. She stood over both screaming men with her blade out.

She knelt down and slit open the front of their trousers. Blood covered the floor, the table, her arms, and her chest. The eleven-inch blade cut cleanly through both penises. The floor was now slippery with red. Their manhood was stuck first in their mouths and then pushed deeper to the back of the throat. Both thugs gagged and then were gone. The one customer in the shop was frozen in place. Sparrow turned to the proprietor and tossed him one of the renminbi bales surrounded by the rubber band. Sparrow walked to the door and into the waiting darkened automobile.

The driver sped off to the back entrance of a known restaurant. It was too early for the dinner crowd and employees were chatting in their break room when Sparrow walked past them to the restrooms. Cooks and wait staff saw her and began to buzz. Immediately afterward the driver appeared at the door to the break room. He just stood there. The employees all crowded into a corner and watched the man blocking their entrance. He motioned for them all to relinquish their cell phones. Sparrow took but only several minutes to dispose of the uniform darkened with blood, wash her face and hands, and put on the second black uniform. She and the driver exited together as seamlessly as they had arrived.

The driver had one last stop. Their intelligence had indicated the superior of the two thugs, with their manhood stuck down their throats, could be found at a competing cabaret on the city's north side, harassing the owners and demanding a blow job from one of the younger girls. As they pulled into the back parking lot, they spotted his motorbike. Sparrow was out of the sedan before it came to a complete stop.

The one triad bodyguard stood by the backdoor. He chewed on a Popsicle stick, which had nothing on it, just rolling it from side to side in his mouth. Occasionally he would take it out and admire his tooth marks and disgusting spittle residue. He was reaching inside his jacket pocket as Sparrow approached from the side. Her knife thrust caught him in the lower throat. He was relatively silent. Blood gurgled out of his mouth, and he fell to his knees. The next blow from the long blade caught him just beneath the ear. She twisted, and it was over.

Most of the girls would be still sleeping at this relatively early hour after putting in a long night of entertaining the local politicians, mid-level military, and the occasional visiting Western businessman. The main hallway remained dark, and she picked up voices and a shaft of light midway down the corridor. With her Glock in both hands, she rounded the corner to the only lit room. Her targeted triad superior had his trousers around his ankles and both his hands on the sides of the girls head as she bobbed back and forth. Sparrow was approaching from the rear. She turned the gun and came down hard on the base of his skull with the butt of the weapon. The triad superior crumbled to the side. Sparrow motioned with her head to Miss Bobble to leave the room—*now*. The Shadow Ops Combat blade slid from its sheath. Sparrow knelt behind the man, and in one smooth stroke, stuck the tip of the knife between his buttocks until the entire blade was gone. The sharpened weapon sliced through the anus, the rectum, and renal pelvis. The angle of the attack caught the urethra and up through the gall bladder, pancreas, and liver. Blood covered her arm, and her knee was in a deep pool of red. She removed the blade, and with the serrated blade, she cut off the victims middle fingers and stuffed them in his mouth. She turned to leave, and the paid courtesan was shaking violently in the hallway staring in disbelief in what had taken less than three minutes. Sparrow raised her finger to her lips to signal for quiet and the damaged young girl nodded and left down the darkened hallway. Sparrow returned to the waiting car.

Sparrow had been efficient, and just now the adrenaline rush subsided as the driver took her to another hotel forty kilometers from the scene. She changed back to her normal clothes while in the backseat. She took another stack of the money and dropped it over the front seat for the driver. "Dispose of my uniform and return tomorrow morning at nine."

He nodded in acknowledgement and said nothing. She checked into the rural hotel and paid cash in advance. All she wanted was a sponge bath and multiple bottles of waters. She had never felt this dehydrated in her entire life.

She lay in bed and imagined the final kill. Alex Cutter: ex-military, ex-intelligence, and ex-lover. She would take nothing for granted. If the timing was not right, she convinced herself to back away. Should the timing be right, she would have no moral issue with pulling the trigger. This man had misrepresented himself to her on so many levels.

Back at her rural hotel room, Sparrow received an encrypted message from the Voice. It simply stated as follows: "Our direct visual surveillance of the subject, Alex Cutter, had him catching an airport taxi in downtown Nanjing at 1834 hours. We lost visuals of the subject past international security at the airport."

Sparrow was both upset and relieved. What did this mean for her? Did they expect her to trot around the globe to eliminate this businessman? With all the blood on her hands in the past few days, did she really need a final kill? When she had first met Alex so many years ago, they were both so young, ambitious, and easily smitten. Since then, she had developed a worldly skill set allowing her to avenge the brutal death of her father. Alex had grown into a respected businessman and had started a family of his own in the western United States. She stared in the hotel mirror. What did she see? A fully grown woman, mature beyond her years, and one prepared to start a new life. A life without the Chairman's mao-tai breath on her neck and one without the crudeness of Ping. Alex Cutter could go on with his life—cheating on his wife and courting the edges of political correctness.

The open issue for Sparrow was the demands from the Voice. Following his instructions to eliminate Alex Cutter, she would be assured of no prosecutions for the deaths of the Chairman and Ping. Nor would there be repercussions for the revenge of her father's death. He offered a clean slate. Was she prepared to kill Cutter? He wasn't the man she thought he was. Their lives had taken radically different paths. He was now a successful family man, who cheated on his wife. Sparrow was a survivor with panache and enough cash to start again.

CHAPTER 39

The top was down on the classic 911 Porsche as Alex wound his way down the mountain road toward Vevey. The wind was blowing his longish hair all around, his favorite rock band was blaring on the superb stereo, and the sports car was hugging the hairpin turns as he descended down the mountain to the quaint Swiss city on the shores of Lake Leman, ringed by the snowcapped French Alps on the southern shoreline. He had just come from Lausanne and a late lunch by the lakeside. He had enjoyed a leisurely meal of melted Gruyère and Emmentaler fondue and a delightful saffron risotto served with *luganighe* sausage. He lingered over the crisp white wine as he watched white dots race across the lake toward the French shore.

As he tapped the brakes and then accelerated around another hairpin turn, he came upon a small herd of dairy cows crossing the pavement. He downshifted and brought the high-end sports car to a safe stop. Two old women in traditional dress walked with the cows, each carrying a tall switch. Over the purr of the engine, Alex could distinctly catch the bells hanging loosely from each animal. The procession took only a few minutes, and Alex politely waved at the two herdswomen, who smiled and returned his gesture.

With the animals safely across the road, he began slowly accelerating expertly through the six manual gears. He arrived at the beautiful lakeside village/city. He passed the multistoried glass building housing global headquarters for Nestlé and continued on to the three-story granite building in the center of town.

Raiffeisen Switzerland was the third largest bank in the country. This satellite bank where he held a safety-deposit box had served him well in the past. They upheld the strict confidentiality the Swiss banks were known for worldwide. Alex was cordially greeted by a handsome older woman with glasses. She had kept her hourglass figure and had a professional air about her. She in turn introduced Alex to another more senior banker, who began a series of validation protocols. With those completed in a satisfactory manner, he was introduced to a third banker, who escorted him to a private room. It was here they completed the final security scrub, including facial recognition technology, and a DNA match.

With all security matters completed, Alex was shown into another private room, which was less sterile and much more businesslike. His initial escort, the older professional woman, entered with his safety-deposit box. Her key matched his, and the metal box opened with a click. She left the room. "Take as long as you wish; the bank does not close for another five hours. Push the button on your left side to alert us when you are done, Mr. Cutter."

He waited until the door had clicked shut behind her and opened the metal box. He removed the contents one by one.

- A current Swiss passport
- Bundles of large renminbi notes bound by rubber bands—each baring the total amount in both local currency and US-dollar equivalents. The four bundles he held totaled RMB 5 million—a notation read US$685,000
- One bundle of US savings bonds. Notation on the band indicating a current value of $250,000. Another bundle of mature Swiss notes valued at US$200,000.
- A numbered banking account in Zurich. When he had last checked, this was valued at the equivalent of US$1,674,000
- Two gold bars and four silver bars
- Forty thousand German marks in large denominations
- Five hundred thousand Italian lira

- A paid-in-full mortgage note for a vineyard in southern Spain
- A paid-in-full mortgage note for a property in southern California
- A paid-in-full receipt for a large tract of land south of Auckland, New Zealand
- An expertly forged document showing Alex Cutter as having diplomatic privilege, issued by the federal government of Switzerland.
- Lock box security passwords and keys for bank boxes in Chicago and Johannesburg.
- Finally, on the bottom of the box, a manila folder holding two photographs. One was his mother, when she was about thirty-nine, and just before the accident that took her life. Her smiling face outlined by auburn hair pulled back into a ponytail. The smile frozen in time for him. Next was the family picture of him and his parents in swimsuits on an old wooden dock. They each held onto a slalom ski as they grinned for the cameraman, a reddish/orange sunset in the background. Alex must have been about fifteen in that picture. The last family vacation before the fatal accident, which took both of his parents. He held the corner of this photograph for better than a minute before returning it and all the contents back into the security box, less several of the maturing Swiss notes.

Alex thanked the private bank officials, cashed his Swiss interest bearing notes, and left written instructions to have the equivalent of US$30,000 transferred monthly to his checking account in Auckland. As the sun lost its battle to the mountains in the west, Alex accelerated at the edge of town and began the short trip back to his hotel in Lausanne.

CHAPTER 40

Just then, on nearly the opposite side of the globe, Sparrow was sitting in the navigator's seat on a military cargo flight from Nanjing. Her departure would not be gleaned from a public manifest, nor would it leave an electronic monetary footprint for the Voice or his minions to follow. Sparrow's relationships with local captains and lieutenants, coupled with HK$1,000, allowed her to escape the city virtually unnoticed. Prior to her departure, she had drafted an encrypted note to her surrogate father, Mr. Tan. She would greatly miss him and his lovely family. She did not want him to worry for her. The note said she had left China and would remain in touch after establishing a new identity.

The large aircraft set down at a military base outside Guangzhou. She settled into a passenger seat of one of the convoy vehicles, dressed as a private in the PRC army, with her hat pulled down on her forehead. No one asked for her papers, and her partners in crime dropped her off at a train station outside the airfield. Traveling in coach class rather than soft seat, she made her way to Hong Kong. By 8:00 p.m. she had shed the drab uniform and checked into the posh Mandarin hotel, which had hosted her and the powerful Chairman on numerous occasions. She was warmly welcomed back and upgraded to a junior suite on the twenty-second floor.

Rather than relax in the luxury of her suite overlooking the storybook harbor, she found the woman's employee locker room on a subbasement floor. She changed into a housecleaner's uniform, tucked her locks under the white cap, and went back to her assigned room. After stripping the bed and throwing all the towels into her hamper, she proceeded back downstairs to the hotel laundry. Nobody paid any special attention to her. A delivery truck was just pulling away from the loading dock. She left her hamper in line with the others and calmly walked to the side of the departing truck, which blocked the view from the dock. She grabbed onto the tarp rope and pulled herself into the empty truck bed. When the delivery truck had made its way from the loading dock back onto the street, she piggybacked for a dozen blocks and then slid out the back when the truck stopped at a busy intersection. She fell in line with a crowd of workers coming off their shift hustling across the thoroughfare before the traffic light would change.

Sparrow used her new identity papers, as Madam Gang, to book an Air France flight to Bora Bora. All first class and business class seats were filled, so she paid cash for a seat in the back of the plane, just happy to leave mainland China.

Upon landing on the island, she took a cab to the port. Several cruise ships were docked, their brilliant white paint jobs stark against the emerald water. One of them, a Norwegian cruise line, was busy bringing passengers back on board after a day trip on the volcanic island. Sparrow fell into the back of the line. As she passed the second mate on the gangplank, she leaned in and whispered to him. He smiled and escorted her to a side passageway away from the seemingly endless line of older white sunburned day-trippers. She passed him two tightly wrapped bundles totaling US$2,500. He continued to smile and opened a nearby door with stairs going up and passed her a numbered key. Moments later, she settled into her new suite for the next stage of the cruise.

Sparrow disembarked at their next scheduled stop: Jakarta, Indonesia. She went directly from the port to the airfield and booked the relatively short flight to Melbourne, Australia. Resting comfortably in first class, she allowed herself to contemplate a life more settled. A soft jazz melody on her earphones helped her relax and fall into a deep sleep.

Anticipating adverse consequences, Sparrow had previously wired funds to multiple international banks in her new identity of Madam Gang. Her associate, from New York, assisted with all the details involved with the large sums moving across cyberspace and security involved with each transaction. With funding issues behind her and a new secure identity in place, Sparrow turned to the next pressing issue. Where would she choose to spend the rest of her life?

She checked into a high-end hotel in downtown Melbourne. Her Madam Gang documents did not raise any concerns from the front-desk staff. She allowed herself several days to evaluate the viable options to live a full life, invisible. After considerable thought, she settled on Saint Germaine, France. This city/suburb of Paris offered her everything on her list of wants. It was large enough to provide anonymity. It was a university town. She could cross the river and enjoy cosmopolitan Paris. Her ethnicity would not be an issue. She would blend in.

In less than a month, she was moving into her flat just off Boulevard St. Germaine. She worked half-day mornings at a café around her block. She studied language at the university. She spent hours at the Louvre and other art venues. On mild evenings she would spend hours lingering over coffee at one of several favorite cafés, a book in one hand. In less than a year, she was Parisian.

Despite her attempts to disguise her femininity, she was frequently approached by young men and much-older gentlemen. She politely declined their advances. She wished no physical or emotional attachment to the opposite sex. There were times, however, when late at night, she would replay that first tryst with Alex Cutter—his warm hands, gently caressing her face, her neck, and her shoulders. He treated her body with almost religious respect. He whispered. He nibbled. She could feel the stubble of his cheeks against her thigh. His light touch on her womanhood sent shockwaves through her entire soul.

She thought about Alex's intellectual curiosity. She respected his drive and purpose. In a short period of time, she recognized his leadership and compassion for others. He had been a single man when she first met him, but she expected he would be a great father. Her memories were of a competent man yet humble. Then her mind raced to the stubble of his cheeks.

Sparrow would frequently lunch outside at Les Deux Magots. Despite her frumpish blouse and flat shoes, men would find ways to catch her eye, say something funny, and finally introduce themselves. Sparrow remained celibate. She learned how to turn the men down without bruising their egos. Many tried a second and third time without success.

Sparrow's life fell into a natural weekly cadence. She worked part time weekday mornings and then focused on art and literature. A late-afternoon swim and a light early dinner followed by a coffee and good book completed her regimen. Weekends found her exploring Paris and the surrounding area. She never took her security for granted. She was always aware of her surroundings and looked for anything or anybody who may appear out of sorts. On rare occasion, she would take an excursion to Lille or perhaps Luxemburg. The trauma she had undergone in China began to lift off her in transparent sheets. She was beginning to feel whole again.

The healing continued for Sparrow. She remained as inconspicuous as was possible for a beautiful woman on the outskirts of Paris. She was careful not to spend too much. She would not argue with street vendors. She was careful not to be caught in the background of a tourist photograph. She was vigilant.

As the years slowly passed, Sparrow looked back at her life and what could have been. She wondered what kind of mother she would have been. What kind of spouse and lover would she have been? How would she have cared for her father had he not been brutally murdered? She had buried the time spent as a courtesan in Nanjing. She did not dwell on her father's revenge or the blood on her hands. She was now in her late thirties and longed for something more in life. A loving husband and a child would make her whole. She would allow herself to think of Alex Cutter. They had an intense brief relationship. What followed was his deception, followed by the Voice instructing her to kill him. Had she followed through with that assignment, her killing record would be expounded, and she would no longer need to live in fear of the triad or the Chinese central government.

Once after a few glasses of chardonnay, she researched Alex Cutter on the web. She found multiple references of his accomplishments. She read on and was stunned to learn of his death in a Tiger Airlines crash in the South China Sea. She put down her glass of wine. She wept.

CHAPTER 41

Weeks after his visit to the Swiss bank, Alex had set up residence in a three-room suite downtown Auckland. He was directly working with a local architect to design his dream cottage just outside the city on rolling land adjacent to Hauraki Gulf, with a meandering creek and ample forage. He learned of his successful lawsuit to gain custody of his daughter. He planned to fly to Los Angeles next week to pick her up. He had learned his estranged wife had moved in with the club's tennis pro—even prior to the divorce becoming final. Nonetheless, Alex looked forward to starting a new life in New Zealand with his young daughter, Alexia.

Finally the big day arrived. Alex had picked up his daughter at the Los Angeles airport. His ex-wife remained stone-faced and did not shed a tear when she handed him the small carry-on luggage and some paperwork.

Their Air New Zealand nonstop flight to Auckland was spectacular. The little girl wanted to tell Daddy about every single thing she had experienced since his departure. She repeated many things and he loved them all. The flight attendants in their first-class cabin spoiled the girl in every way they could think of. Some flirted with Alex, which he politely ignored. After the meal service, Alexia curled up in her seat and was fast asleep. As daylight streamed into the cabin and passengers were stretching and waking up, Alex pointed out the window to his awestruck daughter. Two blue whales were breaching below them as the airplane descended on their approach.

The following week, Alex had her enrolled in a private school, piano lessons, and soccer. Life took on a kind of normalcy they both found comforting. On weekends, he would take her to art museums, a concert, or simply to the conservatory at the Bay. Alex found a young couple with a girl his daughter's age living nearby, and often they would invite the herdsman and his family to join them for dinner and outdoor games. Alex taught her how to care for the animals on his little hobby farm.

Alex focused most of his time on his daughter and his land. He raised sheep. There was much more to it than he initially bargained for. Nonetheless, he studied all there was on the subject and was not too proud to ask his neighbors for assistance. Without the financial need to work, he elected to take on those assignments that did not require travel. Given his expertise in security matters, he was able to pick and choose from assignments he could handle remotely.

When she turned eight, Alex arranged for a birthday party for a dozen of Alexia's school friends. The party had been a huge success. As parents picked up the girls off Alex's massive front porch, a single mother passed him a note and tapped his hand.

"You were wonderful with the girls today. Thank you. May I suggest a little adult time-out. You look like you deserve a break. Meet me at the Harbor Observatory tonight at seven—there's a nearby cottage."

Flattered by the outright flirting, Alex responded, "Thanks for coming to my daughter's party. Today doesn't work for me, but thank you for the kind invitation. Perhaps another time may work out."

Disappointed, the single mom smiled, grabbed her daughter's hand, and joined the other women as they filed out to the circular drive and their SUVs.

Alex released the two hired caterers early and thanked them for everything. His daughter was changing the music to some teenybopper band. She ran over to him, and he bent down to gather her up and fling her high into the air. She shrieked her happiness. "Daddy this was the best birthday *ever*." Alex tossed her again and again. Her giddiness and smile was as genuine as could be.

Alex hugged his daughter and kissed her on the cheek. This is what happiness was all about. He felt a pang of guilt for generally missing her first four years. He would more than make up for it.

"Will Mom call tonight to wish me happy birthday?"

Alex's high was deflated with the enquiry. He knew his ex-wife was honeymooning in the Caribbean with her tennis pro, fifteen years her junior. The odds of a call to his daughter were nil. He picked her up again and hugged her close. "I don't know, darling. She is in a different time zone today. If she should call in the middle of the night, I'll wake you."

"Thanks, Daddy; you're the best." She gave him a peck on the cheek as he tucked her in for the night.

Alex went downstairs to his study. He poured himself a Courvoisier and turned on some soft jazz, keeping the volume low. He reflected on the birthday party and gave it a resounding success. His daughter was growing up. He loved her with every cell in his body. He also recognized, as she matured, she would best have a mother to handle all the girl things a single father was ill equipped for.

Taking another sip of the smooth nectar, he closed his eyes and thought back to those early days with Sparrow. He had truly been smitten with the young woman, and it was for more than her good looks. There was a quality about her, and it was hard to qualify exactly. She was self-assured. She was inquisitive. She was both exotic and interesting.

He fired up his computer. Waiting for the connection, he poured a second glass of the after-dinner beverage. He knew from earlier attempts she could not be found online, so he decided to use his Chinese business connections for any possible linkage. He sent e-mails to managing partners of the Chinese joint ventures he was still familiar with, under the guise of one of their investment bankers. Under the same pretense, he researched various lower level bureaucrats in Nanjing's tax and labor departments for any possible linkage to Sparrow or her whereabouts. He was not overly optimistic. He completed this work, put his glass in the dishwasher, and went to bed.

Nothing came of his multiple enquiries into Sparrow's whereabouts. Alex was pretty much prepared to forget this foolishness. One late afternoon, he dozed off on the coach. A man appeared from deep in his subconscious. It was the other driver from the malting complex—Mr. Tan. The older driver may have had some connection to Sparrow. Alex knew this was a long shot. He, of course, no longer served on the board of directors. In fact, the Chinese national news had confirmed in print all of the victims of Flight 99 who had perished in the South China Sea. He was dead. How could he possibly reach out to Mr. Tan?

Alex woke. His semi dream was still vivid. Now he began to think more rationally. Given the time span, Mr. Tan was likely sixty-eight or seventy years old. Was he more likely retired or dead? Was it worth a try?

There was only one way to find out. The deceased Alex Cutter, now known as Alex Anderson, would travel to China from his home in Auckland and search out Mr. Tan. If he was still living, he may be the only possible linkage to Sparrow.

A certain excitement was building inside him. The mature, realistic side of him saw this as a fool's errand. The lingering spark of a younger man within him urged the attempt. After a few calls and wire transfers, his trip was confirmed. On the following Saturday, he would travel from Auckland to Hong Kong and then to Shanghai. After an overnight in Shanghai, he would travel by train to Nanjing. He could only hope Mr. Tan was still around. It was a long shot. He was excited to try.

The night before his trip, Alex was looking across the table at the young woman his daughter had grown into. He could not have been more proud of her. They were both dressed up. She wore a blue dress that complemented her clear eyes. They splurged on a favorite—Wagyu steaks, truffles, and peanut slaw.

"Something's different, Dad. What is it?"

"You know me pretty well, kiddo. I am returning to China to look up an old friend. I leave tomorrow."

"What's her name?"

There was no reason to deceive the person closest to him. "Her name is Sparrow, and I have not been in touch with her for many, many years now. I have no contact info for her, but I may have a mutual acquaintance that may prove helpful."

"Dad, you've never shared any of this with me. Is this a romantic interest?"

Caught a bit off guard, Alex paused a moment. "There actually was a special young woman I had met prior to dating your mother."

"Oh Dad, this is terrific!" she said as she pushed aside her dessert plate, put both hands below her chin, and leaned forward on the table. Her eyes were laser sharp.

For the next hour, he shared the story, from his professional relationship on several Chinese and US joint-venture companies to meeting Sparrow, a company limousine driver. He skipped over the convoluted relationship with Mr. Ping. He neglected to talk about the assassination attempt on his life in Ireland. He also left out the part of Sparrow traveling to meet him in San Francisco, only to discover he was married with a daughter. He did tell her of the very brief relationship he had with this enchanting woman he called Sparrow.

"Dad, you've held a flame for this woman for all these years. I think it is thrilling and romantic that you wish to track her down."

Alex recounted a few more Sparrow stories, paid the bill, and escorted his daughter from the famous steak restaurant downtown Auckland. He drove her to the boarding school nearby and kissed her cheek good-night.

CHAPTER 42

His Asian flights were on time, and he arrived in Shanghai early evening as the city lights danced off the harbor. After clearing customs as Alex Anderson, with a passport photograph wearing thick black glasses, he took a cab to the Sheraton downtown. The crisp early-autumn evening encouraged him to take a brisk walk along the bund to counter the natural jet lag. Feeling better than he expected, he slipped into a restaurant on a side street. This place was known for its Benbang cuisine. He chose the beggar's chicken—a whole bird stuffed with lotus leaves, wrapped tightly in parchment paper and mud and then cooked very slowly over coals. As he sipped his rice wine, Alex had to wonder if this was indeed a fool's errand. Here he was, a middle-aged man, searching for a woman he had only known as a mature girl. Yes, it was foolish he told himself, but it was also rare to be truly touched by another human being. He finished the wine and walked back to the hotel.

The morning train trip took him through Jiangsu Province's rural rice paddies and fields of wheat. Wheat harvest had just begun, and he witnessed the huge grain fields cut with modern combines and some fields still being harvested by hand with men and women using ancient scythes. The train stopped at Wuxi, known for its university, and he purchased tea and a rice bun. The coal-powered train deposited him in central Nanjing. The ancient capital of China was a contrast between the old and the new. Skyscrapers, similar to Shanghai, stood next to ancient wooden structures dwarfed by the modern architecture.

Alex took a cab to the Xuan Wu hotel. He knew it was silly in a city of over nine million people, but he asked his older cab driver nonetheless.

This hotel was often frequented by Western executives with interests in the adjacent tax-free zone. Mr. Tan, back in the day, would have transported out-of-towners from this high-class hotel. As they drove, Alex described Mr. Tan as best as he could in rather broken Mandarin. The driver wasn't sure and asked Alex a few questions. They sparred back and forth on details. Finally the old driver said he did know of this man. Alex peeled off some renminbi notes. His driver's memory seemed to improve. They stopped short of the hotel's portico, and the driver got out of the cab and approached several other drivers huddled in a circle smoking. He rattled off a series of questions, and Alex noted some positive nods from some of the men. When the driver returned to the cab, he turned to Alex in the back with a smile. Alex peeled off another one-hundred-renminbi note.

Surprisingly, for being in the city for less than three hours, Alex stood in the front of the home of Mr. Tan. He knocked. An older woman answered the door. Alex bowed and introduced himself as an ex-board member of the malting complex who had been driven by her husband a number of years ago. His Mandarin was just OK, and she welcomed him inside.

Mr. Tan was sitting at a wooden table with a steaming ceramic cup of tea in front of him. He recognized Alex immediately and motioned for him to join at the table. The wife brought Alex tea and withdrew from the room.

Nothing was said between them for the first several minutes. Mr. Tan knew Alex Cutter was named in the disastrous plane crash into the South China Sea, yet the man was having tea across the table from him. He waited for Alex to speak first.

"Mr. Tan, thank you for inviting me into your home." Alex removed the heavy dark glasses he was wearing.

Tan simply bowed his head once and then looked Alex Cutter directly in the eye. He remained silent.

"As I understand it, you've retired from driving for the malting joint-venture business—congratulations," Alex said as the much-older man stared at him, unblinking. "You may have heard my name associated with the crash of flight nine nine."

The older man nodded. He continued to stare.

"As you witness, I am quite alive. I have taken on a new name, a new identity. I have come to ask a favor. I hope you can help me."

"Go on" were the first words spoken by Tan, as he lifted the ceramic top off his steaming cup.

"Sir, I am searching for the woman known as Sparrow. I recall, back in the day, you were both drivers for the malting joint venture in the so-called tax-free zone. I wish her no harm. I simply would like to reconnect with her." Alex paused for the man's reaction.

Mr. Tan did not respond for several minutes as he stared off to a distant point outside the window. Then he turned to face Alex. "I have not seen Sparrow for a few years now." This was a truthful statement. He didn't add more.

"Is there any way you could get word to her?" Alex pleaded.

Just then, Tan's wife returned to refresh their tea and offer homemade tea cakes. She retreated without a word.

"Should she contact me, I will tell her you are alive and searching for her. I have noticed you are not wearing a wedding band." Tan left it at that.

"My wife and I divorced several years ago. I have custody of our only daughter," Alex clarified. "Your offer to respond to Sparrow on my behalf is truly appreciated."

Tan's wife pushed a wheelchair into the room. Alex saw a twenty-something man in the chair. He had longish hair and an odd faraway look. Alex got off his chair and extended his hand to the seated man, who did not reach for his handshake. Tan's wife looked older and more tired. Mr. Tan said, "This is our son." It was said in both a sad way and in a way that underscored great love.

After some further small talk, Alex excused himself, thanking Mr. Tan for his consideration. Alex left all his contact info on the wooden table.

When Alex's cab had come and taken him on his way, Mr. Tan knocked out an e-mail to Miss Sparrow. He knew he could contact her in this fashion. He did not know where she lived, in which city, or for that matter, on which continent.

Sparrow received the electronic message in the morning, her time. She was preparing to go to work at her part-time role at the coffee/pastry shop. She spilled her morning tea as she read the message on her screen. Alex Cutter was alive! He had visited Mr. Tan's home in Nanjing hoping to reach her. The message was so very short. She reread it many times in disbelief.

Her life had fallen into a comfortable routine. The part-time work had produced a number of close girlfriends and acquaintances. She had the necessary funds in the bank to live quite comfortably. She relished her exposure to the arts and culture of France. She routinely kept up with her surrogate family, the Tans, in Nanjing. She was well read and took pleasure in her exercise routine. Yet something was missing.

Alex Cutter was alive and looking for her after all these years. Could it be even possible? She banged out a response on her computer and asked Mr. Tan if he had shared her e-mail contact info. Mr. Tan saw the message late in the evening in his time zone. He replied he had not shared her electronic address, as per their agreement for security purposes. His response was abnormally terse, and she sensed something was wrong.

Her fingers tapped rapidly on the keyboard as she asked him what was wrong at his end.

She waited but a few minutes and saw his response. Yesterday, their handicapped son was found in his room not breathing. He and his wife had taken him immediately to the hospital ER. He was pronounced dead twenty minutes after arriving at the emergency room. He did not write any more on his message.

Sparrow tapped out an immediate response to her surrogate parents. She would join them in Nanjing day after tomorrow.

Alex Cutter was relaxing in his Shanghai hotel room the night before his flight back to Auckland. He had Mr. Tan's number now locked into his contacts, and he dialed it to thank him again for his hospitality. The phone was picked up at the other end by a much younger man. Alex had some difficulty with the northern dialect. He remained patient as did the young man on the line. Alex learned his counterpart on the phone must be a relative. He learned of the sudden death of the only son. Using his most formal Mandarin, he left a message that he would be returning for the funeral. Alex cancelled his flight for the next day and left on the morning train back to Nanjing.

CHAPTER 43

Mr. Tan's son's burial was a sad affair with just a handful of relatives and the burial staff. Alex arrived at the hillside grave just as the brief ceremony was beginning. There was a heavy mist coupled with Nanjing's normal pollution, which made it difficult to see further than twenty or thirty meters. He jogged up to join the meager crowd.

Then he saw her; Sparrow was standing between Mr. Tan and his wife. Sparrow's head was bowed, and she did not see him approaching. Alex fell into a fast walk and stopped short of the small group at the gravesite. His pulse quickened. Sparrow's arm reached around the shoulders of her surrogate mother, who was sobbing quietly. The brief ceremony, more civil than religious, concluded, and the meager crowd began to disperse after final condolences to Tan and his wife.

The mist turned to a steady light rain as he approached Sparrow. He was just a few meters away when she looked his direction. She was startled. Alex Cutter had died in a plane crash, yet here he was walking toward her. His hair was more salt than pepper, yet he had retained his trim physique. He stopped short of the family to allow the last of the guests to deliver their last respects.

Sparrow broke free and dashed to him. He smiled and took her into his arms. He spun her as they both did a kind of a pirouette. Her hands grabbed his face, as if asking was this real. He kissed her as gently as she had remembered. The rest of the known world fell away from both of them. She pressed her body against his strength. They kissed again. His one hand held the small of her back, the other entangled in her jet-black hair. They kissed again.

"You're here; you're here" was all that came from her as they continued to pirouette together. The Tans joined them, happy to witness some joy on this dark day. They somehow all came into a group hug. There was a combination of laughing and crying together. Sparrow and Alex joined the Tans at their home briefly after the ceremony. Mr. Tan could not help but notice the attraction between the couple. At any one time, and unconsciously, Alex and Sparrow were in some kind of direct contact. She was touching his shoulder or his forearm or brushing back his hair. He was touching her hand or stroking her hair. After tea, they excused themselves and left together hand in hand.

The cab ride back to the Xuan Wu was frantic in the backseat. The driver smirked. It was more like two teenagers with limited time alone to explore each other. Somehow they made it to the hotel, checked in like two adults under the name Mr. & Mrs. Alex Anderson, shown on his passport. They made it to the elevator. Once inside the elevator, their tongues and hands had a mind of their own. Somehow, they made it to their room, and Sparrow excused herself to use the restroom. Alex stripped the bed of its bedclothes. She came out, backlit from the bathroom night light, in nothing but her bra and panties. She stood there and smiled. Alex reached for her hand and pulled her close. They both attempted to slow things down and the next few kisses were tender. It did not last very long. Alex lifted her to the bed. Things got frantic again.

During their third time, they took time to look deeply into each other's eyes. They teased and laughed a bit. They were completely at ease with each other. The connection was far more than physical. Sparrow fell asleep on his shoulder. Alex stroked her long hair, thankful at this second-chance in life.

When they awoke several hours later, they resumed a more or less teenaged passion. Later, after a shower and catching their breath, Sparrow shared what her new life in France had become. Alex shared his new life in Auckland with his only daughter. They spoke for hours, ordered from the in-house menu, and then made love like two adults. It was the most satisfying twenty-four hours either of them had ever experienced.

They slept holding each other, not wanting to let go. Later Sparrow got up to use the washroom. Alex heard the flush and propped himself up with a few pillows. She returned to the crook in his arm.

"Sparrow, my daughter is becoming of age and needs a mother. I desperately need to spend the rest of my life with you. Auckland is not Paris. But I can offer you a rich life full of love and fulfillment." He paused. "We are not as cosmopolitan as the Parisians; we are simple ranchers, but you would complete our lives."

Sparrow rose up from the crook in his arm and placed both hands on his chest. Looking straight down into his eyes, her black mane touching the hair on his nipples, she paused, then smiled brightly, and said, "Yes, yes; a thousand times yes!'

He held her. She couldn't see the tears welling up in his eyes as he squeezed her close.

Alex and Sparrow worked out the details for her move to Auckland. It was terribly exciting for them both—a second chance and a chance for happiness.

The next important step was for Sparrow to meet Alex's daughter. They caught the first flight they could and upon arriving in Auckland, drove immediately to the boarding school. Alex's daughter was expecting them and immediately gravitated to Sparrow. The following weekend the three of them spent in Queensland, Australia, at a private home Alex had rented just north of Brisbane. The weather was perfect, and they spent most of their time on the beach or diving along the coral reef. Alex made a huge bonfire on the sand on their last night. The three of them stayed up till midnight talking and laughing. Alex went to bed, and the two girls stayed another two hours by themselves by the fire. The natural chemistry between them made Alex very happy.

Sparrow, or Madam Gang as she was known in France, returned to gather up her personal items and closed out her various accounts. She joined her new family a few days later in New Zealand. Sparrow turned out to be the missing piece of the puzzle for Alex and his teenaged daughter.

Alex began to work a bit more on security matters for various clients. All this independent work could be done remotely, and he was successful in bringing his work travel to zero. Sparrow learned about sheep and loved the work the ranch provided. Their daughter recognized the love her new parents shared and the calming effect on her father. During her school break, the three of them vacationed on the South Island.

CHAPTER 44

Alex took a routine call from a prospective client in his den on a late Tuesday afternoon. The prospective customer was actually in the security business as well. They represented the London Metal Exchange (LME). One of the junior compliance people, a math guy employed by the exchange, had run some algorithms relating to high trading volume on a recent afternoon corresponding to extraordinary price volatility. The security guy added the analyst to their call. Alex listened. According to this in-house analyst, the probability of that trading volume and volatility in such a limited time frame was something like one chance in eighty thousand. Alex was intrigued. The analyst went on with his hunch and looked at other markets during the same time period. He chooses the physical copper market, which is also traded on the LME, and he came up with similar results. Intrigued by the highly unusual probabilities, the analyst examined the same time period for the New York Mercantile Exchange (NYMEX), which trades futures contracts for copper. The mathematical results were extraordinarily similar. Alex asked a number of clarifying questions and was impressed with the clarity of the answers from the analyst. The two men on the phone requested Mr. Cutter's expertise. Alex quoted his normal hourly rate of NZ$900, which was eagerly accepted on the other end of the phone.

A cursory review of market activity, during the time frame in question, indicated over sixty-eight million contracts of physical aluminum had traded and another forty-million-plus contracts of physical copper. Both trading volumes were ten to twenty times more than normal. At first blush, it seemed some trader or trading houses were attempting to corner these markets—but it seemed preposterous, given the huge volumes and short time frame. Alex was intrigued.

Alex researched the issue from a security point of view and issued an executive report to his employers. The LME saw merit in Alex's approach and requested he join them in London to brainstorm possible security breaches they had not been able to find themselves. Alex reluctantly brought up the potential assignment with Sparrow, and she encouraged him to go ahead given the uniqueness of the puzzle.

Alex found himself landing at Heathrow International Airport two days later. He had negotiated a US$20,000 retainer and looked forward to meeting this new client face to face. The classic English cab deposited him at LME's administration. The gentlemen around the conference table looked particularly sober. He was thanked for coming, and then the leader of the largest futures exchange in England brought the meeting to order.

Alex learned several new things.

1. The open interest and volatility they had previously spoken of was also clearly evident on the spread activity. For example, the price movement between a July market position relative to a December market position showed the characteristics of potential market manipulation. This was true in a tight time frame of just a few minutes.
2. The NYMEX confirmed their fears.
3. Certain equity markets experienced similar irregularities during this brief time span.
4. Foreign-exchange markets were not immune, but the impact appeared to be less pronounced.

The somber men in the room turned to Alex. "Gentlemen, thank you for including me on this sensitive security issue. As we all recognize, should the public and should industry lose confidence in our open-market system, liquidity vanishes, and honest price discovery is irreparably harmed." Alex paused as his eyes passed over each of the participants in the room. Name cards and titles in front of each told the story of how serious this matter was being taken. Included at the table were presidents of each major commodity and equity exchange, heads of each major brokerage house, and the top echelon from the banks and foreign-exchange markets. He noted senior government officials as well. "I suggest we include management from the Shanghai exchange in our deliberations." There were affirmative head movements of agreement around the table.

"Our large global markets and instantaneous electronic-market executions make it difficult to pinpoint a single saboteur or a consortium of criminals. The very tight time frame also gives rise to the theory this is a random occurrence with no criminal activity responsible." Alex felt a little ridiculous stating the obvious to this esteem group, but maybe they needed it.

Discussions lasted until 1900 hours. A series of unanswered questions were vetted by the group and further assignments given out. Alex passed on a dinner invitation given the jet lag he was experiencing.

In Cape Town, South Africa, it was one hour later, and Primrose had just received another ding on his powerful computer. Another large sum had been deposited in his Luxembourg account. Herr Reins had actually sent him a short encrypted note thanking him for the good work—a first for him to give any sort of recognition.

Primrose called for the eastern European girl.

Herr Reins flew from Brussels to Munich. His driver picked him up at the private airstrip in a new blue BMW. The hour and a half drive took them through the Black Forest. By late afternoon the luxury sedan was silently crossing the moat of his castle.

The gatehouse they drove through was flanked by two octagonal towers. Each was decorated with stone eagles at their peak. The gatehouse itself was a tunnel peppered with murder-holes, from which boiling oil could be cast upon enemy intruders.

Reins had this property completely refurbished five years ago, with the exception of the twelfth-century dungeon and the moat. He immediately climbed the stone stairs to his second floor office, which was decked out with state-of-the-art electronics and laser security. He sat at the oversized wooden desk and tapped a few signals. All the necessary electronic bank transfers were completed without disruption. He checked markets in London, New York, Shanghai, and Frankfurt. Everything appeared normal. He exhaled.

He called the lead person for his castle staff to join him in the office. Gretchen was a statuesque blonde from Stuttgart. She stood almost at attention in the required gray uniform, which did little to detract from her feminine lines.

"We will be entertaining an important guest tonight for dinner. His name is Mr. Goering Damijon. He and his staff will be expected to arrive via motor coach at around sixteen thirty hours. Please arrange to have his staff comfortably set up in the visitors' quarters and arrange for their dinner. As for Mr. Damijon, he is to have the entire west wing. He and I will dine at eighteen hundred hours in the knights' hall. Have the cook prepare pheasant, wild mushrooms, and potatoes. I will select the wine myself from the cellar—have the red decanted thirty minutes prior. That will be all." Gretchen left her boss without comment. It was unusual to host an overnight guest, and she assumed Mr. Goering Damijon must be quite some VIP.

In Stalingrad, the last of the luggage was being stowed on the private Lear jet. Damijon was last to climb the jet's staircase and slip into his front leather seat. He motioned to the captain, and they were rolling down the runway almost immediately.

Solntsevskaya Bratva, known worldwide as the Russian mob, was driven by profits from heroin, human trafficking, illicit banking, and dispute resolution. There were ten quasi-autonomous brigades. Mr. Damijon controlled organized crime from Barcelona to the Black Sea. He had reached this pinnacle of success over thirty-five years. He knew which politicians he could control and whom in the military to trust. He surrounded himself with trusted men, who would lay down their lives for him. He could be absolutely ruthless but found bribery and extortion worked equally as well. He found it did not matter if his partners were Spaniards, Turks, or Slavs—everyone had a price.

"Sir, we will land at Munich's airfield in ten minutes. Your two Land Rovers will be planeside after we complete our taxi," the captain said in military Russian.

Damijon nodded his approval. His five men checked their loaded weapons and deplaned first. The car journey took less than two hours, as they crossed the drawbridge of the twelfth-century castle. Gretchen met the two black vehicles in the circular drive within the walls, greeting Mr. Damijon and escorting him inside to his quarters.

At 6:00 p.m. sharp, Herr Reins met Mr. Damijon in the knights' hall. The all-stone hall had walls that curved up to a ceiling crisscrossed with heavy wooden beams. The side walls were decorated with actual shields from the Crusades. All the light came from overhead candles in iron-wheel bases or from the monstrous fireplace at one end of the room. A small group of musicians performed using original instruments from the Middle Ages. Herr Reins poured the red wine for them both. Damijon sipped and smiled his approval of the thirty-year old Bordeaux.

Small talk accompanied the first course. When the pheasant arrived, Reins motioned for the musicians and wait staff to be excused. He poured another glass of nectar for his guest and himself. Reins did not know this man well. He took instructions from him but usually over an encrypted line. He knew the man to be volatile. One would expect him to be pleased with the windfall profits from the recent trading activity and the market pause. Yet the Russian had yet to mention it. All that could be heard in the cavernous environment was the clicking of silverware on the earthen plates.

Finally Herr Reins decided to engage his visitor. "The final tally on the market manipulation is not completed; however, we estimate the net amount to exceed our expectations. I should have final results prior to your departure tomorrow." Reins sipped the red wine and looked over the glass rim to gauge his visitor's response.

"As usual, you have exceeded the stated goals in a circumspect manner, Herr Reins." Damijon lifted his glass in a gesture of a toast.

"I appreciate your recognition, and I am honored to host you at my home."

"Unfortunately, we may have unforeseen consequences from this brief market pause."

Herr Reins put down his wine glass. He stared intently at his boss across the table.

"There has been called an unprecedented meeting of global market participants in London to address market irregularities. We have a banker in that meeting, who owes his life to us. The market participants include all the major exchanges, major banks, foreign exchange, commission houses, and government. Our insider tells us the group is highly suspicious of manipulation. However, they cannot prove it. They have employed a retired security expert to join in the analysis. Have you witnessed any unusual security procedures at any of the market hubs, Herr Reins?"

Mr. Reins paused a full beat to fully comprehend the ramifications of a consortium of bankers and regulators. He responded, "Mr. Damijon, my review of each of the major commodity and equity markets suggest money flows have not been adversely affected since our brief pause. The same is true for the forex markets."

"My experts in Russia tell me the same. We cannot afford to be sloppy. Sometimes it's the smallest detail that can derail a project." Damijon looked Herr Reins directly in the eyes—neither condemning nor redeeming him. "I fully trust your expertise, Herr Reins and your commitment to Odessa. In layperson's terms, please walk me through the exercise."

"When markets open for business each day, there are existing open orders to buy or sell at specific price points. During their trading sessions, new orders to buy or sell enter the market. Some orders are resting orders—simply meaning they are to be executed if and only if a specific price point is reached. Other orders are to buy or sell at the market regardless of price point. This assures the principles they will have execution on their market orders. Compounding the complexity is the volume of each buy or sell order. A further complication is the spread trade, both intramarket and intermarket."

"OK. OK." The Russian stopped Reins and his simple explanation. "What you are describing is a spider-web of activity, which makes it virtually impossible to untangle."

"Given the speed of electronic trading and the fact we paused the markets for such a short period of time, it would be virtually impossible to untangle the mess and point blame." Feeling better about the situation, Reins took another pull from his glass.

"I understand you have transferred the funds from the operation to more than thirty smaller institutions," said Mr. Damijon.

"Forty one distinct accounts in twenty two countries to be exact, he replied. These accounts range from simple savings accounts to union retirement accounts and brokerage accounts that we have access to."

"Excellent, Herr Reins. I would have expected the attention to detail from you," Damijon replied sitting back in his chair and sipping the fine Bordeaux. "What's for dessert?"

CHAPTER 45

Alex woke early and reviewed the notes from the meeting. It was absurd to believe major markets across the globe would experience a pause in the trading day at the same exact time. Solar flares, backroom computer glitches, excessive order volume, all could contribute to a halt in trading. In fact, all three circumstances had in the past been cited as factors halting trading activity. But to Alex, having circumstances align across all markets simultaneously was too odd to dismiss as random. Others at the meeting had agreed with him, yet no one could pinpoint the cause.

Alex put down his notes and calculated the time difference between London and Auckland. It would be near dinnertime for his wife and daughter. He rang and Alexia answered on the first ring.

"Dad, how are you? We are missing you like crazy. How's London town?"

Alex smiled at her enthusiasm. "Everything is good here, darling. Tell me about the track meet."

"Oh Dad, you won't believe it, but I took first in the triple jump and our relay team took first in the six hundred," Alexia shrieked over the phone. "It was awesome, Dad!"

"Congratulations to our track star. I wish I could have been there. Did you mother attend the meet?"

"She did, and she taped it all for you when you get home. When do you expect to be back?"

"I'm not completely sure. The consortium is meeting again this morning, and I suspect we will assign various aspects of the investigation to the various experts and all work remotely on the project, in which case, I should be home sometime day after tomorrow."

"OK, Dad. Do what you have to do, but that sounds really great! Here's Mom—" as Alexia passed the phone to Sparrow.

"She is really excited as you can tell. How are you doing half way around the world?"

"It's great to hear your voice. I miss you both so very much. It's been a while since I have been out of town, and I don't much care for it anymore." Alex stared out his hotel window to another cloudy, wet London morning. "We should wrap up things here sometime today, and I should be home latest day after tomorrow. I love you."

"That's the best news I have had today. That way you will be here for the slumber party Alexia is hosting here Friday night. Are you prepared for a dozen fourteen- and fifteen-year-old girls in your home?"

"I will be surrounded by women, and I cannot ask any more than that. Do I have any responsibilities for the slumber party?"

"Yes, make yourself invisible. These girls will need their space. They don't need you asking what their plans are for life," Sparrow said teasingly. "I love you."

"I love you too. Bye for now." Alex hung up the receiver.

Alex dressed for the follow-up meeting with the consortium. He chose a dark red tie contrasting his gray suit. The group met in the same room as the day before, but this time a senior representative from the Shanghai exchange had joined.

Alex took his assigned seat and listened carefully to the premeeting conversations going on around him. Representatives were beginning to informally lean away from any public display of an investigation. In fact, as the morning session got underway, a consensus was building in the room not to aggressively investigate the manner. The rationale was simple. Markets had returned to normal across the globe. Yes, money had been made and lost during the market glitch; however, wasn't that the case every day? Bringing too much attention to the incident may have market participants lose confidence in the market exchanges. This could prove catastrophic to the moneymen in this room.

Alex was surprised by the building consensus. By the time morning coffee and tea were offered, a simple proposal to retract the investigation was voted on by a show of hands. The majority of participants had spoken.

Alex was shocked. These men, who only as of yesterday were keen to expose market manipulation on a grand scale, were prepared to forgive and forget. To be fair, they did agree to pass the investigation down to each of their regulatory people, but this was merely whitewashing the issue. With finite resources and working on the problem independently, these regulatory offices had little chance to catch the bad guys in Alex's opinion.

Alex reached for the biscuits and jam that came with the coffee and the realization hit him. These money guys had to protect the franchise. Any hint of successful market manipulation could put them out of business. Their franchise was much more lucrative than any two- or three-minute gap in the trading day. They would go back to their respective market platforms and double down on their future security measures. It was going to be back to business as usual. Alex remained stunned.

In a flurry of formal motions, the meeting was adjourned. Alex shook a few hands and wandered out to the lobby. Professionally he was frustrated. Personally he was happy to be headed home and to be hosting a slumber party for his sixteen-year-old.

CHAPTER 46

Alexia was walking between shops on Chancery Street, downtown Auckland, looking for vintage stores carrying games for her sleepover. The flower truck was parked between a high-end boutique and several vintage storefronts. The white-panel truck fit into the landscape as did the young lovers walking their dog on the opposite sidewalk.

She felt a tug on her shopping bag and turned to look. A large man in white coveralls had spilled some black dirt and plastic flowerpots behind her. She bent down to assist him. She had gathered several pots and scooped up some of the fertile dirt as she held her shopping bag on her wrist. He said nothing but motioned with his head to join him and walk the debris to the white panel truck. With little forethought, she followed him.

The back two doors of the van opened as they approached. The large man motioned for her to go ahead of him to the back of the van.

It happened in an instant. She was pulled into the van by another man. A rubberized bag lopped over her head, and her initial scream was muffled. Doors closed and the van pulled away from the curb. She was struck in the head by something, and her world went dark.

Two hours later she woke in a cellar of some sort. It was daylight, and just a sliver of light filtered through the double wooden doors holding her in. The storage unit was extremely small and seemed to lack oxygen. She could not stand. She held out her arms and could touch the earthen walls. The scent of the wet earth was more like the smell of sex. Her rods and cones began to adjust to the dim light. It was more like a shallow grave.

She was nauseous. Her head pounded. She had soiled herself. The air was thick with dust. She shivered in the cold. She wanted to scream, but her throat was dry, and all she managed was a whisper. She was scared to death.

She could make out men's voices and heard the lock snap open. She was sitting cross-legged, hunched over. Two large men reached into her tiny prison and roughly hauled her out. A third man struck her head from behind, and her world began to spin. The two men holding her stripped her of her sundress. One of them violated her with his middle finger. "You don't have to do this," she screamed. The shortest of the three fondled her breasts. She pleaded for them to stop. With her head pounding and a steady trickle of blood running into her eyes, they tossed her between them as you would a ragdoll. She begged them to stop. Mr. Middle Finger dropped his pants as his partners held her on the dusty ground. All of them took their turn on her. Her world went blank as the third guy struck her again in the back of her head.

She heard the heavy lock snap shut as she was back on her hands and knees in the quasi-grave. The repulsive men could be heard laughing as they walked away. Alexia's lips were bloodied, and there was dried blood on her scalp. She whispered, "Daddy, please help me." She drew up her legs to her naked chest and rolled back and forth, repeating the mantra no one could hear.

CHAPTER 47

Sparrow returned early from chores in the yard, expecting to have Alexia back with her vintage games. She called her cell with no answer. Strange, she thought. The girl spent over half her life on the phone. She left a message.

Late afternoon became early evening, and Alexia was not back, nor had she returned the call. Her friends would be coming tomorrow for the slumber party, and there were a myriad of details to cover. Sparrow became worried.

Early evening became 9:00 p.m. Sparrow called Alex, but he was in the air, and she left a rather frantic message. Without further hesitation, she called the police, reporting a teenager had not returned home for dinner, and it was almost 9:30 p.m. The police response was muted, and she was asked to call all her friends before they became fully engaged. Sparrow reached out to all the girls who were expected at the party tomorrow. No one had seen or heard from Alexia.

Panic set in for Sparrow. This was real panic, where the entire world is crushing down on you. She could not think straight. Some reoccurring thoughts, having nothing to do with the situation, came rolling through her head again and again. Rational thought seemed impossible. The police were talking with her in the living room of the cottage. Everything was surreal. The young policeman looked too young to be taken seriously. She was beyond angry. She looked at the clock on the wall. Alex would be somewhere over the Pacific about now. Why had the police ignored her earlier? She was answering all the questions the uniformed man had for her. The neighboring rancher's wife came over to be with her.

Sparrow thought how, as a little girl, she was not there for her father. He had been tortured and literally cut in two pieces. Now she was not there for her daughter. Her husband was out of the country. Just then, something clicked inside her. She excused herself from the officer and went to get some water. Alone in the kitchen, she made up her mind. Kidnapped victims had little time to live. Seldom were ransom notes received, payments made, and a happy ending for all. Inactivity and panic had frozen her. Then she had complete clarity. Waiting for her husband to land in Auckland and drive to the ranch would take too much time. She had given the police officer all she could. She excused herself.

Downstairs in a worn wooden chest, she searched for the necessary attire and equipment, which included a black vest, black tights, and dark sneakers. The combat blade she purchased online with the eleven-inch serrated blade was in its sheath. Her preferred handgun, the Glock 29SF, was a smaller version of the classic weapon and fit her hand perfectly. It was black square and deadly. The automatic held a ten-round magazine. She loaded nickel-plated brass rounds from Remington.

The police officer had left. She asked the neighbor woman to remain, should there be a call. Sparrow left in the Jeep for downtown Auckland thirty minutes away. She had a phone earpiece and immediately began calling as her mind raced.

Multiple calls pieced together a possible scenario. Alexia was planning to use some vintage games at the slumber party. She wanted to surprise her guests and opted to shop alone. She likely was scouring the vintage shops on Chancery Street downtown. The high-end boutique stores, which flanked the vintage shops, would have security cameras inside and out. She reached the owner of one of the higher-end boutique stores she had frequented. There was absolutely no panic in her voice, only a steely resolve to get her daughter back. The owner agreed to meet her at the store. Twenty minutes later they were both reviewing the exterior security tape from earlier in the day. They both spotted the van almost immediately. They witnessed the abduction, which occurred in broad daylight but took just seconds. She thanked the owner and requested she share the tape with the police as soon as possible.

Using her husband's security-clearance password, she received access to the traffic camera's database. She was successful piecing together the route of the van out of the city. The southwest trajectory suggested a rural destination. Again, using her husband's security clearance, she received access to a military drone, which was taking photos of that quadrant. She did not have more specific information. The Jeep accelerated to the southwest. There were limited farms and ranches in this area. She stopped at two with no luck. The ranchers knew the area well and were prepared to help. Between the two of them, they pretty much knew who was who in the county. She placed a drone photograph on the second guy's kitchen table. Both men studied the picture and ticked off each of the farmers or ranchers they knew by each farmstead. There was just one farmyard neither was familiar with. It was just eight kilometers down a gravel road from where they were. The ranchers grabbed rifles and ammunition. Sparrow pointed on the photo where she would like them to circle-in from. There was no hesitation. They moved out.

Sparrow cut her Jeep lights and proceeded on foot to the darkened farmyard. The white florist van was not concealed. It sat next to a run-down shack with dim lights glowing from within. Sparrow crossed the next three hundred yards in the shadows. She peaked in a side window and spotted two men and a TV showing porn—one of the men was exceptionally large and the other of average height and weight. Her daughter was not in the same room. Both men had weapons. The larger man had a rifle leaning next to his chair, and the normal-sized guy had a handgun sitting on the table next to him. The smaller guy was tipping back a Yeastie Boys beer.

There was no hesitation when she burst through the unlocked front door. She struck the larger man with one round directly in his left eye. Her second two shots caught the normal-sized man in both his knees. He reached for his weapon and spilled the lager. Sparrow had her blade out and thrust it through his outreached hand securing it to the wooden side table. The man screamed, and Sparrow secured a bandana around his mouth. Just then the two ranchers were at the doorway-guns drawn. They witnessed the carnage from one petite woman. She asked them to search the surrounding structures for her teenaged girl. They left. She twisted the knife and pulled it from the table and the hand. She asked for her daughter. The man shook his head. She shot him in the foot. She removed the bandana. She held the blade next to his eye. Now he looked like he wanted to talk. He spit out blood and shook his head once again.

The helpful ranchers returned with a whoop. They had found Alexia, battered and scared and alive. The one rancher wrapped his large denim jacket around her shoulders. They put her into Sparrow's Jeep. Sparrow remained in the house with the lone kidnapper. She had no idea what they had done with her daughter or planned to do. She stood and drew the eleven-inch blade above her head and came down with all the force she could muster. The steel cut through the man's upper spinal cord as if it were a mere chicken bone.

These men likely worked for someone. She wanted that someone to find these men exactly like this. She went to the Jeep and hugged her daughter. They held each other tight as if to never let go. "We got them both; there is nothing to worry about," Sparrow whispered.

"There were three men," Alexia whispered back. "Three."

Sparrow released her damaged daughter and placed a blanket over her lap. She motioned to the ranchers to join her outside the Jeep. Her armed assistants learned of the third abductor.

"Have we checked all the outbuildings?

"No, we stopped checking after discovering her in the shallow storage shed." Needing no further instruction, each of them turned as one and headed to one of three small structures they had not yet examined. The nearest was a decrepit chicken coop-type of wooden structure.

It was nearly dawn, and the better lighting would be of great help. The one rancher reached for the door handle. As it creaked open, a blast caught the door and fragments of the door dug into the rancher's forearm, with some shards peppering his one cheek. The three of them fell to the ground. Another gunshot hit the doorframe. They all rolled to either side of the entrance. The ranchers returned fire from their prone positions. Sparrow rolled further to her right and half-crouching scurried to the back of the building. She saw the top of his head through a distorted window. The third man, who had caused her daughter such pain, was returning fire to the front of the building with his handgun. The ranchers' rifle shots echoed in the tight space.

Sparrow's Glock was set on automatic. She was directly behind the guy and could make out just the top of his head through the milky glass window. She steadied her feet with the Glock held with both steady hands. She squeezed the trigger. An entire nine round clip exploded the man's head and brain matter stuck to the broken glass around his crumpled body.

The silence that followed seemed absolute. After several minutes, the ranchers joined Sparrow in the back of the building. The three of them walked back to the Jeep in silence. Sparrow joined her daughter, who was shivering despite the denim jacket and thick blanket. She turned to her and said, "It's over. Let's go home."

Sparrow hugged and thanked the two ranchers. Without their help Alexia would still be imprisoned and abused. Unbeknown to the ranchers at the time, a sizable cash reward would arrive in each mailbox the following week with a handwritten thank you.

Sparrow drove the Jeep at a high but safe speed to the local emergency room. Her daughter was examined by a young intern, treated, and released. She had big bump on the back of her head. Sparrow was alerted to report any symptoms of a concussion. She was treated for shock. Bruises on her arms and neck would heal as would the anal and vaginal bleeding. Sparrow was much more concerned with the longer-term psychological effects of this brutal attack.

She thanked the doctor and drove Alexia back to their ranch house. Sparrow talked, and Alexia listened. Her daughter remained relatively quiet on the journey home, preferring to have her hair whipped in the wind and nodding to her mother's comforting words.

Alexia stared out the Jeep's window when there was nothing more to share. Her damaged world seemed to engulf her very soul. She wept. Her new world view would be one of skepticism and fear. Who would ever want her after the brutal rapes? The trauma of what had taken place would stay within her forever. As she cried, Sparrow reached over with one free hand to grasp her daughter's left hand. There was nothing left to say on the final few kilometers home.

As the Jeep swung into the long driveway to the ranch house, outlined by Eucalyptus trees, Alexia had an epiphany. She kept it to herself. She would not dwell on being the poor victim. She would not have those thugs define her. She would be strong. She would become hypersensitive of her surroundings. She would learn the martial-arts skills. She would not hesitate to be the aggressor should the situation call for action. She would become completely self-reliant. She wouldn't shut out the world but embrace it with a jaundiced skepticism.

Sparrow and Alexia arrived back at their ranch just moments before Alex. Alexia had stopped sobbing. There were squad cars with lights flashing in the predawn. Alex pulled his vehicle next to the Jeep, and seeing his wife and daughter, he wept tears of utter joy. The three of them spilled out of the vehicles and embraced in a family hug. No words were spoken.

As Alex stood there holding his family close, he began to shake. He had failed to be there when his family needed him most. His linkage to shady men in several joint ventures across China had brought nothing but fear and trepidation. The linkage between the triad and government men at the joint-venture companies was stronger than he ever thought. The Chinese mafia men had failed at their abduction of his only daughter. They would no doubt try again. Could he ever break free from his past? He kissed Alexia on the cheek. He held his heroine wife. She wiped the tears from his cheeks and kissed him lightly on the lips.

A police lieutenant stood off to the side, giving the family the privacy they deserved. After an appropriate period of time, he asked if his medical personnel could evaluate Alexia. Both parents nodded their assent, and Alexia was escorted inside by one of the medical staff. Sparrow related details to Alex of her harrowing ordeal. It was also the first time Alex was hearing of his wife's heroics. His petite wife had found their daughter in a remote rural rundown farmstead. She had killed the three abductors who were heavily armed, dangerous men. She had saved their only daughter.

The adrenaline rush completely subsided, and Sparrow felt drained. She had come incredibly close to losing her daughter. The thought of those men violating her only daughter caused such a visceral response, she found herself shaking and reliving the killings. She cried. Alex had his arms around her holding her close. She felt her body shake against the strength of his. This family trauma and the deep wounds it left would no doubt impact their lives forever.

Alex held his petite wife as she sobbed into his shoulder. The mere thought of his daughter's ordeal left him weak-kneed. How could he bring such pain to his family? Why was he not there for them? Was more professional acclaim and fortune necessary? Had he lost his way? What long-term impact would this trauma have on their family? Some of his tears mixed with Sparrow's on her cheek.

The police lieutenant was reticent and allowed the couple their embrace. He gave them private time in their kitchen. The lieutenant visited quietly with his sergeant. They both agreed that a middle-aged smallish woman had circumvented the system with her own detective work and reconnaissance. Without her initiative, a young girl would be gone. The senior officer shook his head and asked the couple for a moment. Alex and Sparrow followed him into the living room. He told the couple he and his men would follow up with the two ranchers to corroborate the story and would send another team to restrict access to the rural crime scene. They would be returning in the morning for further reports and forms that were required.

When the final squad car had left, Alex and Sparrow tucked Alexia into her own bed. The mild sedative she was given would help her rest.

"How on earth did the triad find us? I felt we were all safe." Alex sat at their kitchen table staring into a cold cup of coffee. "And why would you tackle this alone?"

Sparrow's head was in her hands as she stared down at the table. She waited for several moments before responding. "The police did not have the same sense of urgency that I had. I felt I could not wait hours for your arrival. Our daughter was abducted. I had to move. When I saw her on the security camera being dragged into that white van, something snapped inside me."

"You could have been killed," Alex said reaching for her hand.

"I wasn't.

Alex stared into her eyes and a tear formed in his own. "We're not safe here anymore."

"I know that," she said.

"You were incredibly brave," he said, patting her hand.

"Let's go to bed."

They both stared at the bedroom ceiling. Alex finally said what they both were thinking. "They know where we live."

"I know," she said simply.

"We'll leave early in the morning," he said as they both stared up at the ceiling in the pitch dark.

"No, we should leave now." Sparrow said with absolute conviction as she got out of bed.

CHAPTER 48

On a cool sunny morning in southern Germany, Damijon and his staff departed the castle after a hearty breakfast of sausages, heavy crusty bread, and dark coffee. Herr Reins's boss was satisfied with the outcome of the market pause and the subsequent movement of funds, leaving no viable trace for investigators.

Herr Reins was pleased to see Damijon's party go. He changed after breakfast to his hunting clothes and chose his favorite shotgun from storage. In the barn he released his two black labs, who barked enthusiastically when they recognized the gun. He bagged two pheasant and killed one large jackrabbit before lunchtime. The visit from the Russian oligarch had gone extremely well. Herr Reins had his staff prepare an Aperol spritz as he relaxed on the western-facing deck as the sun drenched his barley fields in an orange haze.

Jerry Primrose chose to remain in South Africa. The security around Aqua-Sian was better than he could expect elsewhere in the world. The young women were relatively inexpensive, and he still found them exotic. What they would do for some additional South African rand was truly astounding. He had developed a taste for biltong, the finest quality cured and dried-beef sticks, washed down with a Delheim Vera Cruz Shiraz. His instructions from Herr Reins were to stand down. Cape Town's moderate climate fit his new lifestyle. Life was good. He would await further instructions.

Mr. Tan and his wife continued to receive packages from Sparrow at least twice monthly. They typically would be routed and repackaged through Singapore or Kuala Lampur, Malaysia. This gesture was greatly appreciated by the Tans given their minimal retirement pay from his military days.

The triad and the central government, suspicious of the Chairman's activities for several years, each conducted its own investigation. The Voice coordinated both but unbeknown to the other. Postmortem, they followed the money. Three months after his death, they both discovered the accounts in Nanjing and Beijing. Two months later they found the Hong Kong account. One junior analyst, working for Mr. Xin, in the politburo's central office, doggedly worked the financial system to uncover one offshore account held by the Chairman in the Bahamas. The analyst brought his discovery to Mr. Xin. The banking protocol in the Bahamas was rather strict, and Xin's financial team was unable to penetrate the security to get access to the account. Plan B for Mr. Xin involved straddling the government's influence with the unrestrained muscle of the triad. The Voice was instructed to use all means at his disposal to secure the Bahamian account.

A rather proper British citizen, by the name of Mr. Bloomtree, was responsible for the security protocol for the Central Bank of the Bahamas. Bloomtree lived in a three-story luxury condominium high on the hillside overlooking Nassau's Cable Beach. He had held his position at the financial institution for over the past eleven years. His bank, with external reserves of over $980 billion, was the largest of the big five on the island. Bloomtree never caught on to the laid-back island style of some of his peer group. He preferred a bow tie with a seersucker suit Monday through Friday.

On this particular Friday, Bloomtree chose to walk home from work. The air was relatively cool given the unusual north breeze. His plans for the evening were simple. Undo the bow tie, slip from the wingtips to his flip-flops, and enjoy a Scotch on his lavish third-floor deck.

The tie came off; naked feet found their rubber matting, and Bloomtree was sipping his third Scotch and water when there was a knock on his front door. Highly unusual, he thought, given the security his compound had around their buildings. It could only be a neighbor looking for a favor, perhaps catching the mail and paper for a few days. Nonetheless, Bloomtree was always cautious. Next to his front-door jamb was a red security button. Should any issue arise, this silent alarm was linked directly to both the local police and a private security firm. Bloomtree placed his cocktail glass on a glass table and peaked through the eyehole. He witnessed one smallish man with his back to him, obviously holding a bouquet of flowers. His first thought was flowers for a neighbor not home, and he opened the door.

A second man appeared from the side and expertly kicked Bloomtree in a kneecap, crushing him back into his hallway. Both men entered and silently closed the heavy door behind them. One of the men head bumped him and then looped a yellow plastic tie around his wrists. The second assailant did the same around his ankles. Three seconds later they had hoisted him up and carried to the living-room couch. The first assailant pulled a screen from his backpack and logged on to a live phone call. He held the electronic screen such that Bloomtree could see it. The young girl on the screen was near hysterical, her clothes torn, and hair disheveled. Bloomtree's only niece was attending college in Manchester, England. She was his only family. She shrieked on the phone hook-up as her eyes fixed on something just off screen.

Bloomtree was a smart man. The liquor haze was now completely gone. His niece screamed something unintelligible. He looked away from the televised phone call and asked the assailant, not holding the screen, for a private moment. They put the televised call on hold and placed the electronic instrument on the table.

"Gentlemen, you are holding the upper hand. What are you after?"

The smaller assailant smiled. "You have frozen an account of ours, which we require access to immediately. Your only niece is joining us remotely to underscore the importance of our request." The man sneered, happy with his rather proper English response.

"You will have to be a bit more precise for me to help you," Bloomtree responded almost as if he were in his office environment.

The smaller assailant released the bounds on Bloomtree's wrists and handed him a handwritten note with a numbered and lettered account. His niece screamed something from the electronic screen. The second assailant placed the instrument on mute.

"We need access to our funds in that account now."

"We will have to wait until the bank opens Monday morning," explained the rather calm banker. The blow to his eardrum knocked Bloomtree nearly unconscious. The other assailant reached into his backpack for a syringe. The needle penetrated the carotid artery in the lower neck, releasing a mild sedative.

Bloomtree was groggy and not in control of the situation. He vomited on the teak floor.

"Mr. Bloomtree, you have three minutes to remotely access our account. Should you elect not to assist us, your niece will be in the hands of our colleague. He will certainly kill her, but knowing our colleague like we do, he will repeatedly rape her first. You have two minutes forty-three seconds from now."

"My computer is in the study upstairs. Bring it to me. You must understand there are certain account protocols even I cannot circumvent."

"We have no time to waste, Mr. Bloomtree. Get us what we came for."

It wasn't done in two-plus minutes, but Bloomtree had accessed the account on his screen. It showed US$50,000 as a balance. It showed a withdrawal of $9 million a little over a year and a half ago.

The one lead assailant unmuted the long-distance call and instructed his associate to release the girl unharmed in the morning somewhere in the English countryside without her phone. He turned to Bloomtree and said he had done the right thing. He explained they would be giving him one more injection, which should put him out for six to eight hours. They would untie him. They would be off the island when he recovered. He had not stolen funds and should not feel ashamed. They had not taken funds from the account. He could return to work Monday as the bank's lead security man. Any further adverse response from him would immediately put his niece in harm's way.

"What did the Americans say?"

"No harm; no foul," Bloomtree muttered and allowed them to inject him with the second sedative in his left arm.

The Voice had the information of the sizable withdrawal within minutes. He focused a team of top forensic analysts to follow the funds.

CHAPTER 49

Alex, Sparrow, and Alexia grabbed a few personal belongings. Alex went to his personal safe and grabbed what was there. They were headed southeast of their ranch to a neighbor with his own airplane and airstrip. The flight to the South Island took forty-five minutes. From Wellington, they flew commercially to Perth, Australia, on doctored passports, which disguised their true identities. Two gold bars changed hands, and the family found themselves in the second mate's quarters on an iron-ore vessel bound for Fukuoka on the southern-most island of Japan. The voyage would take just over two weeks. Over this time Alex and Sparrow went over and over again their activities, which may have led the triad to their door. They had successfully stayed off the grid for nearly two years and were stymied on how their enemy had a fresh scent on their trail. They reviewed their international travel. They revisited their financial footprint. They considered gaps in their various interpersonal relationships. They walked through each scenario and continued to come up blank.

Seas were rough just north of Okinawa Island, and Alexia and Sparrow were sick. The storm lasted one full day. They still had two days ahead on their voyage.

The Aussie captain wished them well as they descended the gangplank. An old-fashioned rickshaw shuttled them into the city proper. The three of them rested in an old hotel frequented by lonely sailors and paid companions. The mattresses on the floor seemed much more comfortable than the swinging hammocks on the boat.

More favors were cashed in, and a fishing-boat captain took them from Fukuoka to Sapporo in the far north. They stayed in a downtown hotel for foreigners. Next was an international flight using their doctored passports to Vancouver, British Columbia.

They had to restart their lives. Alex recognized a certain disconnection with his daughter for the first time since they had been reunited. Sparrow was not herself either. To be sure, Alex was more distant and seemingly self-absorbed. They needed to reboot.

Alex outlined his proposed next steps with Sparrow to reach a kind of family consensus. She agreed and added some detail to his outline. First, they would enroll Alexia in a girls prep program in Edmonton, Alberta. Surprisingly she agreed and thought it wonderful. Next they would rent a cabin on Vancouver Island as a sort of base camp. Sparrow and Alex would split up and retrace their respective routes to New Zealand. They would routinely regroup via encrypted communications each evening regardless of where they were in the world. He would reenter the People's Republic of China through Tibet, retracing every aspect of his journey to the ranch in New Zealand. Sparrow would return to New York City where she and her old partner had successfully transferred funds internationally. The decision, from a macro standpoint, was to uncover the snake that was following them and cut it off from the head. They never could hide from the serpent and be truly happy and content.

Despite the trauma Alexia had been through, she seemed to flourish at the new school. She did well earning all A minuses and B pluses. There was a boy interested in her from a prep school just a few kilometers from hers. She made friends quickly. Indoor track season had begun, and she earned a spot on the varsity team in two events. She looked forward to each Thursday evening when her parents would call her from anywhere they happened to be on the globe. Alexia was at the age when everything revolved around her. She did not dwell on her horrid kidnaping. She rationalized that her father was in the security business and may have enemies.

She was caught in the middle, but her stepmother had miraculously found her in the Australian outback and saved her. The only lingering impact for Alexia was a real fear of confined spaces. Her time spent in the dark trunk of a vehicle and a smelly cellar had changed her forever. She needed to sleep with a nightlight on nearby and preferred wide-open spaces.

Alexia had a fondness for fashion. She did not wear Levi's and sweatshirts to class as most of her peer group, preferring print dresses and scarves in the spring and a sophisticated après-ski look for winter. In the fall she tended toward black slacks and woven sweaters with colorful patterns. She preferred sandals for spring, black boots for winter, and highheeled burnt-orange half boots with fringe for autumn. Minimal jewelry was her style with the exception of a small gold cross-held by a thin gold chain. Her long blond hair was typically held back on one side by a brooch, and she had dozens of them.

Alexia had another distinguishing characteristic not known by her new girlfriends at school or the young man at the prep school across town. Her father had introduced her to the martial arts at a young age. She was a quick study. She was very limber and lighting fast with her hands as well as her feet. Her father had her study Shaolinquan, the oldest institutional style of Chinese martial arts.

The circuitous route her family had taken to Canada was certainly odd, but she trusted her father to keep them safe. She knew only bits and pieces of her stepmother's past. Sparrow had shared that her biological father had been discredited and murdered by the triad. She had loving quasi-parents in the Tans, who had also been tortured and killed. She had no siblings.

Sparrow had told her of another death of a friend at the malting complex she had worked at. He had been more like an uncle to her. The night before his murder, she had driven the acting general manager to a park. There he had collected a vial from an unknown man. The inference was this held a potent poison of some kind. The following day the acting GM had her uncle, who had been previously fired, visit his temporary office. Her uncle was found dead moments later. The inference was of deliberate poisoning, which she had heard the acting GM brag about to one of his subordinates. She had noted how deliberate and careful the GM had been with the deadly vial.

Alexia loved how her stepmom moved with such confidence and grace. Her stepmom had so much to teach her. And she absolutely loved how her parents were deeply committed to each other. She couldn't wait for Thursday night and the chance to tell them of her upcoming date with the boy from the adjacent all-boys' school.

Sparrow landed at JFK airport and took a taxi into town. A clear fall night in New York allowed the city to look its best. Her friend Chang met her in the lobby of the Waldorf Astoria. Her encrypted message had him worried. From his perspective, he had left the triad and central People's Republic of China government on the other side of the world as he pursued his dreams in the Big Apple. Sparrow arrived in the hall looking spectacular in a cream-colored Halston dress that accentuated her feminine form. Her black pumps accentuated her athletic legs and clicked across the tiled floor to Chang's table.

Chang reached for her hand, pecked it, and offered her a seat. "I am both surprised and a bit nervous seeing you back in New York. Your last message suggested you had found real contentment on a ranch in the middle of nowhere. What can I possibly do for you?"

Sparrow raised her hand to capture the eye of a young waiter, who was only more than pleased to be called over by such a woman. "A Campari and soda for me? What would Mr. Chang care for?"

"Make it two, please." The waiter left with the order but lingered just a moment too long in hopes of capturing Sparrow's attention. That not being the case, he retreated to the bar. "I must say marriage looks good on you, Sparrow," Chang said convincingly.

The busy and noisy lobby bar was a perfect place to have an intimate, confidential conversation. "My life was splendid until it was interrupted by men sent by the triad to intimidate and destroy me," she said as the cocktails arrived. The young waiter lingered again a bit too long in hopes of catching Sparrow's eye. She didn't, and he left. "Our daughter was abducted. Men who took her were ultimately after me. I need to know why."

Mr. Chang sipped the red cocktail. "I have some close friends who are forensic auditors. It may not sound sexy but these guys are well compensated and revered in the financial community. I trust these guys. A team of three of them will cost seven hundred thousand dollars. I think they will be well worth it. They have the skill set to reconstruct all the transactions and codes used for the money transfers. They are also skilled at recognizing any and all attempts to follow your money trail."

"If that is your recommendation, let's get them started. I can have the necessary funds lifted to their accounts tomorrow morning."

"I do not believe you will be disappointed, Sparrow. I will call their lead guy tonight and get the wheels turning. It's all about following the zeros and ones across cyberspace at the end of the day," Chang said as he raised his glass in mock salute.

CHAPTER 50

Alex met with a major in the Russian army and a major in the Chinese army at the same canteen a mile from the Soviet-Sino border in the north. The three men shared several shots of cheap vodka. Alex passed the envelopes respectively to each officer. Both men paused to count the multiple stacks of US hundred-dollar bills in each envelope. After one last vodka toast, Alex was hustled under a tarp of a Chinese-army garbage truck crossing the border without incident.

With impeccable documentation, Alex eased into his soft seat on the first rail car. The trip was long and boring. Alex slept in an awkward position and awoke with a neck ache in central Nanjing.

As was prearranged, Alex met Mr. Tan at the southwest corner of the massive Central Park. They greeted each other and then walked across the busy six-lane street to a quiet teahouse. Tan choose a table on the third floor overlooking the sports complex in the park. After the tea service had arrived, Alex brought Mr. Tan up to speed on the kidnapping of his daughter, his wife's heroics, and their hasty departure from the sheep ranch.

Mr. Tan shook his head. There had been such trouble for his friend and his family. "I can think of only one reason the triad would have any interest in your family. They must believe you have access to their illegal funds—either under the Chairman's name or Mr. Ping," Tan explained in his Mandarin dialect. "Another possibility is a more personal vendetta given the deaths of three local triad members, which they may link to

C. R. REINERS

Sparrow. I do not believe this is a real possibility. The triad today is all business. Risking personnel to simply even the score, when there may be no financial gain, is not their style any longer."

"Sparrow had access to the Chairman's personal offshore account in the Bahamas," Alex shared with the much-older man. "She transferred the lion's share of the account after she killed him."

Mr. Tan showed no surprise on his face. "She is a strong woman, who was placed in a very difficult position. I say we focus our attention on the funds transferred and who may have any line of sight to the banking details. Let's get to work."

That evening Sparrow in New York communicated via encrypted message her suspicions and next steps. Simultaneously, it was the next morning for Alex, given his time zone, and he shared with her his results to date. Both of them were now focused on any financial miscues they may have missed in the past. Almost immediately the triad had tracked down the Chairman's ill-advised gains tucked away within the country. Later, it seemed, they had become aware of the offshore account in the Bahamas. How would they link the offshore account to Sparrow? One would have thought, given the strict banking protocol and confidentiality of the British-style banks, it would have been near impossible to link Sparrow with the numbered account.

The Voice met face to face with his forensic financial staff. He now had the information from the security manager for the Central Bank of the Bahamas. The ex-chairman's account was infiltrated by someone to the tune of $9 million. There was nothing unusual with the withdrawal from a banker's standpoint. All the correct passwords and passcodes were flawlessly executed. To date, all the Chinese forensic staff concluded was a withdrawal to a US account, and the transaction had been completed online. They could not decipher more detail than that. The Voice was not impressed with the team's meager conclusions, and he made that feeling known to all in the room.

Chang and Sparrow meet with the three forensic experts they had hired two days later in a New York bagel shop. Sparrow was taken aback by their youth. The three geeks in front of her looked to be just out of high school. All three wore thick glasses and each sported a beard of sorts. The scraggily facial hair, the T-shirts sporting grunge bands, and the sixties-style headbands did little to install confidence in Sparrow as they were introduced to her.

The oldest of the three, and apparently their leader, started right in with their analysis. There was no small talk and certainly no social graces evident. Sparrow was instantly lost with the technical jargon and algorithms used by the boy-man. She allowed him to continue, hoping her friend Chang could interpret for her later on. The geek-squad she had hired seemed to be on the right track. She politely nodded and allowed the presenter to continue.

They answered several of Chang's questions, also in a technical language Sparrow failed to understand. Then they left.

"What was that all about?" Sparrow asked shaking her head a bit.

"These guys are brilliant. They did more than we asked. Let's grab a bagel and a cup and grab that open table outside."

Finally situated with their carbs and black coffee and scoring the table on the sidewalk, Mr. Chang began his interpretation for Sparrow.

"These guys surfaced more information than I expected." Chang began by holding up one finger to indicate the initial point and subsequent digits to underscore each additional take-away.

"One, the account under question in the Bahamas has been accessed since your withdrawal a year and a half ago. Two, it was accessed by a local-bank official on the island using the bank's strict confidential protocol. Three, the account information was shared electronically with a senior official in Beijing. Four, the balance of $50,000 in the account was not touched. Five, the Chinese official has accessed the account multiple times since the security breach using the bank's proper protocol. Six, they pinpointed the breach coming from the private residence of the bank's head of security. Seven, the Central Bank of the Bahamas is not aware of this breach in their security. Eight, security cameras in the hallway of the banker's private residence captured two Chinese men departing from the security manager's home moments after the account had been breached. Nine, our geek-squad followed the electronic footprint to the politburo's offices in Beijing. Ten, they actually pinpointed the owner of the receiving information in the capital city. He is quasi-government and quasi-triad. Reverently, he is referred to as the Voice by senior men from both organizations."

Sparrow was dumbfounded and a bit shaky. The investment in these cyber detectives had more than paid off. She thanked Chang and began to leave the table without touching her buttered bagel. "Wait a moment; there's one more thing." Chang held out one fist in one hand and his index finger in the other. Sparrow returned to her seat. "Point eleven; our geek squad uncovered a short recording of an initial conversation between this Voice and the Central Bank of the Bahamas. It seems on his initial foray into the banking system, he went through a junior person at the bank prior to engaging the necessary passwords and passcodes. All these conversations between bankers and customers are recorded. It's a rather short exchange between the Voice and the bank employee, but I have it here." Mr. Chang said as he searched his bag for the recording device.

Sparrow sat mesmerized. Chang played the tape. The conversation was short and businesslike, but she turned ice cold as she recognized the same voice that over two years earlier had instructed her to kill Alex Cutter, and, as a result, her past killings would be expunged from the record. It was undoubtedly the Voice from her past. She asked Chang to play the short tape a second time, which he did. She was convinced a second time.

She thanked Chang for everything and left the table. She returned to her hotel. Tonight on their international call, Sparrow would share with Alex this secret she had kept from him. The Voice was the head of the serpent, which was after them. In the past, the Voice had searched her out, offering to erase her record for having killed the Chairman, Mr. Ping, and several triad members, in return for her killing of Alex Cutter.

Alex would now recognize he was sleeping in the bed of a killer. She was not simply a company driver for the malting complex. She had been a courtesan. She had been a kept woman. She had rubbed elbows with some very powerful people in China. She had a long and clouded history. She wished she was on the other side of the world with Alex right now. Delivering this message over the phone would be too impersonal. Was her world, she thought while in the hotel elevator, falling apart? She cried when she closed her hotel room door behind her. Suddenly she felt very alone.

She placed the international call at 10:00 p.m. her time, which was 9:00 a.m. the next morning at Alex's Nanjing hotel. Alex had Mr. Tan join him for the call with his wife.

Sparrow relayed all the incredible detail her geek-squad had dug up—focusing on all points one through ten. She could sense the excitement from the two men on the other side of the phone. Alex and Mr. Tan reported their meager findings to date, which were not anything as exciting as Sparrow's.

Sparrow said she had one more thing. Both men blurted out "What is it?"

Sparrow played the short taped conversation between the junior banker in the Bahamas and the Voice. "What does that actually mean, Sparrow?" Alex enquired.

"I know this man," she said. "I had dinner with him over two years ago. He represents a shady side of the Chinese government. He has ready access to the triad's senior leadership and has one foot in the federal government. When the government cannot accomplish what they want through political means and the military and police are too structured, they turn to this man. He is quasi-federal government and quasi-triad. He is known in powerful circles as the Voice."

The men at the other end of the phone remained silent, expecting more. "He approached me after the death of the Chairman and Mr. Ping. He had given me permission to avenge the brutal murder of my father. In fact, he had pointed out which triad members were directly responsible for my father's murder. As for the Chairman, he had collected many internal enemies over time and had padded his own pockets to excess. Party leaders wanted him gone. I staged his fatal heart attack and those in powerful positions were actually grateful. The death of Ping was more of a nonevent for the powerful men of Beijing." Sparrow paused to see if there was a reaction on the other end of the phone. There wasn't.

She continued. "The Voice instructed me to kill you, Alex." She paused again but could only hear her own breathing in the mouthpiece. "I, of course, left China to start a new life outside Paris. Alex, please forgive me for not sharing all this with you. I wanted to have a normal life. I love you, and I love Alexia. Please forgive me." She began to cry.

Alex, hearing all this for the first time, wanted to be there. He wanted to hold her and stroke her hair and tell her it would all be all right. But with multiple time zones separating them, all he could do was whisper "I love you" over the long-distance line.

Mr. Tan spoke for the first time. "I recognize the man's voice you played on that recording. I am certain of it. On several occasions, I drove him from the airport to the malting complex and sometimes to several of the other joint ventures along the river. I know this man."

Alex looked at the older man next to him on the conference line. "Are you sure?"

"Absolutely, I do. One time, when the tracks were being replaced for the high-speed train between Nanjing and Shanghai, I drove him to his office just off the bund. I know this man," Mr. Tan said with great conviction.

Sparrow stopped crying. Alex stared at his older partner in the room and smiled. "I have an idea," Alex said.

"We will trap the snake in a sack and have someone else remove its head," Alex said. Both Sparrow and Mr. Tan were listening intently. "China is undergoing tremendous change—political change, social change, business change, and class change. Even the family structure is changing. Some are getting rich as the society adapts to a more open financial system. Many are skeptical of those who may not have the Party's best interest in mind. Those at the top of the pyramid are beginning to welcome the twenty-first century. However, those in leadership positions will not compromise their own influence and subsequently their own power. The Voice straddles two worlds. One is the established power base of the Party, and the other is the cruel world of the triad. I believe we can use the system to entrap him and ultimately eliminate him."

"What do you have in mind?" Mr. Tan looked ten years younger to Alex. He looked excited to be part of the plan.

"We hack into his private account. We plant misinformation. We make him appear to be potentially a liability to the politburo. We make him a potential liability to the triad. We cast doubt on his credibility. We place him in compromising positions. We get his current host of supporters to begin to doubt him and challenge their allegiance. We get powerful men to want to place distance between the Voice and their offices. We create such distrust there is only one logical outcome from the powers that be."

Both Mr. Tan and Sparrow were excited about the plan to discredit the Voice and ultimately destroy him. Tan spoke first. "Allow me to use my resources from my old army days to infiltrate the cyberspace he occupies as well as his physical office in Shanghai."

"I will tap into my resources from the Nanjing cabaret," Sparrow added from her phone line half way across the world. "I too have some midlevel military men who may prove useful in gathering the type of intelligence we will require."

The excitement was building on the phone, and Alex added, "I have contacts from my days on the malting-complex board who may prove useful as well. Briefly, I served on two other boards in the Nanjing tax-free zone, which I will tap into."

"Gentlemen," interrupted Sparrow. "The Chairman was particularly close to a Mr. Xin, who serves on the Standing Committee of the Politburo. Allow me to tap into that senior resource in some fashion."

Alex added he would continue to pursue activities at the Caribbean bank. They all agree to touch base again the following evening. There was much work to be done.

CHAPTER 51

Alex led the conference call the following evening: "I have tracked down the security manager at the Central Bank of the Bahamas. At first he was not willing to cooperate much until I explained we had linked the breach of the account with the video of the two Chinese men leaving his private residence last Friday evening. He is frightful given the scare they put into him by threatening his only niece in Manchester, England. I have hired for twenty-four seven protection for the young student, which has encouraged our security manager to assist us.

"Next, we had half of the remaining fifty thousand dollars in the account withdrawn as cash with electronic fingerprints coming from the Voice. We had the actual cash, in small bills, sent overnight mail to the office in Shanghai used by the Voice. It was a bit old school, but no one can dismiss the intent. We show the Voice changing passwords and passcodes for the account. We have passed on an encrypted message to Mr. Xin, at the politburo, that all the remaining funds in the account have vanished. The chief of police in Shanghai has been informed he will no longer be receiving a monthly stipend. Water pipes at the Shanghai office of the Voice have mysteriously burst, damaging some hard-copy files. Mr. Xin was also informed by one of his trusted assistants that some confidential information held by the Voice was given directly to another branch of the politburo, by-passing Mr. Xin's office entirely." Alex stopped there to allow the others on the line to comment.

"That is outstanding news, my friend." Mr. Tan was piping in from his own secured line. "I have identified two captains, in active service, who

216

have been damaged by the Voice career wise in the past and are more than willing to participate with us. I did offer them the necessary compensation we had agreed too, which they both felt was adequate. I have also identified a disgruntled driver he uses when in Beijing. This driver can pinpoint all the usual destinations he frequents while in the capital. I should have more for you by this time tomorrow."

On this follow-up call, Sparrow was the last to contribute. "The Chairman and Mr. Xin from the politburo were at one time quite close business associates. That relationship seemed to have faded drastically prior to the Chairman's death, primarily due to the Chairman's greed. I have learned from some of Mr. Xin's closest staff members that the politburo executive wanted some time to distance himself from the Chairman before eliminating him once and for all. The Voice has access to the politburo exclusively through the office of Mr. Xin. I have placed numerous rumors with his staff indicating his allegiance may not be what it seems." Sparrow took a sip of her tea and allowed her news to sink in.

Alex was next on the phone line. "In less than forty-eight hours, we have successfully disrupted the Voice. We have also identified the two triad members who victimized the Bahamian banker from the townhouse security video."

CHAPTER 52

The recoil from the rifle slammed him backward. The kick came from a 458 magnum Winchester 500-grain elephant-gun. Primrose had researched the weapon prior to his foray into Tanzania. To drop the beast in its tracks would take a frontal or side brain shot. The bullet would travel through at least eighteen inches of structural bone and sinuses and then break through super hard tusk roots on its way to the mammal's brain. Primrose's shot however glanced off the skull as the beast charged down the path toward the small hunting party. The competent guide Primrose had engaged for the hunt calmly lifted his weapon, the scope catching the animal's frontal lobe; the trigger squeezed one round. The large male seemed to buckle, its front legs tipping forward onto its knees. A moment later the magnificent specimen lay awkwardly forward, its trunk across its forehead, as if to bellow a final warning.

Primrose was nonetheless pleased with himself. The professional photographer took numerous shots of Primrose and the beast. Primrose enjoyed posing with his elephant-gun cradled in the crook of his arm, with his bushman's hat set at a cocky angle. After a few more photographs, catching the setting sun as a backdrop, Primrose had the lead Jeep take him back to camp. He looked forward to reliving the hunt with the eastern European girl he had brought along.

Alex's team had worked numerous angles over the course of several days to discredit the Voice. They remained patient and allowed the drip-drip-drip of a barrage of misinformation to take its toll. By the week's end, Mr. Xin's office had collected enough damaging evidence to warrant a face-to-face meeting with their boss to outline their growing political concerns with having future engagements with the Voice and the office of the politburo. Similarly, the three lead men of the Chinese triad had reached a conclusion that this dangerously efficient man had outlived his usefulness. Once these independent conclusions were reached by the highest powers from each organization, the outcome was never questioned.

The assassin came from the sixth Special Warfare Group prior to his final training in the Naval Commando Unit. He was of average height and was rather senior at thirty-two years of age. His muscles were toned as three wires looped together to add strength. His eyes were razor sharp yet camouflaged behind thin clear-framed glasses, which gave the appearance of an aging athlete at the backside of his career. The assassin was reached by a representative of the politburo directly, who was accompanied by a senior representative of the triad. The assignment was clear. Kill the man known as the Voice. There were no restricting rules of engagement. This could look like a suicide, an accident, or even a murder.

Coincidently, the assassin had trained under the command of the Voice in his previous life and the men knew each other well. The assassin did not question his superiors. He had no emotional attachment whatsoever. Although he was military, he knew he would be compensated with multiple political favors bestowed on the very few in China. He also would enjoy the luxury offered by the triad at one of their Macau gambling resorts.

During this time, the Voice was becoming increasingly suspicious. He had picked up various bits and pieces of misinformation referencing his involvement in non-sanctioned quasigovernment activities. He had learned from other informants there was a segment of the government attempting to link him to illegal personal accounts offshore. The Voice was not naïve. He called in reciprocal favors owed to him. The maize of powerful and influential men in China residing in both the party government and organized crime made it difficult to pinpoint the source of his nemesis. He continued to call in favors and paid out bribes but could not pinpoint his enemy from within. One of the calls he made was to his trusted apprentice from the Naval Commando Unit.

The assassin had not heard from his mentor for over nine years. The man he was assigned to kill had invited him to an intimate dinner party the following evening. He graciously accepted the invitation.

CHAPTER 53

The exotic courtesan rolled off Primrose for the second time that evening. She retreated to the bathroom now that they were back at Aqua-Sian. He knew she would then retreat to the balcony for a smoke and then to her separate bedroom down the hall.

Primrose was getting a bit itchy for some further action. It had been quite a while since he had been instructed to stand down by Herr Reins. He had filled his time with various outings, such as the hunt in Tanzania, but was getting antsy for some real work. Given his idle time, Primrose tinkered some more with the complex algorithms he had used to assist in pausing the Shanghai equity market. It occurred to him to freelance a bit. He had the tools to have the market pause, and he had the capital. Perhaps he could duplicate the ruse on another marketplace and keep the profits for himself. He considered several possibilities:

Tel Aviv Stock Exchange
Gre Tai Securities Market, Taiwan
Copenhagen Stock Exchange
Yanger Stock Exchange, Myanmar
Bursa, Kuala Lumpur

These five exchanges offered Primrose opportunities. All were rather obscure relative to the massive market participation in the major exchanges. All offered enough opening and closing volume to allow for manipulation, if managed within volume limits. All had limited security protocols relative to the one Primrose had already breached in Shanghai. Primrose had nothing but time. Now he filled it with a project of his own. Boy, this was going to be fun again.

CHAPTER 54

The Voice greeted his protégé in the lobby of the downtown Beijing hotel where there was a private dining room reserved. After a warm and rather formal greeting, the Voice had his guest frisked by two armed men. The awkward social pause while the assassin was being examined for weapons was filled by two more dinner companions arriving nearly at the same time. Both new entrants were subjected to the same procedure.

The four men walked up one flight to their waiting table on the hotel's second floor. The two armed bodyguards remained outside the door as the guests took assigned seats at the intimate table setting. The small talk revolved around family matters and the upcoming Olympic Games.

After the first course was delivered and the wait staff had left the room, the Voice shared with this intimate circle of associates his speculation of a conspiracy to discredit him in some way. He asked for their advice and counsel.

The assassin remained stone-faced as was his custom and personality. The other two guests appeared nervous that such a topic was openly being discussed. The inference was some party, very senior in the government or the triad, was attempting to smear the Voice and blemish his career. No one touched their first course. The Voice paused as he clicked his water glass with a fork. The room remained otherwise deathly quiet. The Voice reformulated his enquiry as he asked each man of anything they may want to add. The assassin was first, and he shook his head no. The second man stumbled with an explanation of his being out of the country for the past three weeks. The last guest, the only banker in the group, looked down at his plate and shared he had been approached by senior government officials recently to examine financial records associated with the Voice. The clinking of the glass stopped. The Voice asked for further details. These were shared somewhat reluctantly by the nervous banker. The wait staff returned to the room, but they were waived away by the Voice. There was a degree of tenseness in the room. More questions were addressed to the banker. He continued to stumble with his answers. It got more uneasy in the room. The Voice quietly requested for the banker to remain and excused his other two guests to remain out in the ornate hallway.

When it was now just the two of them, the Voice continued. "I have trusted you with delicate financial matters for years. I have made you a rich man, a very rich man. I always believed I could trust you."

There was silence in the room. The banker continued to stare at the plate in front of him. He began to physically shake. For the first time, he looked up into the eyes of the Voice and said nothing.

"Calm yourself. I expect you to assist me going forward. By this time tomorrow, I want a detailed accounting of whom you talk to, what they expect from you, and what they are offering you. Is that clear?" The Voice got up and opened the door to the hallway and asked his other guests to join him.

The assassin recognized the tension that remained in the room. He also had assessed the competency of the two armed men the Voice had at the door. This was not the venue to eliminate his target. He would remain patient. The small talk at the dinner table continued, and he added minimally to it, true to his personality.

The Beijing duck was superb. At the evening's conclusion, the Voice toasted his guests with a fine Cognac and thanked them for coming. As everyone prepared to leave the dining room, the assassin leaned into his host and requested another moment in private. The Voice nodded his agreement and coaxed his other guests to the door.

When they were alone, each stood opposite from the round dining room table. The assassin thanked his host once again. The two men remained in their places hands on the backs of their chairs. Both looked directly into each other's eyes. Both sensed a further tension building in the small room.

"I must admit to being caught a bit off guard when I received your formal invitation to join this group for dinner. We have not spoken for many years. I am curious why you elected to reach out to me. How can I be of service?" The would-be assassin shifted his weight from one foot to the other.

"You are here because I trust you and consider you a highly skilled professional," the Voice responded as he continued to stare unblinkingly at his protégé. "The banker and politician you met tonight may not be the close associates they appear to be on the surface. I have good reason to believe I have been targeted by some faction in either the government or the triad to be discredited in some fashion. I intend to root out this cancer and deal with any and all responsible parties." The Voice added, after a brief pause, "There is no room for two dragons in one pond."

The assassin smiled and responded with another classic Chinese proverb. "Look to your enemy for a chance to succeed." The assassin nodded again. "I am at your service, sir."

The two men shook hands as they exited the room. The assassin turned to go down the stairs, and the Voice remained with his two bodyguards.

The assassin climbed into his cab under the hotel's portico. He had less than eighteen hours to eliminate the man who had just engaged him to dig out the cancer creeping into his storied career. He instructed the cab driver to circle back to the hotel and drop him off a block from the entrance.

The Voice was aware of the cab's U-turn just as it happened—his paid informant was on keen alert. He instructed his men to position themselves with clear lines of sight in the hotel's lobby bar. Their orders were clear. The Voice called the cell number of the assassin, who picked up and thanked his host once again for the evening, never mentioning his return trip to the hotel.

The Voice was convinced of the deception. He chastised himself for not recognizing the signals. First there were his other dinner guests who did not show any real surprise when introduced to his protégé. Second, this military man would have developed strong bonds within the government given his advanced rank. His loyalty would be placed with those directly responsible for his standing in the elite naval force. Those bonds would likely be stronger than a relationship he had with the man nine years ago. And finally, his reluctance to participate in any of the dinner conversation around the current politburo's leadership gave him pause.

The assassin entered the hotel through a side door, brushing aside a janitor cleaning the tile floor. He had released his Glock from its holster and held it tightly against his right thigh. He was entering the large hotel lobby from its southwest corner.

The second bodyguard for the Voice heard it in his earpiece. The hotel janitor called in the approach of the assassin. He relayed the message to the Voice and his partner on the other side of the room. Just as the Voice caught movement behind him in the bar's mirror, the second bodyguard had pulled his weapon and fired two automatic rounds into the back of the assassin's head. A woman screamed. Patrons fell to the floor. The Voice took a final pull from his Scotch and soda and left the lobby. He walked deliberately to the man lying face down in a pool of blood. Convinced of the man's final demise, he continued walking to a waiting sedan with darkened windows.

Alex, Sparrow, and Mr. Tan heard the news from one of their confidants in the state department. The Voice had escaped the noose. The news had already been digested by Mr. Xin at his politburo office. He was quickly erasing all ties with the Voice. Certainly this was a dangerous man. Besides, he was turning his attention to the increased market volatility experienced at the Shanghai exchange, which ultimately reported into his office.

Alex and Mr. Tan called Sparrow on a secured line after they had some time to digest the news of the assassin's failure to eliminate the Voice. They knew they were in a compromised position. There had been too many linkages to various sources connecting them to both the government and the organized crime syndicate as they attempted to discredit the Voice at multiple levels. The Voice had won. They had lost.

A decision was made for Alex to leave China with Mr. and Mrs. Tan that same evening. Sparrow was to leave New York and join them at their safe house in Vancouver, British Columbia.

Sparrow left on a United Airlines flight direct from LaGuardia to Portland. She would drive north from there. It was not so simple for Alex and the Tans. Mrs. Tan's travel documents were not updated and in proper order. It would take a minimum of two to three weeks to have all the necessary stamps on her passport. Collectively they decided Alex should leave without them and join Sparrow. There was a degree of risk for the Tans to wait and receive the proper exit docs, but it was felt the risk of attempting an unauthorized departure would be far greater. Alex departed using his forged passport on a Dragon Air flight connecting in Hong Kong and then on Canadian Air to Vancouver, British Columbia. He hated leaving the Tans behind. Mr. Tan assured him they would be fine. They would stay with relatives thirty kilometers outside the city until his wife's international travel would be approved by the authorities.

Primrose sat back to review his handy work. He had initially isolated his efforts on breaching market security at the Gre Tai in Taiwan, the Yanger in the former Siam, and the Bursa in Malaysia. He opted to concentrate on the rice-processing businesses represented in Taiwan and Malaysia. He had already established trading accounts in them both. He orchestrated another manipulation at both exchanges, but this time he chose to do so at the market opening. There was adequate market volume of both buyers and sellers. The market pause of just less than three minutes was enough to cause outright panic selling and the unwinding of bull spreads. The result was a total windfall profit of well over US$3 million. Primrose left a few open orders in the market for window dressing. He transferred most of the trading profits to private off shore accounts previously established. He sat back, pleased, and thought of his ignorant father now back in prison for another botched armed robbery. He called for the eastern European lady to join him for cocktails downstairs.

CHAPTER 55

Herr Reins heard of the market disruption in the two rather obscure markets the following day. The modus operandi was too similar to what they had successfully pulled off months earlier at the major exchanges. He immediately expected Primrose. This kind of cavalier behavior could expose them all. He was beyond angry. He called Primrose on the emergency line they had established. He let it ring multiple times and never reached a connection. He left an encrypted message for him to call. Next he made a call to his boss in St. Petersburg. Damijon answered his cell on the first ring. Herr Reins brought him up to speed with the independent heist on the Taiwanese and Malaysian markets. The modus operandi appeared eerily similar to their successful pause in the major markets a few months ago.

Damijon's first reaction was to kill the copycat. But this man's expertise, if indeed it proved to be Primrose, was too valuable. He decided to spare him. He instructed Herr Reins to threaten the man if necessary but to focus on what protocol he used in the successful ruse and report back to him as soon as he could.

CHAPTER 56

The Voice sped away in the nondescript sedan with both of his henchmen. The driver took them to a safe house in the port city of Tianjin. He would have preferred to have captured the assassin and learned of his handlers. The situation did not allow for that degree of precision. He did not second-guess the reaction of his bodyguard. In fact, the bodyguard had saved his life. The quick, decisive action may have given those responsible for the assassin's assignment reason to pause. The Voice scoured his contact list both within the triad and across multiple government agencies. He was willing to pay triple for information linking his would-be killer to the killer's handlers. This was a significant premium. A more typical payment for sensitive information would garner the source enough to subsist in their two-room apartment on the city's outskirts. A triple payment would assure an informant of a luxury apartment overlooking the bund in Shanghai. Word quickly spread among those who worked in the underbelly of society. Those coming forward with worthwhile information would have to clearly distance themselves from any inference of assisting the foe. These were crafty people, and for a triple incentive, they could figure it out.

As one would expect, the worthwhile information came in snippets.

1. An elderly Chinese man with a northern Mandarin accent had approached an army sergeant to secure the whereabouts of two retired captains, who had served under the Voice years ago.

2. A secretary for the Standing Committee of the Politburo was asked to forward an updated dossier of the Voice to her boss.
3. A clerk from the Bank of China (Xiqu Square Branch) was aware of a strange transaction involving US$50,000 in hard cash being converted to small renminbi notes, which were subsequently mailed overnight to an office in Shanghai. (The Voice recognized his office address.)
4. A security guard at a Nanjing whorehouse, called the Wild Bunch Cabaret, was approached over the phone by a woman he knew as Sparrow. She was searching for any dirt on the Voice or his office staff.
5. A board member from the malting complex in Nanjing was approached by an ex-Board member, Alex Cutter. The conversation was cordial, but the inference was of potential improprieties, not only from the deceased Chairman, but also from the man known by all as the Voice.

Other bits and pieces filled out the puzzle. Alex Cutter, who had left China some years back, was out to discredit him. The woman known as Sparrow was no longer working at the cabaret and appeared to be working her best to cast doubt on his loyalty to both the triad and the federal government. An older Chinese gentleman, whose name he did not catch, appeared to be out to cast doubt on his character.

The Voice had the informants handsomely paid and set out a net to his colleagues involved with passport control and exit visas. Initially there was nothing of particular interest from this governmental body. The Voice pushed them for more than nothing. A very junior staff member brought three items forward, which he thought may prove interesting. First, there was the wealthy banker with lymphoma who was requesting an urgent visa to have a surgical procedure done in Singapore. Next was a young student from the Han clan looking to make a four-day trip to Vietnam to visit his girlfriend. Finally, there was an expedited request for an elderly woman to join her husband on a trip to Vancouver, British Columbia. She had never been out of the country. They were not in a tour group. They were not with a sanctioned party. Their request, coincidently, came the day after the aborted mission of the assassin. The Voice zeroed in on this last visa request.

The underling's supervisor was only too willing to cooperate with the Voice. In a matter of minutes, he shared the details of the visa request from the woman who wanted to travel to Vancouver. Her last name was Tan.

The Voice called ahead. He told his people in Nanjing he would join them in the morning. With the details offered by the visa request, he expected his crew to have this woman available for interrogation when he arrived. A small government plane was at his disposal. He would fly from Tianjin to Nanjing at first light. His minions found no one at the address listed. They also knew their boss. They needed answers. Sprinkling some rather large renminbi notes to neighbors confirmed the woman had left with her husband for a relative's home just north of the city.

By the time the Voice landed with his small attachment at Nanjing's massive overbuilt airport, they had local police round up Mr. and Mrs. Tan on some trumped up tax evasion charge. The couple was under guard and awaiting the Voice at the Xuan Wu hotel downtown. The top four floors of the hotel were booked by the Voice. Those expats and visiting businessmen in the upper floors were escorted to new quarters either in the hotel or in suites in the adjacent hotel.

The Voice recognized the older man the minute he stepped into the guarded suite on the hotel's top floor. The old man looked fit and alert. Mr. Tan immediately recognized the younger officer. They had not served together in the People's Army. Mr. Tan had been fifteen years his senior, but they had completed several officers' training courses together. On the other hand, his wife looked weak and miserable, and she was visibly shaking.

He had them taken to different rooms, each at the opposite end of a central living-room space. He chose to join the whimpering older woman. He kept the door open to the hallway. He clicked on the recorder resting on the credenza. The two men who had accompanied him on the Nanjing flight motioned for Mr. Tan to the room down the hall opposite. Each man carried a black leather satchel. They closed the door behind them.

The initial scream heard was subhuman; a sustained scream with no pause for a breath. What followed was more a whispering plea. A grown man was crying in agony. More whispers. The next scream was louder and seemed to go on forever. Man's inhumanity to man knew no bounds. Next she heard her name called at a pitch almost unintelligible. Then the screaming simply stopped. The entire suite was silent other than the whir of the recording device.

The Voice turned to the elderly woman. "Your husband, unfortunately, will never be the same. He will live, however, if you tell me where I can find Mr. Alex Cutter and the woman known as Sparrow. You have thirty seconds to make up your mind and save your husband an unspeakable death."

She tried to speak. Nothing came from her mouth. She was frozen. She couldn't think.

The final scream she heard from down the hall was of a man reduced to mush. She fainted. When she was revived, the two men with the black leather satchels sat across from her. The Voice stood at the door. In very formal Mandarin, he simply looked at her and asked, "Madam?"

Mrs. Tan rolled onto the floor and into the fetal position. She cried out again and again "Vancouver, Canada; Vancouver, Canada," until her voice became a whisper, "Vancouver, Canada." The Voice nodded to the two men, who picked her off the floor and carried down the hallway. She was crying so hard she had difficulty catching her breath.

The Voice turned off the recorder. His team had recovered the cell phones from both Mr. Tan and his wife. There were only a few calls under the Recent category. The Voice was curious and redialed the one with an area code of 780 and turned on his recorder once again.

"Hello, Mom; Hi, Dad" came the cheerful greeting after just two rings. The young woman was met with silence on the other end of her phone. Her demeanor instantly changed as she literally screamed "What's wrong!" Given the deathly quiet response, she hung up and the line went dead.

Next the Voice dialed a 604 area code and was connected to a number in Vancouver, British Columbia. He began the recorder. The call was answered on the first ring.

"Mr. Tan, thanks for calling. How are you two?" Sparrow's voice was cheerful and full of life. Her greeting was met with silence on the other end of the international line. She tried again. "Mr. Tan can you hear me?"

The Voice recognized Sparrow's distinctive inflections. After a moment Sparrow had hung up, and he stopped the recording.

Initially Sparrow panicked as she stared at the dead phone in its cradle. She waited five minutes and tried to call the number listed as last on her phone. After ten unanswered rings, she gave up. She wanted to reach Alex, but his plane was somewhere over the Pacific right now.

Ten minutes later her phone rang, and she ran to catch it. She heard a click. "Hello, Mom; hi, Dad." A pause and then "What's wrong?" Sparrow recognized her daughter's distinctive voice.

Next she heard subhuman screams, then nothing, followed by uninterruptable whispers, and then a horrific primal scream, followed by the whirl of an old recorder. Next she heard the whimpering of an old woman and the refrain "Vancouver, Canada; Vancouver, Canada" and then almost in a whisper "Vancouver, Canada." She recognized Mrs. Tan's voice.

"Mr. Tan, thanks for calling. How are you two?...Mr. Tan, can you hear me?" Sparrow's own voice gave her chills on the recorded line.

She looked at the wall clock. Alex was not due in for another three hours. She could not wait that long. She was immediately out the door and dialing the private hangar at the local airfield. She reached the right guy after being transferred to his home phone. She remained calm, but the pilot caught the urgency in her voice. She claimed her daughter in school in Edmonton had taken ill and she needed to make it to her immediately. A one-way fare was suggested by the pilot, and she agreed. She would meet him at the hangar in thirty minutes. She made it in twenty-two minutes, and he was just completing the flight plan. The two of them were airborne in less than an hour since Sparrow had heard the fatalistic recording on her phone. They should land at YEG in less than two hours. Sparrow had alerted her husband with a detailed phone message he would get upon landing. She had called ahead to reach Alexia but only got her voice mail. She attempted to remain calm, but the message to her stepchild was underscored with nervousness and urgency.

CHAPTER 57

The Voice had two men in Edmonton that worked for the triad. He had never met them before, but he knew the proper protocol to reach them and confirm his identity. These men were intimately involved in the oil-trading business. They did not question the Voice or his credentials. They would follow the instructions and knew the payoff for them personally was more than fair. A few quick key strokes and several telephone calls were able to pinpoint Alexia Cutter's prep school. They in turn had two of their street men on campus looking for the young student. Calling the phone number they had for her from the Tans' contacts, they successfully triangulated her position at the boy's prep school in the north section of the city. Within minutes they pulled up to a dormitory on Chancer Street. They entered the dorm, which had no security, and found a young couple making out in the shared living room. They confirmed it was Alexia given the photo scanned to them on their phones. It took the two thugs less than a minute to untangle the teenagers and knock the young man unconscious. Alexia's mouth was taped, and she was in the back of their van and in a large black woven bag in less than three minutes. The text to the Voice confirmed the heist of the girl.

She found it absolutely pitch dark in the bag. She had trouble breathing with the tape over her mouth. Her hands were bound behind her. The woven bag scratched at her back and against her legs. Real panic set in—the type of panic that recognizes utter helplessness. She could hear her own scream in her head. She was not getting enough oxygen. She began to roll back and forth. A strong hand caught her upper arm and squeezed hard—real hard. She stopped rolling back and forth. She listened to the two men in the front seat. She didn't understand a word. They were speaking a southern Chinese dialect she was not familiar with. The van continued to roll and pick up speed. She sensed they were out of the city limits and the stop-and-go traffic pattern.

After what seemed to be an hour, the van stopped. She was unceremoniously dumped from the bag onto her shoulders. The gravel cut through her dress and into her skin. The bag over her head was removed. The two men each had holstered weapons. The one man grabbed the plastic ties holding her hands behind her and pushed her forward to follow his partner up a rather steep path to a building at the top. The first man led the way, and Alexia was pushed after him by the second guy. She breathed deeply through her nose. She pushed back lifting herself against the chest of the man behind and simultaneously viciously kicking the man in front at the base of his neck. The man forward collapsed. The impact and the steep incline pushed her captor backward losing his grip on her. Alexia turned, pirouetted, and placed a kick to his throat. Her captor fell backward on the steep incline. She took two steps and kicked his solar plexus and then aimed a follow-up kick expertly at his neck. The man's head snapped back, and he fell lifeless on the dirt pathway. The first man was just struggling to get up and was fumbling with his gun. Alexia jumped toward him feet first and saw his neck snap back in an awkward motion. She found a knife in the first guy's jeans and cut herself free. She left the two captors where they lay and took the keys to the van. Alexia was some twenty minutes down the road when she spotted a truck stop.

Several grisly truckers turned from their stools to witness a young girl walking to the ladies' room. Her dress was torn at the shoulder, and she was bleeding through the cotton material. Her hair was disheveled, and she had marks around her mouth. She wore no shoes. One trucker was getting off his swivel stool to help her when his partner reached out to pull him back. The pretty girl emerged from the rest room a short time later. She confidently strode up to the counter where the men were finishing their lunch and asked if anyone was heading west. Two guys immediately raised their hands. She chose the older guy and walked barefoot with him to his cab.

Alex's plane landed twenty minutes late on a rain-slick tarmac. As the plane maneuvered to the gate, Alex listened to his phone messages. When he tapped on Sparrow's voice message, he could sense the terror in her otherwise calm demeanor. Was he late again when his daughter needed him most? Alex ran down the Jet way into the main terminal, and the necessary customs and immigration lines had built as several international flights had arrived at nearly the same time. He coaxed and cajoled those in front of him to allow him to move ahead in the snakelike lines. He was only partially successful. He did not clear all the protocols until fully an hour had passed. A young customs official, sensing Alex's nervousness, kept him far too long with a list of questions. Nonetheless, Alex breached the airport's final security and headed to the adjoining business terminal for private aircraft. He reached the central desk and explained his personal situation and need to get to Edmonton and his daughter as soon as possible. An older pilot overheard the dialogue at the desk, put down his magazine, and approached Alex. He could see the anxiousness in the eyes. He said he was free and could help. The cash traded hands, the flight plan submitted, and they were off to Edmonton in a Piper 350. Alex was now four and a half hours behind Sparrow.

The wheat fields of the Canadian prairies seemed to stretch as far as the eye could see in all directions. The wind danced through the almost ripe fields. The trucker was sailing down the open road. Alexia considered using her phone to reach her parents. She thought better of it prior to pushing the connect button. This must be how they had located her. She threw her cell out the window to the utter surprise of the driver. She asked the grizzled driver if she could use his. She tried both private lines for Alex and Sparrow. Finding no connection, she left a message for each. She was fine. She was safe. Do not try her cell phone. She would join them at the Vancouver cabin. She put her bare feet on the dashboard and leaned back. The open window had her hair flying around in all directions. She shut her eyes. The truck driver could not help but notice her hair color matching the mature wheat fields all around them. He stole glances at her tan toned calves and thighs as her dress whipped around in the windy cab.

Alex received Alexia's message just has he landed in Edmonton. His relief was beyond expression. He reached Sparrow. She had gotten the same message from her daughter and was overjoyed. It was a bittersweet call, as she had to inform Alex of the call she had received from the Voice. It was all just a recording—her voice, Alex's voice, Alexia's, and finally the screams from Mr. Tan and pathetic moans from his wife.

Alex could not immediately respond. He had been so overwhelmed with the positive news of Alexia's safety; he could not immediately compute the tragic news of the Tans' torture and murder. He pulled his rental car to the shoulder and placed his head on the steering wheel and wept.

Sparrow heard her husband's howl over the phone, which came from his very soul. She waited. Alex pulled himself together. They resumed their conversation and agreed to a plan. Sparrow and he would return to their British Columbia cabin and remove all objects that may hold clues to their whereabouts. They would relocate. It was imperative to secure a safe house for their daughter. Next they must hunt down this madman and eliminate him once and for all. They agreed to hunt the snake down and cut off its head.

The Voice had not heard from Alexia's kidnappers for over two hours, and he was concerned. He had never worked with these men from Canada prior. Were they professional? He reached out to the two oilmen, who had been his primary Canadian contact. They promised to follow up and get back to him with any update.

The oil guys got back to the Voice with the news of their men found on the steep path. Both were found dead from spinal injuries. The girl had disappeared. The men still had their weapons secured in their holsters. The plastic cuffs were left on the pathway. The van they had used was discovered twenty minutes away at a truck stop. The girl had vanished.

The Voice was not used to this incompetence. Had this happened in China, the men would have never let an eighteen-year-old girl get the better of them. He hung up from the oilmen's call to take an inbound one.

It was from his handler in Beijing with several assignments, which the political elite would prefer to be addressed in a more clandestine fashion. The Voice listened intently. The three new assignments would pay handsomely. All were in areas of his known expertise. The handler listed them each with an expected time line for completion.

1. Guangdong Province: A joint-venture company by the name of Latimeir Inc. was doing particularly well financially. The joint venture had installed a new chief executive officer the prior year and offshore sales had nearly doubled. Net profits were improving, and the new company was expanding production. The new headman simply did not understand how the real game was played. Repeated references to the required protection the triad could provide were met with deaf ears from the new management. The Voice had to smile to himself. This was exactly how he had earned his reputation seven years ago. His handler wanted this to be resolved by next week. No problem.

2. Gansu Province: A rouge Tibetan monk was stirring up the 650 workers at a state-owned slaughterhouse in the north. Rumors of starting a quasi-union were spreading. The open question was whether this could be solved without the monk's untimely death. Due to the potential international sensitivities surrounding this relatively straightforward assignment, his handler preferred this be addressed by the Voice himself.

3. The last assignment was a bit more complex. A French industrialist had made significant investments across China. They were building fighter jets for the Chinese Air Force on one hand and middle class cookware on the other. Their interests spread from mining, to smelting, to consumer products, primarily electronics. This successful firm had three young Chinese interns working

for them in various capacities—all in Hong Kong. The problem was all three of the interns were slated to be fired next week for insubordination, lying to their supervisors, and creating a great deal of rework. The problem was all three of the individuals were nieces and nephews of the most powerful men in China. These men served on the politburo. They did not wish to bring disgrace to their family names. They had specifically requested the Voice to manage the delicate situation personally. The Voice grimaced as he recognized the necessary time commitment this assignment would take. Alex Cutter would have to wait.

An hour later the Voice received another call. This call was from his senior triad contact who showed no interest in the goings-on in Canada. He had two items he needed the Voice to address as soon as possible. In typical fashion the items had the preferred outcome, with no background as to the fundamental issue.

1. An entrenched gang in Hong Kong, calling themselves the Dragons, had independently moved to offer their protection services to many of the international banking groups. The Voice was instructed to eliminate the Dragons' leadership.
2. An offshoot of this Hong Kong gang had established a secure supply chain for offshore drugs distributed within the greater Shanghai area. The assignment was to destroy the lucrative competitor and leave a message for any future entrepreneur.

The Voice sat back in the leather chair and stared out to the bay. He had time to reflect now that he had numerous initiatives underway. He took a sip of steaming tea.

His Canadian counterparts were busy tracking down the whereabouts of Alex Cutter, Sparrow, and their daughter in the greater Vancouver, British Columbia, area. The issue of Alex Cutter and Sparrow would have to be put on hold for the time being. He had booked his flight to Hong

Kong for the following morning to address both the French entrepreneur and the gang calling themselves the Dragons. He planned to cross over into Guangdong after his visit to Hong Kong. He had instructed his lead lieutenant to infiltrate the drug cartel canvassing the Shanghai market and report back within the week. The pesky Tibetan monk in Gansu Province would be discredited by bribed monks just across the border. This would give the Voice the necessary time to address the Gansu issue personally when he could get back up north.

CHAPTER 58

Alex and Sparrow met at their British Columbia cabin, arriving almost simultaneously. "Alex, I am so scared." Sparrow ran into his waiting arms.

Alex hugged her as if he would never let go. "It's going to be all right," he said, stroking her hair. "We know Alexia is OK. We have to assume the Voice has men searching Vancouver given the ungodly screams from Mrs. Tan. Let's gather up only what could be traced and leave. We will inform Alexia on the line she used to contact us. I have a safe house across the border in Portland, Oregon." Alex released his hold on his wife.

Sparrow left for the bathroom. She closed the door and just stood there with one hand on the back of the door and the other on her hip. The sobs came in bunches. She had witnessed her father literally cut in two. She had killed four members of the triad. Because of her, the only real family she had known was brutally murdered. She could still hear the screams from Mrs. Tan. There was more sobbing. Because of her, their daughter had been kidnapped—twice! She had killed a very powerful man, the Chairman. She had left Mr. Ping in a pool of blood. She had married the love of her life and started being a real family in New Zealand. The long tentacles of the slick-talking Voice were following her family around the globe.

She stopped crying. She used the bathroom. As she washed up, her reflection in the mirror showed, once again, a steely resolve. Discrediting the Voice had not worked. A proven assassin had failed to bring down the Voice. Sparrow silently vowed to complete the task and bring closure to this living nightmare. She dabbed at her red eyes and went to join her husband.

Alex heard the crying coming from behind the bathroom door. He too felt lousy. What kind of man was he? He had placed his only daughter in grave danger twice. In one case Sparrow had saved her. In another she had fared for herself. Where was her father in all that? He had cheated on his first wife. He had condoned that indiscretion given his wife's aloofness and wandering eye. Did that make it OK? He had engaged the lovely Mr. and Mrs. Tan, and now they were dead. Was he a selfish bastard or incompetent? He was moving his family from safe house to safe house. Could they run all their lives? He thought back to his brief engagement with Mr. Ping and cringed. Could he bring himself to share that episode with Sparrow? He was not proud of himself. Was he the man his wife and daughter thought he was?

Alex went to the kitchen and splashed cold water on his face. There was little time to dwell on the past now. It was time to move his family to a safe place. Where was truly safe? How long could they run? He gathered himself and joined Sparrow in the living room.

The two of them scoured the cabin, gathering a few essentials and wiping any trace of their occupancy away. They called and reached Alexia on her new borrowed phone and instructed her on meeting at the new safe house in Oregon. Alexia estimated she could be there sometime the following day.

CHAPTER 59

Alexia napped for an hour with her bare feet on the cab's dashboard. The truck's windows remained open, and her hair and dress whipped around. The older driver could not help but take furtive glances at the beauty sitting next to him. She had taken a call on his phone a little over an hour ago, which seemed to calm her down. Now she was just beginning to wake up as she stretched her arms and wiggled her toes. She opened her Pacific blue eyes and stared directly at him. "How much longer to Vancouver?" she asked.

"Two and a half hours, I reckon," the driver replied as he leered at her.

"I have to pee. Let's stop just ahead there," she said, pointing.

The driver nodded and slowed the big rig down as he downshifted and flipped on his turn signal.

Alexia got out of the vehicle after the whoosh of the air brakes being released. She walked to the diner. A waitress caught her eye and motioned with her head nod where she could find the ladies' room. She was finishing up at the washbasin when she looked at herself in the mirror. Something wasn't feeling right. Her father had always told her to listen to her gut. The older man she had ridden with for the last six hours had gotten her out of Alberta. They had only shared a bit of small talk. She had borrowed his phone. It was just the last few interactions that seemed odd and somewhat uncomfortable. Could she trust this stranger to deliver her safely to Vancouver? Her gut was telling her it was time to bail out and secure other transportation. She returned to the idling rig. The driver was leaning against the cab sipping on a Coke. He handed her a second bottle. She took a long swig. He was staring at her. It was uncomfortable. He kept staring at her chest.

"Thanks for the ride this far and the use of your phone. I am going to rest here a bit and catch another lift going west. Thanks again for all your help."

The older man noticeably winced. He moved closer, into her personal space. She could smell him, his sweat, as he leaned in. "Darling, that won't be necessary. I can have you to town in less than two hours." She said nothing, and he remained close to her with one arm leaning on the cab, as if to block an exit route.

When he dropped his Coke bottle and reached for her with that hand, she reacted. The Coke bottle she held crashed into his forehead. Her right foot slid behind his, and she pushed at his chest. The trucker man fell awkwardly backward. Her next kick landed directly on his Adam's apple. He was struggling to catch his breath. She used the Coke bottle and came down hard on the back of his head, and he went limp. It was much more difficult than she could have imagined, but somehow she pulled him to rest under the trailer. He had parked a distance from the diner, and she doubted he would be discovered in short order. She shut off the rig and walked away.

Alexia returned to the diner, and the friendly waitress gave her a piece of lemon merengue pie with her coffee. The adrenaline rush was gone, and Alexia felt awfully tired. She confided in the waitress. Could she catch a safe ride to Vancouver? The waitress moved across the room to a red vinyl booth. After a brief discussion, she returned to the counter with Alexia. It had all been arranged. She knew the driver. It was her son. She would be in safe hands all the way to her destination. Alexia thanked her and left huge cash tip under her saucer.

The eldest son of the friendly waitress was about her age. She joined him at the fuel pumps. His back was initially to her. He looked about six foot two with a shock of thick wavy auburn hair, a bit on the longish side. He wore faded jeans and a white tank-top T-shirt. He turned her direction.

She caught his eyes, which were an aqua blue. Then he smiled in an aw-shucks kind of way. Perfect white teeth made for a dazzling look. His T-shirt was tucked in a narrow waist. His arms and face held a healthy sun kissed tone. The hair on his forearms had been bleached by the sun. "Hi, you must be Alexia."

He measured her in the first glance—about his age, white country-style dress, which complemented her hourglass figure. Her legs were well toned. She was barefoot. Her long blond hair was messed up in a rather sexy way. She stood maybe five foot six or five foot seven. He held her gaze perhaps a bit too long. Her hazel eyes appeared intelligent and worldly.

"I am," she said as they both awkwardly shook hands. "And you must be...?"

"William Stanford; my friends call me Bill," he said as he finished fueling the rig. "I guess we are both off to British Columbia. I am happy for the company." He opened her cab door. As she climbed into the truck, her forearm nudged his hand. She felt an electric current.

"Thanks for the lift, Bill," she said with a smile that could not come off her face.

There was an unmistakable attraction for them both. He pulled slowly away from the pumps, expertly going through the manual gears. The grin on his face could not hide his enthusiasm for this assignment. "Thanks, Mom" was going through his head as he brought the rig to cruising speed.

The highway was wide open. They both shared backgrounds, turning to each other more than was necessary. There was no mention of the older truck driver Alexia had dispensed with and returned to his cab unconscious. The conversation flowed naturally. Nothing seemed forced. They both silently wished this trip was longer than the two hours it would take. A song came on the radio, which was a favorite of both. Simultaneously each reached for the volume control to turn it up. Their hands touched. Neither pulled their hand away. There was palatable electricity in the cab. The big truck rolled on. Years later they would both vividly recall that exact moment. For now, after some nervous laughter, they resumed the get-to-know-you conversation.

Alexia borrowed Bill's phone and called for her dad. He answered on the first ring and told her of the aborted plan to meet at the Vancouver cabin. He gave her specific instructions on reaching the safe house in Portland, Oregon. She agreed and signed off saying, "I love you, Dad."

She told Bill of the change in plans. He was more than pleased. It was getting late, and he pulled into an all-night diner. They split a meal of oven-baked chicken, whipped potatoes, and green peas. Both ordered just ice water. The conversation flowed effortlessly, as if they had known each other for years. There was absolutely no rush to return to the road. They lingered over a split order of banana cream pie and black coffee. By the time they returned to the road, it was getting late and was just starting to drizzle. The road was slick and glossy looking. It went from a misty drizzle to a hard rain. The windshield wipers thumped hard with each cycle. Bill suggested they stop for the night at a hotel he was familiar with about an hour ahead. Alexia agreed. After that exchange there was silence between them. They both looked ahead through the headlights splitting the highway between his and hers.

The motel sat adjacent to the main highway. Bill pulled the rig up to the main office. He returned with just one key. "Are you all right with this? They seem to be full-up this evening. I can sleep in the cab."

"Don't be foolish. We can share the room."

Nothing could have been more perfect. They entered the standard hotel room facing the highway. Alexia used the restroom first and then returned to look out onto the highway through a crack in the drapes. Bill returned from the bathroom and stood directly behind her. Nothing was spoken. She felt his clean breath against her neck and his warm hands on her hips. He kissed her gently on the neck and next to the strap of her dress. She shivered unexpectedly. She turned to face him. They kissed as if they had known each other for decades. It was sweet and tender. They did it again and again. There was no teenage groping and no hurriedness. As a few lone truckers sped by with their headlights glancing off the drapes, he slid her dress straps over her shoulders. Again she shivered, and the white country dress fell to the floor. His hands discovered her. They were warm hands. He touched her as if she could break. His kisses then began to cover her shoulders, her breasts, her firm tummy, and finally to her womanhood. She held his head there. He held her buttocks. She shivered once again.

The lovemaking continued, usually in slow motion, sometimes accelerated to the point of near exhaustion. Somehow they always caught their breath and continued. The occasional truck roared by, its headlights casting their shadows on the smooth ceiling. Hours later Alexia curled up next to him under the crook of his right arm. He held her like that as they both slept.

The early light snuck into the room through the crack in the green hotel drapes. She awoke first and lay quietly, watching him rest. Minutes later he awoke, kissed her, and held her close. Alexia now understood the look her father gave Sparrow. They made love once again. Alexia had never felt so whole. William vowed to never let this young woman be alone again.

They crossed the Canadian–United States border by late morning. Conversation in the cab was effortless between them, and the trip seemed to fly by. Following her father's directions, they arrived at the safe house midafternoon in Portland.

Alexia introduced her young man to Sparrow and her father. At first Alex was not pleased to have someone privy to their exact whereabouts. That sentiment changed as he learned more from the young man. They insisted he stay for dinner and then the night, before returning to Canada.

CHAPTER 60

He despised disobedience. He abhorred poor judgment. He looked down on the slovenly practices of Mr. Primrose. Herr Reins appreciated discipline and loyalty.

Herr Reins was sitting in the front cabin of a private aircraft bound for Cape Town, South Africa. Had he had his way, Primrose would be tethered to a four-hundred-pound weight at the bottom of the Black Sea. Damijon, his Russian boss, had instructed differently. Primrose had apparently successfully hacked into the exchanges in Malaysia and Taiwan. The man had value.

Ten hours later Herr Reins's aircraft taxied to the private terminal at Cape Town's international airport. He disembarked wearing white linen trousers and a short-sleeved khaki shirt under a dapper brown and black checked sports coat. The Oxford dress shoes matched the black of his Armani sunglasses. It was casual yet screamed "I am in charge." Primrose met him at the bottom of the jet's stairs.

"You've been busy, Mr. Primrose."

"Welcome to South Africa, Herr Reins. I have indeed dabbled in a couple of Eastern markets of late. I am excited to share some of the results after you have had time to freshen up. I booked you at the Cape Royale. I trust that meets with your approval."

Reins nodded to the affirmative as they both slipped into the back seat of the waiting limousine. The driver sped off and their conversation ceased. Primrose remained in the downstairs lobby and was joined by Herr Reins shortly after checking in.

Reins took charge of the conversation when they had settled into an alcove and Tiger beers had been poured. The young black waitress retreated, giving them utmost privacy.

"I was not pleased to learn of your independent foray into foreign markets. It has the distinct possibility to be linked with our role in Western markets several months ago." Herr Reins took a long pull from his pilsner glass.

Sensing this was the fundamental purpose of his trip, Primrose was prepared for the expected confrontation. "I developed some different algorithms and tested them on two obscure market platforms. They were successful, and they cannot be traced," Primrose stated as a fact.

"Go on."

"I developed a mathematical labyrinth using multiyear market data, which does several interesting things." Primrose paused, waiting for a reaction. Getting none, he continued. "I have purposely developed a model that more likely than not will show market losses forty-seven percent of the time."

This statement forced Reins to place his beer back on the cocktail table.

"The model doubles down on the other fifty-three percent of expected market movements. The result is highly correlated daily and quarterly profits net profits, with more than adequate market losses to disguise any ruse." Satisfied with his rudimentary explanation, Primrose took his first pull on the cold beer in front of him.

"And this so-called test you ran in Malaysia and Taiwan—what did you learn?"

"The initial test was highly successful in both markets. I masked the volume in the markets opening rather than closing bell. I believe we can use the same protocols on the markets closing as well."

With that the men retreated to Herr Reins's suite. Primrose had a detailed report to share with his German colleague. Indeed the results were every bit as good as was indicated in the cocktail lounge. Herr Reins was a detail guy. He spent the next two hours going over the data and financial results. When he completed the review, he took off his glasses and smiled for the first time during the visit. He called St. Petersburg with the positive report. Damijon was very pleased. Reins smiled for the first time. Primrose returned to his digs at Aqua-Sian and the exotic eastern European woman.

CHAPTER 61

Alex Cutter, Sparrow, and Alexia stayed in the Portland safe house just two weeks. Alex found a ranch in Wyoming for sale by the owner. He traveled alone to the site, which was off the grid 120 miles southeast of Cody. He purchased the property under his assumed personal credentials from an elderly lady with a cashier's check. There would be no paper trail linking the real Alex Cutter.

The ranch house was built on a solid rock foundation, but the structure itself was dated back to the late 1940s. Over their first year, Sparrow had transformed the three-bedroom home into a spectacular cabin-style luxury abode. There was warm hickory flooring throughout, an oversized updated kitchen, and original Western art. She added a front courtyard facing west where they would enjoy the sunsets in comfortable rocking chairs. They had installed skylights in the master bedroom. Alex had taken on the assignment of updating the outbuildings.

Alexia enrolled under an alias in the University of Wyoming in Laramie. She made the varsity soccer team. Her boyfriend Bill would spend every long weekend between school quarters with the family at the totally renovated compound.

Two years passed without interference from the Voice or his minions. Certain normality began to set in for the Cutters. Alex gave up his security business and concentrated on his family. They were financially secure and emotionally satisfied. Then the call came in for Alex on the encrypted line.

It was both the security guy and sharp analyst working on the London Metal Exchange. They had last spoken nearly two and a half years ago during the query into potential market disruption and manipulation on several key international markets. This time, they explained to Alex, there were abnormalities in some of the more obscure markets. Alex asked a lot of probing questions of the two. It was intellectually intriguing. After a lengthy call, Alex promised to get back to them.

He was surprised with the reaction from Sparrow. She told him to go to London and take on the security assignment. She recognized he was getting antsy with the slow pace at home and may need some outside stimulus. Alex was on the first leg of his international trip the following day.

CHAPTER 62

In the two-plus years that had intervened, the Voice successfully completed the assignments given to him by both the central government and organized crime. His reputation as someone who could get things done continued to grow. He was now forty-nine years old. His father would have been proud. Today he lived on the one hundredth floor of China's tallest building in Beijing. He overlooked the beautiful green park directly below and the blue bay outside his other floor to ceiling window. He now selectively took assignments, including legitimate ones from the commercial tycoons of the People's Republic.

A few years back, his men had discovered the Alex Cutter safe house in Vancouver. The trail had grown ice cold after that. The Voice dismissed the hunt for Sparrow, as his universe had grown exponentially since.

The second and third foray into the secondary markets proved highly profitable for Herr Reins and his people. They used legitimate brokers in each marketplace placing massive buy and sell orders according to the algorithms developed by Primrose. They scored both wins and losses in each brokerage account, but the gains continued to exceed the losses per Primrose's calculated outcome. Net gains exceeded US$32 million. These gains were reinvested in New York real estate, a desalinization project in Saudi Arabia, and various telecommunications in the developing world.

There were no internal securities investigations at any of the markets they participated in. It was easy money. The Russian boss man directed them to expand the trading platforms and the time frames for each market foray. Primrose was skeptical. Why kill the golden goose, he mused.

Nonetheless, the idea of doubling their profitability was simply too enticing. Primrose went to work on a new set of calculations.

Alex Cutter's plane set down at Heathrow at 1820 hours. He would join his associates for dinner at Gordon Ramsay at the Chelsea location. Alex was famished. He started with sautéed foie gras and roasted veal sweetbreads—a specialty of this restaurant. For his main Alex chose the roast pigeon with fennel, lavender, honey, and apricot. Alex selected a Château Pichon Longueville Baron classic. He felt the red would complement what his dinner companions had selected. With coffee came the lemonade parfait. The premeeting conversation remained on the light side. When the dessert plates were cleared, the waiter closed the door of their private meeting room.

"Alex, our counterparts in several of the secondary markets in the Middle East and Asia have reported increased volume bubbles and volatility. We sensed this was similar to our market experiences on the LME and NYSE a few years ago. Statistically our analysts have confirmed activity well out of the Bollinger waves."

"Wait a minute, guys," Alex Cutter interrupted as he placed his coffee cup down. "Let's not get too technical on day one." He adjusted his chair in order to look the young analyst directly in the eye. "What does that all mean?"

"Statistically there are trades at certain times of day that are way out of bounds given the mathematical probability. They have occurred at a frequency also well outside statistical expectation."

"What you are telling me, gentlemen, is someone is manipulating certain equity markets—but in this case, what most traders would recognize as secondary markets." Alex readjusted his seat to face the other man at the table. "If they are so good at this, why focus on the smaller marketplaces? The big fish is caught in London or New York."

"We speculate their market fingerprint is much easier to disguise, and these markets do not have the sophisticated cyber security as we have in the West."

The waiter returned to pour more coffee, and Alex waved him away. After the door to their private dining room was secure, Alex continued. "You must admit, this is brilliant to focus on secondary markets, if this is indeed what is happening."

"We concur, Mr. Cutter." The young analyst adjusted his glasses. "Our modeling has been reviewed by experts in the secondary exchanges, and they have agreed with our hypothesis. They have readily asked for our help. Can you join us in Kuala Lumpur day after tomorrow?"

They spent the next several minutes finalizing contract terms for Alex Cutter. Alex sent an encrypted e-mail to his wife in Wyoming from the hotel that same night. He would contact her from his hotel in Malaysia.

The Malaysian Airlines flight to Kuala Lumpur was smooth, and the attractive flight attendants made the first-class travel extremely comfortable. Alex elected to spend the flight time reading the security reports from the various secondary markets. He did not understand all of the technical trading jargon, or even all the mathematical modeling, which was included. What he did understand was human greed.

The flight got to KL, as the locals called it, in the early evening. The tropical humidity had his shirt stuck to his back, and he elected to carry his sport coat separately. The arranged dark limousine deposited him at the Mandarin Oriental. He took a quick shower and changed into a tropical suit.

He joined the local security people of the Bursa exchange in the hotel lobby bar. The recap was discouraging. Indeed they could identify abnormal market volumes and extreme price fluctuations. At issue was the fact the exchange had added a multitude of new products in securities and derivatives. Superimposed on the volume complexity was a new Islamic market team offering shari'a-compliant capital markets and trading platforms. This was a new wrinkle for Alex to consider. He asked for further clarification.

The lead investigator explained what was meant by shari'a law. "It is the body of moral and religious law derived from Islamic prophecy. In other words, the exchange developed a religious investment team that assures investors they are complying with their Islamic faith."

"So what you gentlemen are describing to me is a market that has morphed into a multitude of investment offerings. These include company securities, futures, options, and now, Islamic derivatives true to their faith. Is that basically correct?"

"You are absolutely correct, Mr. Cutter," said the lead investigator. "Nonetheless we have identified several abnormalities we cannot account for. I assume this is why the exchange has called for your expertise."

The group talked some more over stale pretzels and tonic water. Alex excused himself when the group ordered the first round of beers.

The next morning Alex began to develop a computerized model with several of his colleagues from India. Over the next four days of nonstop work, they had a model that could capture abnormal market behavior. They engaged the suspect markets with full approval of their respective boards. What they discovered was market distortions occurring in just the opening bell and closing bell of each of the suspect markets. These two periods would typically have the greater trading volume and subsequent volatility. They also concluded the distortions did not occur every trading day.

Herr Reins's group continued to cash in on their market manipulation. They had become more sophisticated as time passed. Now their largest trades were intermarket spreads, which would be incredibly difficult to trace. For example, they may purchase call options in the Malaysian market and sell put options in Tokyo. Primrose was getting seriously rich.

Charlie Leong, the Indonesian man who had assisted Herr Reins and Primrose years earlier, was taking note of the wild market volatility in many of the secondary markets. The $9 million he had collected from this group a few years back must be chicken feed to them now.

Leong wanted back in the game. He and two of his musclemen traveled to the castle outside Munich to pay a visit to Mr. Reins. They were met at Munich's Franz Josef Strauss airport by the limousine service frequently used by Herr Reins and his staff. The trip took less than an hour through the Black Forest.

Herr Reins's assistant, Gretchen, met the entourage in the circular drive just as the sun was setting. The castle's gargoyles were casting their medieval shadows across the lush green carpet of the promenade. She showed them their individual accommodations and confirmed dinner for Herr Reins and Mr. Leong in the knights' hall at 1900 hours.

The two men sat down to herbed leg of lamb with olive butter and roasted tomatoes. From the cellar, a 1959 Cotes Du Rhone offered an earthy briny accompaniment. Dessert of espresso shortbreads was served with Cuban coffee. The business was discussed after the second cup of coffee was poured and wait-staff excused.

Leong was first to broach the obvious topic. "Herr Reins, you recognize why I have traveled half way around the world to see you."

Reins smiled and lifted his left over wine glass. "Your skill set was put to very good use in several of the major markets, and I believe you were amply rewarded for your unique skill set and confidentiality."

"It now appears the algorithms used in the primary markets may be in play in some of the secondary markets," Leong interrupted.

Again a knowing smile from Herr Reins. "You are correct in recognizing some interesting fluctuations in several of the minor market exchanges; however, I assure you the mathematical models you provided to access the NYMEX, CME, and London Metal Exchange several years ago are not the same we are leveraging in the Eastern markets."

Leong was prepared to interrupt again but was waved off by Herr Reins. He continued. "Nonetheless, the timing of your visit is fortunate for us both. The exchanges we are engaged with are employing much more sophisticated monitoring systems, and I believe your expertise may be required to circumvent them." Reins finished his wine and waited a response.

Leong paused a moment to connect the new dots. "I think I should listen to your proposal, Herr Reins, keeping in mind I feel my contributions to direct-market manipulations deserve a percentage of profits rather than a flat fee one might pay to a technician."

"I could not agree more. There is another complication, and your direct involvement may prove most useful. It's my sense, the Mr. Primrose you previously met, may have become a bit sloppy. I could see how you could replace him in our consortium."

"I would expect thirty-five percent of the profits for this hands-on work." Leong pushed his coffee cup aside.

"Mr. Primrose is collecting twenty percent today and has become a wealthy man."

"I propose to deal with Primrose and direct the hands-on market manipulations myself and will expect one-third of the proceeds."

"Done," said a relaxed Herr Reins. He rang a bell. The service staff appeared, and he requested a second bottle of the same vintage from the cellar. After his guest shook his hand and retired for the evening, Reins called St. Petersburg with the news of a new technical man joining the team. Initially, Damijon, his boss, was skeptical. Given the new guy's background and expertise and the fact they had successfully used his insight to crack security at the major exchanges, the move to replace the slovenly Primrose made sense.

CHAPTER 63

Primrose was enjoying his morning coffee at Aqua-Sian, overlooking the magnificent view of the Indian Ocean when security buzzed him. The lady—who, the security was aware, had spent many evenings with him in the past—was at the main gate. Without a thought, Primrose told the guard to let her pass through.

The Indonesian assassin waited silently in the car's truck. The well-paid Eastern European woman pulled her car into the driveway and disengaged the car's boot. As instructed she waited at the front door and buzzed for entry. The maid Primrose employed caught the familiar figure on the video feed and released the double locks on the stylish teak door. The courtesan stepped aside and the assassin slipped into the tiled entry. The silenced weapon popped once striking the black maid in the face, and she folded at the waist.

Primrose heard nothing but the roar of the ocean's surf pounding the rock shore below. He was dressed in a beige smoking jacket, and his bare feet were nestled in white fleece. He was tapping on his computer.

The hired Indonesian, having received the layout of the building, cautiously moved toward the glint of the computer screen reflecting off the wall at the end of a long tiled hallway.

The silence was broken by the crystal-clear statement coming from the home's intercom system. "Mr. Primrose, this is the main gate. We have noted an unidentified person leaving your companion's automobile and reaching your front door. Your female companion remains outside. Is everything all right?"

Primrose froze for just a moment. He did not turn off his computer. He took four long strides to the special door in the room's corner. It looked like a closet. He shut the door behind him as the independent lights and ventilation systems kicked in. All high-end homes and condos had a safe room in South Africa. Primrose hit the large red panic button at shoulder height. The silent alarm rang at the main gate of the complex as well at a private security service. Response times were typically under five minutes. In this case, the first jeep carrying three security personnel arrived in less than four minutes. The men were heavily armed as their vehicle screeched to a stop on the driveway. The well-trained men all carried automatic weapons and wore gas masks. Their passkey allowed quick access. Their red-laser scoping lights danced off the walls as they stepped over the crumpled maid. Two more jeeps arrived moments later, securing the perimeter.

The assassin heard the commotion at the front door and turned over the computer desk to secure a defensive position. The first stun grenade tumbled into the room and disoriented him. The second flash grenade was followed by a full out assault by the security men.

The lone assassin caught one of the security men in the thigh before he was peppered with automatic fire that nearly decapitated him. The entire episode took under one hundred and forty seconds from the time they entered the home.

Primrose was instructed to remain in the safe room while security fanned out to check for other assailants. Later that morning, with the coast being clear, Primrose left his condo for a downtown hotel room where he informed Herr Reins by phone of the attempted assassination.

Surprisingly, it struck Primrose as odd at how relatively businesslike Reins had been on the line. The seriousness of the incident hit Primrose later that night. He was targeted and nearly killed. He decided he did not need more money. He needed to extricate himself from Herr Reins.

Herr Reins immediately called his handler in Russia. Damijon was extremely displeased with learning of the failed attempt on Primrose's life under Mr. Leong's direction. Reins agreed fully. Both agreed to disengage with Leong. Damijon agreed to dispense with the Indonesian man as soon as was practical.

Primrose left Cape Town thirty-six hours after the break-in at Aqua-Sian. He traveled under an assumed name and an expertly forged Swiss passport. He had over US$20 million spread across multiple accounts. He planned to disappear in Lausanne, Switzerland. He checked into the Hotel Schönegg in the southern Swiss city. After a short week, he had booked a luxury loft in the village of Ropraz, just a few kilometers outside from the city Centre. The French-speaking city was large enough to disappear into.

He severed all his contacts in South Africa. He moved all his funds to a numbered Swiss account. He left behind the two models he had known in Cape Town. His new wealth would draw more ladies to his bed, and he did not have to take orders from anyone.

CHAPTER 64

The humid air hung like a blanket over Bangkok. Leong knew something was terribly wrong when he did not hear back from the assassin sent to Cape Town. Leong wondered what could go wrong. The target was middle aged and grossly overweight. The assassin was highly regarded and a true professional. He found himself repeatedly looking at his cell phone for a message, and there was none. His new partners in Germany and Russia would not be pleased with this initial failure on his part. He had made a promise to them and had come up far short. These were men who would not condone failure. He made up his mind to leave Thailand and disappear. He had adequate funding to go anywhere. He chose Burma, where he had senior contacts in the military, which still ran the country. Relatively minimal bribes would have him disappear into Naypyidaw, the capital city of Myanmar. Initially he stayed in the Aureum Palace Resort and Hotel. Later he switched to a country home, with two boy servants and four beautiful girl helpers, which was several kilometers from the outskirts of the capital.

Alexia was completing her senior year of college at the University of Wyoming, majoring in criminal law. She and Bill were planning their wedding for this coming June. Her future husband had completed his political studies and was hired by the Saskatoon Prime Minister's Office. He had started his new role last week in Regina. He drove back to be with Alexia every other weekend.

Life seemed back to normal. Sparrow was happy to help with the nuptials. She was planning a shower for all of Alexia's college girlfriends. It would be wonderful to have the whole family together this coming Saturday afternoon when Alex returned from Kuala Lumpur.

CHAPTER 65

Sparrow and Alex had no contact whatsoever by the Voice or the triad for over two and a half years. Alex was starting to talk privately with Sparrow that the past was the past. Perhaps they were no longer being targeted. Perhaps the Voice had woven a net even he could not extricate from. Nonetheless, they seemed to have their lives back.

Sparrow had listened to the rhetoric and wanted to buy into it. Outwardly she did. In her private moments, she could not escape the reality of the man's actions, which had so impacted her and her family. He had pitted her against the man she would ultimately find true happiness with. He had arranged for her daughter to be kidnapped—twice! He had been directly responsible for the cruel torture and murder of her surrogate parents, the Tans. No doubt, he was involved through the triad of the brutal dissection of her father in Jiangsu. His influence and tentacles spread beyond China's borders. He had made his presence known half way around the globe to rural Saskatchewan when he had Alexia taken by two armed men. She could find no complete closure to this chapter in her life without his death. She no longer wanted to look over her shoulder or wince at a stranger looking out of place. She had formulated a plan and would return to Beijing to complete the task herself. She fully recognized the dangers of such a plan. Living with the thought this man could crush the life she had made for herself was simply unacceptable.

She had never lied to her husband. She rationalized it was better he not know she could be putting her and their family in harm's way. She decided to act.

Prior to Alex's return from Kuala Lumpur, she sketched out a text he would receive the middle of his night. It read she would be making a short trip back to China in order to assist the Tans' oldest daughter, who had fallen on bad times. She expected to be gone no more than three days and without question return in time for Alexia's wedding shower. She promised to be safe. She closed the message by saying how much she loved him.

With expertly drawn up travel documents, Sparrow proceeded first to Hong Kong and then by boat to Guangzhou—a city whose metropolitan area was double that of Beijing. Her many past contacts came through for her with the exchange of several thousand in renminbi notes. It was an easy city in which to become nearly invisible. A facial artist reconfigured her profile with temporary wax, plastic, and hairs. Coupled with peasant clothes, the new profile was one of a rather destitute older woman shuffling down the crowded street in hope of a handout from visiting Westerners.

The next morning she was on a train to Beijing. Her third-class car smelled of urine and tobacco. Even the few young male travelers in her compartment gave her no notice. She lit off the train on the city's outskirts to meet a few more of her old associates. The items exchanged for cash were crucial for her success. An elderly pharmacist had the poison and pills she requested. An old customer, now in midmanagement for social services, provided the necessary paperwork to proceed past security. Initially he wanted more than cash from Sparrow, but when it became clear that was not a possibility, he simply doubled his fee. Another associate provided the eleven-inch blade she would carry strapped to her calf and hidden by the burlap trousers she wore beneath a dirty peasant oversized blouse. The final piece was just as critical. The captain, she had known years before from the cabaret, was now a major in the air force. He had the means to smuggle her on an outbound cargo only flight to northern Gansu. From there, she would connect with local tribesmen who frequented into Mongolia to trade. This planned exit from China came at a steep price. She peeled off the US$1,000 notes until they totaled US$200,000 into the waiting palm of the newly commissioned major.

A motorbike picked Sparrow up at dawn and drove her to within blocks of the building. The service entrance in the rear was crowded, and she fell in with a group of men she identified given their red bandannas. The dishwater blond wig was held in place by her own red scarf. The men she was joining were in on the ruse and had been paid handsomely. Their crew was cleaning and repairing the massive building's sewer system. Prior to joining the other two dozen sewer workers, she was given a vial of stench. Sparrow covered herself with the disgusting brown fluid. Initially she had vomited and allowed some of that spittle to remain on her work boots. When they got to security, the young officers waved the group through without a body check and only a cursory peak into some of the pails and toolboxes.

Sparrow was in the bowels of the second tallest manmade structure on the planet. Her intelligence confirmed the Voice was in his penthouse office on the one hundredth floor above them.

Alex was surprised when he logged on in his hotel room in Kuala Lampur. His wife was bound for mainland China to assist the daughter of Mr. and Mrs. Tan. Admirable yes, but they had not been close to her and her husband and had no contact with them since the funeral of her brother over six years ago. Alex was also deeply concerned with Sparrow returning to China for any reason. They had successfully created a life of their own. Why screw it up?

Alex got on the phone and reached the Tans' only daughter. She surprised him saying she had not heard from Sparrow and thanked him for his call. Alex reached out to his wife on several occasions only to be diverted to voice mail. Stunned and afraid, Alex immediately left for the airport and, with expertly drawn documentation, caught a nonstop flight from Kuala Lumpur direct to Beijing. He left a message for Alexia. He was leaving Malaysia with a quick business stop on his way home. He expected to make it to the wedding shower—at least to meet all her friends and then to exit and let them have some fun.

He checked his phone for messages prior to disembarking the plane in Beijing. There were none.

He struggled to remain calm as he waited on his one checked bag. It would appear somewhat awkward and attract unwanted attention to be traveling internationally with only a small carry-on. His bag appeared on the carousal, and he proceeded through customs and passport control without incident. His forged documentation worked flawlessly.

On his fourteen hour direct flight, Alex had reviewed all the potential possibilities for his wife to lie to him and return to the People's Republic of China. He addressed each analytically. The conclusion he reached scared him to the core.

Sparrow and her covey of sewer workers climbed the maintenance stairs within the towering structure. Lugging their equipment had them all perspiring and breathing heavy. They had reached floor eighty-one and were forced to take a breather. Some of the group remained behind in groups of two or three to create the illusion of opening up clogged drainage pipes on other floors.

Sparrow and her reduced cadre made it to the desired floor. The proper tools opened various ductwork and piping. Sparrow attached her eleven-inch blade and the vials of poison and pills to the inside of the metalwork and iron piping. Her assistants closed and only partially sealed the two hiding places, just steps from the maintenance door behind the plush executive elevators used by the Voice and his entourage on the hundredth floor of the magnificent skyscraper.

Sparrow and her band of sewer-rats retrieved all their tools and descended the stairs. In the half light, the endless spiral of stairs seemed to lead straight to hell.

CHAPTER 66

It was typical Beijing traffic—a combination of luxury government sedans, countless motorbikes, and the occasional cart pulled by an ox creeping at a snail's pace. It took Alex nearly two hours to arrive by cab into central Beijing. He paid the driver with the tobacco-stained teeth. He was at the base of the super structure, which held the Voice. He walked into the lobby.

Ten hours behind in Laramie, Wyoming, Alexia had become worried. Her wedding shower was just a few days away, and she could not reach her stepmother or Alex. Messages were not returned. This was uncharted waters. The three of them were always connected. The real threat that hung over their heads, demanded Alex, Sparrow, and her to be vigilant and always readily available. Something was just wrong, terribly wrong.

Alexia, like her father, was prone to action. She postponed her final test in Criminal Law II, Insanity Defense. She reached out first to the junior bank analyst, who her father had talked about and was impressed with. The young man, after convincing himself this was Alex's daughter, shared with Alexia the abrupt departure from Kuala Lumpur of her father the day before. He also shared the market disruptions they were concerned with had faded. He said the unexplained market volatility had ceased as the international team ramped up their investigation. Her father had not shared any details of his itinerary.

Next, Alexia checked all outbound manifests from Kuala Lumpur and spotted her father's alias on a nonstop flight to Beijing. Her father's international-security clientele gave her immediate and ready access to the necessary databases. She tracked his credit card to the downtown business hotel in the capital city. Finally, she reached her only known contact in China—Mr. and Mrs. Tan's only daughter. The married woman confirmed a pleasant phone conversation with her father, but that clue seemed to lead nowhere.

Alexia's rudimentary detective work coupled with her intuition concluded her father had followed Sparrow to Beijing. The most likely conclusion was a final confrontation with their sworn foe—a powerful man, she had only heard referred to as the Voice.

Given her deep financial resources and professionally doctored travel documents, Alexia traveled by private plane to San Francisco. She barely made the connection on a United Airlines direct flight. In just under thirty-four hours since missing her final school exam, Alexia found herself checking into the Beijing Sheraton.

Sparrow and her sewer entourage made it to the subbasement of the super structure. They were all exhausted. She thanked the group's leader and paid him their agreed upon final installment. They all exited through the security checkpoint with the same cursory pat-down, given their disgusting smell.

Her motorbike companion delivered Sparrow to the Golden Sun Commercial Hotel on Xibianmen Inner Street. The businessman's hotel was four kilometers from the gleaming superstructure she had just breached. Her associates had prebooked her a suite on the sixth floor. Her new persona was hanging in the closet. She removed the wig and red scarf in the establishment's back lot and disposed them in a trash bin. She covered herself with a calf length coat and stylish hat, provided by her scooter driver, before entering the hotel's lobby. She took the stairs to the suite.

Sparrow emerged forty-five minutes later in the lobby. Men, huddled in deep conversation ceased their animated dialogue and stared at the incredible woman walking confidently through the tiled lobby. Hotel staff, both men and women, stopped their busy work to watch her stroll by. Arriving guests cut their cell phone conversations short and watched the beautiful woman pass next to them. A visiting Japanese businessman snapped a photo.

Sparrow was wearing a simple black dress, cut with a low back. The cashmere-like material hugged her frame. Diamond earrings and an understated jade necklace spoke of wealth and privilege. Her high-heeled boots clicked across the tile. She wore her hair up with a few strands leaking down to her earlobes. A prearranged black limo picked her up under the hotel's portico. She gave the driver the address.

The cosmopolitan group in the lobby of the tallest building in Asia seemed to give her the same respect. Two security men approached and were to accompany her to the suite on the prestigious one hundredth floor.

One of the security men was rather large and bulky. The other man was slight and lean. Both looked extremely capable. They took positions on each side of her as they entered the private elevator. There was no need for a search as Sparrow carried no purse and her dress left little to the imagination as it hugged her feminine form. These men had delivered numerous young women and young men to the top floor.

Both professional security men held their eyes forward, only taking furtive glances at the beauty they were charged with. The three rode up the elevator, which would take six minutes to reach the top executive floor. For the first three minutes, all three stared at the electronic floor monitor over the door; then Sparrow relaxed and took a pace backward to lean against the walnut backing. Her security companions stared at the monitor as each ascending floor clicked by.

The next few motions were captured in milliseconds. Sparrow dropped her lipstick from a closed hand. The larger of the two men bent down to retrieve the article. Simultaneously Sparrow's knee caught the man's head on its upswing, and her left elbow bent and crushed the smaller man's larynx. A follow-up twist of the larger man's head completed the task. Her lipstick tube with a concealed black paint spray shrouded the security camera in the corner of the elevator.

Sparrow lit off the elevator on floor one hundred and pressed the Hold button. She walked behind the elevator bank and tapped the security panel to enter the Employee Only maintenance door. It took her several brief moments to secure the poison and the blade from their concealed tubes. The contraband was taped inside her knee-length boots.

Sparrow took a calming deep breath before buzzing on the door marked one hundred in classic Mandarin. She heard a metallic click and from overhead speakers a familiar confident tone.

"What an unexpected pleasure, Miss Sparrow; please come in. I am out on the veranda." With his back to her on the terrace, the Voice was sprinkling and spraying some rare blossoms. He wore a Western cut suit sans tie. He turned to face her when she reached the double doors opening to the spectacular one-of-a-kind terrace overlooking all of Beijing. "It's been far too long; please have a seat, and I will have tea delivered," he said as if they had seen each other last week and not six and a half years ago. "Sparrow, you have not changed and are as beautiful as ever."

She noted his extreme self-confidence. As she walked the length of the suite, her eye caught original artwork of heralded artisans from both the East and the West. She greeted him at the doorstep of the terrace with a respectful bow. Just then a male servant was bringing tea service. He silently poured the beverage, bowed, and left them alone.

"It's been a long time," she said, reaching for her cup. "You have done quite well."

The Voice smiled. "As the world has become smaller and more complicated, my services have become more sophisticated and surgical for a broader range of clientele." He sipped his tea. "It's very good to see you again."

Internally Sparrow cringed. Having tea with the man responsible for so much pain in her life seemed surreal. She smiled and bowed her head. "I acted cowardly when you had offered me complete forgiveness of several triad killings for simply delivering the head of one, Alex Cutter. I have come here to ask for a second opportunity." Now she raised her head and looked him in the eye. The internal clock in her head seemed to tick faster.

With the security men disabled in the elevator, she likely had only a few minutes to kill this man. She waited patiently for a response as her internal time machine raced ahead.

After a full minute, the Voice studied her face and placed the teacup in his saucer. She heard footsteps on the tiled floor behind her. "It was bold of you to search me out but not surprising given your history for action."

Sparrow leaned forward reaching inside her stylish black boots with one hand. She glanced behind her to find two massive men, shaved bald with the exception of one long ponytail-like feature. The one man held a *jian*, "a double-edged sword used only by the most skilled warriors in ancient China." The second bodyguard held a *dao*, a single edged sword with a wood wrapped handle, used in ancient times by the Chinese cavalry. A third man appeared in Sparrow's periphery vision with a Glock, its red scope trained on her heart. "Don't be foolish, Sparrow; these men are quick to kill. They are not of the same cloth of the security men you disabled in the elevator."

Her whole world came crashing down. How could she be so self-absorbed to believe she could circumvent security around the Voice? He had prospered in the ever-changing world of politics, organized crime, and commercial espionage. "You win" was all she could think of saying.

She was taken to a back bedroom and given a tranquilizer. Her world went dark as she thought about the family she had failed.

CHAPTER 67

His rudimentary Mandarin coupled with his charm had the center island female desk staff grinning behind their demure exteriors. He learned who was occupying the top executive suite. His reconnaissance confirmed several levels of security surrounding the man whose suite was more of an impenetrable castle. Disappointed, Alex left the tallest building in China to return to his hotel. He was convinced the only access to the Voice would come when his quarry was out of the stratosphere and back on ground level.

He was walking back the few blocks to his hotel when a military jeep pulled aside and stopped. The young officer pointed at Alex and motioned to join him in the passenger seat. Alex had little option but to climb in. From behind a small caliber pistol was shoved into his rib gage. The vehicle took a U-turn and headed for the underground garage of the superstructure he had just come from.

Unceremoniously Alex was hit from behind and lost consciences as the double garage door closed behind. He awoke with the scent of Sparrow's perfume a few hours later. His head hurt. His vision was blurry. He was bound and in the same room with Sparrow. She remained unconscious. Three alert armed men were in the same room. Through the fog in his head, Alex realized he had failed to save his lovely wife. The thought of imminent death gave him a metallic taste in his mouth. One of the large guards walked up to him as he sat up from the floor and leaned against the wall for support. The blow to the side of his head sent him back to complete darkness.

It was midnight, and the Voice was in his lushly appointed home office. The desk lamp was the lone source of light. He had Sparrow's and Alex's passports on the green desk protector. Tomorrow he would have a document expert review them. He was impressed with the level of sophistication—surely a costly implementation. Since the Chairman's death in Hong Kong over six years ago, his analysts discovered the offshore accounts and the one significant withdrawal. Sparrow, as the Chairman's number-one concubine, may have had certain proprietary access. He would find out. Her companion, Alex, also had exemplary forged documentation. He would find out why.

The Voice would employ another expert as well. This man had proved his usefulness many times over in the past. His field of expertise was interrogation—using any means necessary. The Voice learned he was in Lithuania and could return to Beijing early next week after his current engagement with the Russian mob. The Voice would wait. He wanted the very best and proven man for the job.

By one o'clock in the morning, the Voice had considered various scenarios and concluded Sparrow's and her companion's visit may indeed prove very profitable. He instructed his men to move the two prisoners down to the forty-first floor of the building, where he had two holding-cell rooms. They were to be kept apart but not to be beaten. He would wait for the professional from Lithuania.

CHAPTER 68

Alexia reached out for a second time to her only known mainland China contact. The Tans' only daughter answered on the second ring. She was most pleased to hear again from Alex's family. Alexia shared what little detail she had. At the mention of the Voice and his likely involvement, Alexia sensed the steely resolve in the Chinese woman from Nanjing. She was prepared to do anything to help.

Alexia enquired about securing a weapon. She was told it would be nearly impossible in the brief time frame she had outlined. Alexia was crestfallen. Had she come this far to be of no help? It seemed foolhardy to have come all this way with no real plan in place. She felt stupid.

"There may be another avenue to pursue," suggested the woman from Nanjing. She paused for a reaction. There being none, she continued. "The man we wish dead is constantly being shadowed by highly professional bodyguards. My husband and I have been studying him since the cruel death of my parents a number of years ago. We have observed one potential weakness."

Alexia could not contain herself and interrupted. "My God! What is his Achilles's heel?"

"The man believes he has no equal. He is egotistical. His ego has no boundaries. To him, all humankind is subservient. His clientele, even those in senior government positions or powerful triad bosses, are mere mortals compared to his intellectual prowess."

"Let's use this to our advantage." Alexia agreed. "What's next? We don't have much time."

"Since the horrific death of my parents, my husband and I have collected information on the Voice. We have watched as his notoriety has expanded. He surrounds himself with professional bodyguards and smart analysts. He grants favors to many powerful men in politics and business. In return, he collects many extraordinary favors from the triad, the government, and foreign commercial enterprises. He is arguably the second most powerful man in China, after the premier. Nonetheless, we believe his extreme ego may prove the fatal flaw we should exploit."

"Do you and your husband have a specific plan?"

"We do." The Tans' daughter suggested she and her retired husband would join Alexia in Beijing the following morning. She hung up.

Alexia booked an adjoining room at the Sheraton for her guests from Nanjing. Utilizing her father's security contacts from around the world, she requested their reviews of the security tapes from the lobbies of the top Beijing hotels and the superstructure housing the Voice. The agencies were only too happy to assist given the exemplary relationships her father had forged over many years.

She received the two key reports back within the hour. Sparrow was observed in one businessman's hotel twice. The first incident showed her entering the hotel from a side door and using the stairs. She was dressed in a long topcoat and floppy hat. The second observation came on the same afternoon. On this tape, Sparrow was dressed in an elegant black evening dress making her way through the lobby and catching everyone's eye. The second report came from the lobby of the second largest skyscraper in the world. There was another sighting—this time of Alex spending time at the central desk and then departing alone. Sparrow was not included in that sighting with Alex. On that same day later in the evening, Sparrow could be seen dressed to the nines and accompanied by two security personnel to a private elevator. Alexia concluded her stepmother had gone directly to the top floor and an encounter with the Voice. Although not in the security frame, she suspected her father was close behind, but he had not entered through the main lobby.

Alexia met with her two contacts from Nanjing early the following morning in the Sheraton's second-floor restaurant. They all ordered tea. She shared the details of her clandestine review of security camera tapes in the two lobbies. She was convinced Sparrow was still in the superstructure, and she suspected her father had followed, entering the skyscraper but avoided the lobby. She was anxious to hear of her contacts' plan for the Voice.

Tan's daughter's husband spoke. He was older than she and spoke with confidence and some authority. "As my wife has shared with you, the Voice has an ego second to none. We have explored various scenarios to exploit that flaw and believe we have one which could work."

Alexia nodded as she placed her cup back down, indicating for him to continue.

"What truly motivates the Voice is his belief of his superiority to everyone else. Yes, money and influence are important to him, but they are merely a way to keep score. We believe we can exploit his ego and get him away from his heavily protected castle."

Alexia nodded again and inched her chair closer.

"Prior to my retirement a few years ago, I was assigned to cyber security for the politburo. I am proposing sending a message from their proprietary server to the Voice. The communiqué will request a clandestine meeting with two of the members of the standing committee. The message will infer his unique skill set is required in order to avoid an embarrassing international incident." The older man took a sip of his tea and continued. "In order to breach the server's security, we will require a significant sum to be placed in the palm of a young man charged with the politburo's information-technology safekeeping."

"What will it cost?" Alexia asked.

"We suspect it will be one million renminbi, deposited into an offshore account."

"That can be done," Alexia replied immediately, knowing of her father's wealth.

"OK, let's get to work," the Nanjing couple said in unison.

The two unconscious prisoners had been transferred to floor forty-one. They were placed in separate soundproof rooms. When Alex came too, he realized he was no longer bound by the plastic cuffs. His head hurt, but now he felt a bandage had been applied when he was out. There was water left for him. The inside room was without windows and held just a bed and a single chair. Sparrow awoke in her own room with identical furnishings. A small meal had been left for her as well. Their captors resided in a sort of living room between them but there was absolutely no verbal or written communication.

CHAPTER 69

The following afternoon the Voice received the abbreviated electronic message direct from the politburo. He personally knew the two men from the government's top echelon and was not taken aback by their request for extreme confidentiality. They proposed to meet privately the next afternoon in the tea garden on the northwest corner of the central park. Bodyguards would not be necessary or welcome. The Voice tapped back his response to agree to the meeting. Upon pushing the Send button, he had to enjoy the moment. With over one point three billion Chinese, the heads of government turned to him for sensitive assignments. This sort of thing gave him great pleasure.

With the Voice confirming the clandestine meeting, Alexia and the Nanjing couple had to do two things. First, they needed a kill that would not attract attention. Next, they needed to locate Alex and Sparrow in the superstructure and rescue them. It would be necessary to leave China as soon as possible. They had less than twenty-four hours to pull it off.

Alexia had two ideas. First, she needed assistance to locate her imprisoned parents. She elected several simultaneous initiatives.

1. Bribe the hotel's normal security staff for information.
2. Check with housekeeping for any leads.
3. Monitor the kitchen and room service staff.

The first two initiatives were proven worthless. However, when she checked with the room-service staff on any unusual requests, she hit pay dirt. The head of that department shared two very recent odd requests from the high-end hotel guests. A room on the forty-first floor had asked for two food trays—both with stale two-day old bread, a cooked cabbage, and tap water. The same room ordered three full-course meals from the high-end restaurant. The wait staff was told to place the orders outside the room, and they would be compensated appropriately. No one had gone in the room.

A note worth RMB 500 passed hands, and Alexia was given the room number. Alexia was betting room number 4104 held her parents.

Alexia's second idea was to secure some of the fast-acting poison used by Ping on her adopted uncle. She was prepared to take the gamble and hopefully source from Ping's old office at the malting complex. The company driver, who had replaced Sparrow and Mr. Tan, was more than willing to track down the vial and deliver it to her in Beijing for a hefty fee. He returned her call after he found the vial to be worth more than he originally thought, and renegotiated his fee with her.

The deadly vial of bird flu virus was in their hands the next morning. The Nanjing couple were able to have it mixed in the tea served to the Voice at the agreed upon rendezvous spot as he waited for the two members from China's standing committee. The Voice sat back smugly at the second-floor table overlooking the magnificent garden. He was dressed in a dark suit with a blue tie. His colleagues should join him soon. This next assignment would solidify his reputation in the country for being the go-to guy.

The waitress bowed politely and served him tea in an ornate cut glass. She retreated, and he took one sip. A moment later the Voice became dizzy, and he felt warm urine passing down his leg. Next he attempted to push his chair back and stand. In a half-sitting, half-standing position, his bowels released. He attempted to cry out but found it difficult to even breathe. Ironically, known as Yuyin in traditional Chinese, or simply translated as the Voice, he had nothing to say on this last day. He grabbed for the tablecloth and dragged it to the floor as he collapsed. Other diners in the teahouse left their tables and distanced themselves from the infected man.

The Nanjing couple watched from a distance. When the outcome was certain, they left the restaurant to join Alexia at the downtown superstructure.

CHAPTER 70

The lobby of the second tallest building on earth was ornately decorated with ancient Chinese weaponry. Each relic was displayed behind protective glass. The walls were covered with art from the Zhou Dynasty and written proverbs from Confucius, its most famous citizen.

To create a diversion in the lobby, the Nanjing couple had each carried a full tray of ceramic tea services. They stumbled near the security guards' desk and the crash of kettles, cups, and spoons rang throughout the doomed lobby. With that sound in the background, Alexia had broken into one of the display cases and pulled out a dao. She wrapped the leather cord around her wrist. The smooth wooden handle fit her hand. The single-edged sword seemed well balanced. As she stepped into the elevator, other guests withdrew at the sight of the deadly blade. She hit the button and then moments later stepped off on the forty-first floor. In her left hand, she held the housekeeping pass key, which she had received in return for three crisp US one-hundred-dollar bills.

The key clicked open the tumblers, and Alexia was in the room's tiled entry. Two men sat in the living room. One was in the kitchen with the fridge door open.

Alexia dipped low and swung the sword through the exposed ankles of refrigerator man. The blade cut cleanly through the tendons and flesh. The large man fell sideways like a tree being harvested. Alexia rolled into the living-room area and caught one of the men just below the kneecap, separating his upper body from his legs. The second living-room man was pulling out his weapon when Alexia chopped his hand off at the wrist.

The screaming of all three men would not be heard in the hallway or adjacent rooms given the soundproofing. Methodically, Alexia finished off each neutralized guard with a blow to the head. Blood soaked through the white carpeting in the living room and pooled on the kitchen tiles.

She released her mother first from the adjoining room and next her father. Both had been drugged and were somewhat incoherent. By this time the Nanjing couple had joined her. The group took the staff-only elevator to the basement garage. The arranged laundry truck bounced over the last speed bump at the garage exit. The getaway vehicle wound its way through the heavy midday Beijing traffic to the military base north of the city.

The arranged military cargo plane lumbered down the runway with all five of them onboard. Sparrow was the first to come out of the drug-induced state. She unbuckled her belt and knelt next to Alexia with her head in her lap. Alex came to just a short time later. He too unbuckled and knelt next to his wife. He had one arm around Sparrow and the other around Alexia's waist. The adrenaline rush was gone for Alexia. The three held each other. They sobbed tears of joy. By then the plane was leveling off on its flight to a military outpost in northwest Gansu Province.

After refueling in the middle of the night at a Gansu Province military base, the plane took its weary passengers over the Gobi Desert just as the sun was rising over the endless waves of sand. Four hours later they were just outside Ölgii in western Mongolia. From there the journey was by camel to Kazakhstan with a spice trader and his family.

More money changed hands, and the five of them were safely stuffed in a garbage truck that serviced a monastery on the Mongolian-Soviet border. They remained at the ancient monastery for a night and a day, leaving the following evening via a military truck convoy. The string of trucks crossed the Ural Mountains sixteen hundred kilometers later. The grueling journey took the group to the docks on the Caspian Sea, where a grizzled captain agreed to take them south with the sixty thousand metric tons of wheat he had on board. Numerous bribes and numerous vehicles brought the group back to the United States over the course of several weeks.

Sparrow's contact in New York, Mr. Chang, arranged for the Nanjing couple to resettle in a condominium just north of San Francisco on the bay in Sausalito. He had gotten them the necessary documentation to fit in and satisfy the authorities. This included social security numbers, past tax filings as expats, and a supermarket debit card. Sparrow had transferred a significant sum to a local bank that would cover all living expenses for the rest of their lives.

Sparrow and Alex decided not to move again. They would remain in Wyoming. They had beheaded the serpent that had plagued their family and now could live out their days in peace. Sparrow spent her time tending to a large garden and fixing up the outbuildings on their property. She had friends in Cody and rancher wives from closer in. Alex loved working the small ranch. He still took the occasional security-related call, but most of that work he passed along to associates. Alex heard back from the Bahamian banker and thanked him for the safety of his daughter. Alex purchased some cattle and one bull. In the evenings the couple would typically watch the sunsets from their rockers on the terrace. Both Alex and Sparrow anxiously awaited their first grandchild.

Bill and Alexia married on a late-spring evening in Cody, Wyoming. The Nanjing couple joined their numerous college friends, who traveled from across the country for the intimate outdoor ceremony. Alexia looked absolutely stunning in her white gown with trimmed lace. The reception lasted well into the night, and no one left the party early. Bill had retained his interest in politics and served on the city council in Laramie, Wyoming. Alexia's passion was protecting unwed mothers and children without a home. Their first home was a three-bedroom colonial on a cul-de-sac next to a park. The couple was expecting their first child in March.

Two more years passed. Alex received a call late one evening in his ranch office. "We believe to have cracked the code that has been responsible for market manipulations in multiple exchanges, and we need your help." The nearly breathless analyst from the London Metal Exchange was excited to share the breakthrough with Alex. They spoke for another thirty minutes before Alex rang off.

He approached Sparrow, who was watching her favorite taped television show. She placed the remote on pause and curled her feet beneath her as he entered the den. Her dark hair cascaded down to the dark green V-neck sweater. The first hints of gray were beginning to show. In the half light of the room, she looked beautiful.

"I know you have not come in to join me to watch my favorite cooking show. What's up?" Sparrow readjusted herself on the half sofa and tapped a spot next to her.

Alex was serious. He sat next to her and spent more than an hour revisiting the tale of the global-market manipulations the authorities had tracked over time. She asked excellent follow-up questions, and Alex responded with highly technical answers. She had recognized certain uneasiness with her husband over the past several weeks. Now he seemed focused, engaged, and excited. He completed the review shared by the LME analyst and looked Sparrow in the eye. "What do you think I should do?"

"Go," she said.

_____THE END____

Made in the USA
Lexington, KY
27 September 2017